GRAKOFF & GARIKOFF

One's an extortionist, the other slightly defective. They're brothers, sort of, and they run a fly-by-night interstellar trading company. They need pilots willing to risk their lives taking ships through foreshortening fields—the only way to travel faster than light; pilots who're not picky about who they work for.

Panglor Balef, pilot and certifiable paranoiac, is stuck working for Grakoff-Garikoff, Shippers and Traders Inc., Veti. Aside from a little trouble with a stowaway, a falsified flight plan, and the bombs that his bosses rigged to guarantee his obedience . . . he has hardly any reason to be paranoid! But even paranoiacs can have enemies, and Panglor is in weirder company than usual . . . heading for a planet that doesn't exist!

To survive this adventure, he might just have to reinvent faster-than-light travel. Either that or go crazy.

It promises to be a *very* strange trip.

"Jeffrey Carver imagines wonders and allows us to share his vision."

—Terry Carr

"An interesting and different novel. A fun read."
—*Future Life*

Books by Jeffrey A. Carver

Seas of Ernathe
*Star Rigger's Way
*Panglor
*The Infinity Link
*The Rapture Effect
Roger Zelazny's Alien Speedway: Clypsis
From a Changeling Star
Down the Stream of Stars
*Dragons in the Stars
*Dragon Rigger

The Chaos Chronicles:
*Neptune Crossing (Vol. 1)
*Strange Attractors (Vol. 2)
*The Infinite Sea (Vol. 3)

*denotes a Tor book

PANGLOR

Jeffrey A. Carver

TOR®

A TOM DOHERTY ASSOCIATES BOOK
NEW YORK

This is a work of fiction. All the characters and events portrayed in this book are fictitious, and any resemblance to real people or events is purely coincidental.

PANGLOR

Copyright © 1980, 1996 by Jeffrey A. Carver

Cover art by Alan Gutierrez
Edited by James Frenkel

A Tor Book
Published by Tom Doherty Associates, Inc.
175 Fifth Avenue
New York, NY 10010

Tor Books on the World Wide Web:
http://www.tor.com

Tor® is a registered trademark of Tom Doherty Associates, Inc.

ISBN: 0-812-53446-8

First Tor edition: July 1996

Printed in the United States of America

0 9 8 7 6 5 4 3 2 1

For Kathy and for Chuck

Introduction to the New Edition

THIS BOOK is a modest revision of a novel that was first published in 1980. In certain ways, *Panglor* is the foundational novel of my Star Rigger Universe.* It's not the first book that I wrote in that future history, but it's the one that sets the stage for all the others. This is the story of how it all came to happen: how starfarers first learned to navigate the streams of space** among the stars—the Flux, that strange realm where intuition and imagination, meshed with the objective topographies of spacetime, create fantastic images through which pilots can navigate their ships. The adventures of pilot Panglor Balef provide the first glimpse of the Flux, without actually naming it.

Panglor has been out of print since shortly after its publication in 1980. It was first published by Dell Books, just prior to Dell's closing down its science fiction line. It appeared without promotion, with a dreadful cover, and sank like a stone. I am delighted to see it return to print. And to celebrate the occasion, I have done some of the editing on the prose that I might have done in 1979, if I'd had the skill then. James Frenkel, the book's original editor and its present editor as well, has assisted me with the job.

---

*Other books in the Rigger universe include *Dragons in the Stars*, *Dragon Rigger*, *Star Rigger's Way*, and *Seas of Ernathe*. (That's in chronological order within the future history.) A new, still-untitled novel is presently in the works.

**Just to keep matters straight, I should point out that my novel *Down the Stream of Stars* is not a part of this universe, but rather another future history altogether—the Starstream Universe, also home to the books of *The Chaos Chronicles*.

It's a curious experience, looking back on work first done sixteen years earlier. These days, it's not that uncommon for a writer to dust off an early work, and to revise and expand and generally recraft a new novel out of old cloth. I have not done that. I *liked* the story I'd told and had little further to add to it; but it was clear that it could be made a better book with a little help from a more experienced hand.

I suppose any author mutters quietly to him- or herself, looking back on work done a goodly time before—especially work done in the formative years, when his or her craft and narrative voice were just emerging. In my case, the muttering is often but not always critical; sometimes it's astonishment at a line or paragraph that seems to sparkle with unexpected originality. Once, when perusing a book of mine after a long absence, I was particularly startled by one scene—*a scene I had no memory of having written*. Suddenly, paranoiacally suspicious that a fast one had been pulled on me, I dug into my files, found the original manuscript, and checked to see if someone else had snuck in those sentences. No one had but myself; such is the ephemerality of memory.

In rereading *Panglor*, I found an energy and exuberance that I didn't want to lose. I also found some pretty clunky prose and painfully awkward bits of characterization. And so, vorpal red pencil in hand (no word processor for this one), I set out to snip back the thickets of purple prose here, to straighten the garbled sentences there, to stamp out the redundancies everywhere—and in general, to provide a better read without needlessly altering the book that a promising younger writer had created.*

---

*I did the same thing with my earlier novel, *Star Rigger's Way*, when it was reprinted in a Tor edition a couple of years ago, and found the process—and the results—satisfying.

That's what I've tried to do, anyway, and I hope I succeeded.

I had a good time rereading the book while I was at it. I hope you enjoy it, too.

Jeffrey A. Carver
November 1995

P.S. For information on the Internet regarding my other books, drop in on Tor's World Wide Web site, or my own home planet, at:

http://www.oneworld.net/SF/authors/carver

Author's Note

Panglor is pronounced *PANG-lor*,
ou-ralot is pronounced *OOH-ruh-lot*,
and
Alo is pronounced *AY-lo*.

1

ANY MOMENT, Panglor Balef knew, it could be over. His mouth felt gritty, and his stomach hurt. If the goddess of fate smiled upon him, he would soon see the star. But if her smile turned malicious . . .

There was nothing to do but wait. He glared at the instruments, which told him nothing. The sequencer chuckled annoyingly. He sat forward and cursed savagely: "Whore!" Then he sat back. "Ah—" he grumbled. His voice was not as acid as he'd hoped. Two weeks in this ship, and his curses were losing their bite. That worried him: loss of the cutting edge, failure of cynicism. He was tired.

"You aren't worth the bile eating my gut," he told the ship, and it was nearly true. This ship, *The Fighting Cur*, had once been a stout freighter, but it had lived its years. Still, it was a spaceship and the only thing standing between him and the vacuum of space. He had other worries caged in his thoughts at the moment, such as whether he would survive foreshortening. "Talk, sweethearts," he pleaded of the instruments.

Fear gnawed at him. "LePiep!" he barked. There was a scuffling noise behind him, and the ou-ralot poked her head up beside the center instrument display. Panglor glared at her. "Trying to toss me out, hang me on," he gargled. The ou-ralot looked at him perplexedly. A prairie dog-sized animal, she had soft, tufted fur and round eyes. Her wings were concealed in the fur on her back, but her bushy tail twitched nervously. "Dope," Panglor said, in a sudden swelling of affection.

The ou-ralot was smart and empathic, better company than a human; but certain things were beyond her understanding. One of them was the incredible nervous strain of foreshortening, of flight between the stars. There was nothing a pilot could do while in foreshortening; the cards had already been played, in the instant of the ship's insertion into foreshortening, through the collapsing-field near the star of origin. The joker was that not all ships that entered foreshortening came out at the other end. *Where* the losers emerged, or if they emerged anywhere at all, was one of the unanswered questions of star travel. The statistical chances of failure were small but well established, and there was no known way to improve them.

As he often did, Panglor considered where his ship might emerge if the uncertainties went against him. His mind filled with images: Misty wastes, veils of darkness closing around *The Fighting Cur*, sealing it forever from the view of stars, planets, or any references at all of the known universe; an infinity of darkness and emptiness, beyond space and time. Limbo. Or . . . adrift among the stars, the ship speeding at a sublight snail's pace in the vast interstellar reaches, prematurely emerged from foreshortening and doomed to spend eternity coasting, missing its target by billions of miles, centuries late, its pilot long since dead.

It was the emptiness behind the uncertainty that terrified Panglor. He didn't want to end his days alone, in some nether realm of emptiness, in limbo.

He glanced at LePiep. "Over here," he said, whacking the cushion beside him. The ou-ralot sprang up and settled in the seat. "Good," he said. The control bay was still. The bridge of *The Fighting Cur* was a shallow, curved section bending back on both sides to the exit passages. The compartment was gloomy, the sensor-fringe viewscreen in the front wall lit dimly by the midnight-blue glow of foreshortening.

Panglor felt twinges in his chest, a hint of hysteria. He rubbed his forehead and then his temples, fingering several days' grease and sweat.

The EMERGENCE light clicked on, amber.

Lying thief, you taunt me! he accused silently, his blood rising. But he swung to look into the binocular scoopscope. The image he saw in the scope was a gray background with two clusters of white pointillist dots, swarming crazily. The clusters existed only on two specific planes, which danced toward convergence. Murdering mothers! he thought. His eyes ached. The dots swam. They fell into a three-dimensional contour, an obliquely aligned cone.

A muted tone sounded from the console. Beside him LePiep panted raspily in echo of his own excitement. He held his breath, banished his demons . . .

He felt a tremor in his gut and his groin and his ears, and the ship dropped out of foreshortening. The viewscreen darkened completely and filled with stars. He blinked at the star pattern, then switched to a stern view.

There it was, an aurora-red glow, hanging in space and retreating like a debtor. It was the capture-field that had snared him from foreshortening. He cackled, shaking a fist in triumph. "We beat it!" LePiep squirmed madly beside him. "Peep!" he cried, ruffling her fur. "We're there. You can relax." He touched the ou-ralot under the chin. After a moment she stopped squirming and stared at him with wide, wet eyes.

He had made it through. He was free.

Free to see human beings again. Free to continue his job and his life.

Free. For all the good it would do him.

But, whatever else—the danger of disaster in foreshortening was behind him.

The capture-field was still shrinking in the viewscreen. The *Cur* was moving at a hell of a good clip, probably about .01*c*. Panglor scanned the instruments and disengaged the safety to the drivers. That started the sequencer, and the ship immediately began rotating into the proper deceleration attitude. A golden-white G4 sun moved into a corner of the viewscreen, a bright disk. It was an ordinary G4 sun, no different from any other, except that it was the *right* G4, Dreznelles 3, the third-named sun in the Dreznelles star group. Panglor noted the spectral ID coming in, confirming the star's identity, and he smiled. He could afford to smile, to feel a touch of gratitude before the baser emotions took over.

The drivers kicked on, jarring the ship until the internal grav field compensated. What a creaky old can this ship was. Like him. In another day or so the ship would rest. But not him; his troubles were just—

"God, it's already started," he muttered. His nerves were shot; he had to make himself relax.

LePiep hopped down from the seat and disappeared, whistling, into a pile of junk near the exit. "LePiep!" he yelled. She remained in her burrow. Eighteen, maybe twenty hours to relax, to get ready to deal with people again. The thing was, he knew he'd be watched—probably from the moment he arrived. "LePiep!" he bawled. "Get out here!" He groped under his seat for a brew packet; he snapped its activator until the liquid moke was steaming hot, then he sipped it and brooded.

He recalled Garikoff's face, rough-hewn and dark, his eyes piercing as he gave Panglor the orders to fly. Blackmailing bastard. For a cent Panglor would have killed him and walked out, but at that point he didn't really have much choice; they had him outnumbered, and they had guns. So he'd gone along with the orders—not that he'd had a better offer in sight, anyway—and Garikoff's goons weren't likely to leave him unobserved now, so he'd have to carry the orders through. There was just one question: What kind of work did the bastards have up their sleeves for him at D3, and what were his chances of coming away from it alive?

He studied the star field in the viewscreen, not comforted much by its beauty. "Peep?" he growled. The ouralot poked her head out of the junk pile and stared at him with pulsating brown eyes.

"Hy-ooop?" she whistled. "Hy-ooop?"

The Dreznelles 3 Waystation, population approximately half a million, circled its sun in a Trojan orbit following D3's second planet. Manmade, it was the only human-inhabited world in the D3 system. *The Fighting Cur* was about twelve hours out when it entered the Waystation's real sphere of influence, the long-range linear-shift field. The ship began decelerating in a new mode. The field interaction produced a glowing halo several hundred kilometers out from the ship: radiant loss of kinetic energy that the field couldn't absorb. The image in the viewscreen was now fringed with orange light in the fore and aft displays, but totally washed out to the sides. Panglor switched the sensor-fringe to radar/UV composite, and that restored some clarity to the view.

Waystation Control beeped him shortly after he entered the linear-shift field, asking for registry and flight codes. "Never give you a break, do they?" he grumbled to LePiep, disguising his relief at hearing a human voice. He returned the information in a telemetric pulse, and Control fed him back some orbital numbers and then went away and left him alone with his thoughts again.

Hours later, the waystation actually became visible, a cluster of sparks shifting slowly against the stars. The cluster of sparks grew and multiplied; he was closing fast, still decelerating. "LePiep, look at this." The ouralot rooted some wafers out of a broken package and tossed her head disdainfully. Panglor, disgruntled, watched the approach alone.

The first thing to resolve visually was the floating spaceyards, a jumbled assortment of liners and freighters and large haulers and police vessels and station shuttles, all moored in orbit a dozen kilometers from the station proper. The *Cur* stopped its deceleration and drifted by the outer yards. They passed the marshaling and loading area, where large cargo haulers were swallowed by the entry ports of enormous warehouses. Behind the warehouses, several of the spiderweb radiators of the linear-shift field glittered impressively across the panorama of stars. Though they were a mere fraction of the entire system—comprising hundreds of radiators, f-s field generators, and the vast solar converters and relays much closer to the sun—they were nevertheless awesome, winking and glittering against space. The sight was appropriate for a station that was a trade center and interstellar crossroads. The D3 Waystation served several of the busiest trade routes of southern Sagittarian space, particularly the routes connecting Veti, trans-Cygnus 34, and the outworlds of the Boreaum Matrix.

Waystation Control came on-com, telling him to relinquish control to beacons blue-two and blue-three, and to prepare for rendezvous with the tugs.

"Christ, anyway," Panglor grumbled, locking the *Cur*'s sensor-fringe to the beacons' lasers. He and his ship didn't need tugs. But what could he do? Couldn't fight the guild and union regs. "Ought to just let a man do his job," he growled. LePiep, startled by the anger in his voice, jumped up onto the console and gazed sympathetically at him, eyes wide, her small ears standing upright. He stared back at her. "What?" he said, in exasperation. The ou-ralot had caught him off stride. She blinked. She was trying to help, trying to calm him. "Ah hell, Peep," he said guiltily. "Right; okay."

Four tugs approached *The Fighting Cur* like glittery eyes slipping across the starfield. They latched without fuss, and forty minutes later, the *Cur* was docked at a mooring station. Panglor secured the ship. Waiting for the shuttle, he located his duffel in his cabin, stuffed it quickly, then sat down with LePiep. "Friend," he said, stroking the ou-ralot's back, "what I really could use is a strong drink and some time to figure this thing out." He had tried to figure it all out during the flight, but he never could think properly during foreshortening transit.

The shuttle arrived: time to be off. He zipped LePiep into her quarantine bag, and with that in one hand and duffel in the other he boarded the shuttle and took a seat at the very rear of the cabin. LePiep huddled against him inside her bag as the shuttle broke from the *Cur* and accelerated.

The waystation proper came into view when the shuttle passed the mooring area and pitched over to change course. The view was spectacular. The station was a fabulous, articulated jewel filling half the heavens.

Sunlight spilled over its surface in intricate patterns of darkness and brilliance. Passing behind one angular wing of the station, the shuttle darted into shadow, leaving the station's nearest section etched in blazing fringes and outlines against the night. The shuttle decelerated, wheeled, and scooted toward the upper edge of the wing. Minutes later, they docked, and Panglor looked up at an open port.

LePiep cried softly in the confinement of her bag. She stared at him through the clear plastic with fearful eyes. "Hey, Peep," he said, feeling sudden pressure in his throat. He blinked mist out of his eyes, then lifted the bag and the duffel and moved to the port.

Arrival inspection was a bloody nuisance—customs, decontamination, medical. Eventually they were released and sent on their way down a concourse, Panglor decontaminated and in clean clothes, and LePiep decontaminated and fluffy, perched on his left shoulder, her tail hooked under his arm. They followed a pair of floating electric blue lines that converged in the distance like parallel rails arrowing to a horizon. It was a psykinetic directional—personalized, supposedly, to his own intended destination and visible only to him. Despite the number of concourses he had to walk through, at least he didn't have to worry about getting lost.

Each new hall was a shock of stimuli: people swarming and gliding in every direction—spacers, transient passengers, locals. He saw an enormous variety of clothes, tight and bulging and bright and subdued, people chattering in unfamiliar languages and reeking of pungent smells. None of these people seemed quite real to him. He couldn't help thinking of them as ghosts—just like the ghosts who had put him out of work, and the ghosts who were blackmailing him now—as something less than human, not to be trusted.

He reached up to stroke LePiep, comforted by her

warm presence against his neck. "Peep-o," he said—but couldn't finish whatever it was he wanted to say. His stomach was all knotted up, and so were his thoughts. It was those ghosts . . . He felt like an alien among humanity. Peep didn't care; Peep *was* an alien. But he wasn't. He was human. And what about the rest of these people? They were supposed to be human. So why were they all so unreal?

The directional led him to one of the many privacy-shadows, clustered at the edge of a guest lobby. He stepped inside. From within, the privacy-shadow shimmered colorfully, cutting off external sight and sound. A silver-haired woman smiled from behind a console. "I hope you had a pleasant transit, sir. May I help you with your accommodations?" She seemed almost seductive, with moist lips turned up slightly at the corners.

"Yah," he said. LePiep was buzzing in his ear, but he was captivated by that smile. He ignored the ou-ralot.

She asked what accommodations he would like. Basking in the sound of her voice, he barely followed the gist of her words. Luxury or standard? LePiep hissed, prodding him with her paw; he patted and shushed her, and nodded *yes* to the luxury.

"No!" he said an instant later, coming to his senses. LePiep had been warning him; he had fallen prey to the woman's hypnotic smile. But his credit wouldn't cover a luxury room.

Her smile collapsed to a frown as she asked for his credentials. He muttered, "Pilot Panglor Balef, flying for Grakoff-Garikoff, Shippers." She worked at her console, then gave him a room confirmation—economy single. There was a message waiting for him in central communications. "Right," he said. Her smile had lost its magic; she was now only a purveyor of information. Was that how they sold high-priced rooms? "Listen—"

But the woman, the console, and the privacy-shadow vanished. He was left standing, astonished, in the chaos of the lobby. God damn. A holacrum—the bitch was nothing but a holacrum.

Worse than a ghost.

What the hell kind of place was this, anyway? They came at you with illusions, went straight for the glands, tried to sell you something you couldn't afford—and if you refused, you were just baggage?

LePiep chirruped, nuzzling him. He exhaled and started walking, shifting the ou-ralot down into the crook of his arm. One day they would push him too hard—and someone would pay.

A psykinetic directional blinked, pointing out of the lobby. He followed it up several floors and down a corridor, then stopped where it pointed, glittering, through a door. He touched the edge of the door with his fingertip. It paled, and he stepped through. Economy single. It wasn't really all that spartan: small, but fitted with selectable holo-décor; a chair that seemed designed to discourage him from spending too much time here; single sleep bay; mistshower. Not bad, actually, by most standards.

LePiep fluttered around, making her own inspection. Panglor watched her for a moment, then frowned, remembering the message that was waiting for him. His orders, no doubt. He went to the com-console and activated the query line. "Message for Pilot Panglor Balef, *The Fighting Cur*. Please display," he said. He touched his fingertips to the ID scanner. LePiep was making vulgar, throaty noises as she squirreled about, making it impossible for him to think. "Hey, bud," he grumped. "Knock it off, huh?"

The ou-ralot landed on the counter and stared at him sullenly—a transparent play for sympathy, which he ignored. The message appeared:

"SENIOR PILOT PANGLOR BALEF, GRAKOFF-GARIKOFF DRISCOLL CLASS FREIGHTER #B387. AUTHORIZED, LAY-OVER D3 WAYSTATION, NOT TO EXCEED TEN DAYS. PURSUANT TO ORIGINAL ORDERS, RECEIVE AND CARRY OUT INSTRUCTIONS FROM CURRENT LESSEE OF SHIP, BARRACU TRANSPORT AND DISTRIBUTION, INC KRAZEL. PROCEED TO SKY LORE LOUNGE FOR MEETING AT 2130 AFTER ARRIVAL. AWAIT CONTACT. APPROVED, GRAKOFF-GARIKOFF, LTD, SHIPPERS AND TRADERS INC VETI."

Well, that didn't tell him much. But it told him something. If the *Cur* was being leased to a company incorporated on Krazel, which was a lot like not being incorporated at all, then the company was most likely a front for Grakoff-Garikoff themselves. Why? To insulate them from the law?

He had expected something like that, but it dismayed him nonetheless.

"Peep," he said, "I don't know exactly what's happening, but I don't think it's going to be good." His voice cracked, and he turned away from her until his feelings had a chance to freeze solid. Then he looked again; the ou-ralot watched him with consoling eyes.

"Okay, now," he said, blanking the com-screen. "I've got two hours before I have to meet those rat-buggerers, and that's plenty long enough for a strong drink." He turned and tickled LePiep under the snout. "Want to come along or stay here?"

"Whooee!" she pleaded, eyelids dropping. She ruffled her wings under the brown fur of her back and settled down into a comfortable position. Her eyes blinked slowly.

"Okay." Panglor rummaged for a packet of wafers, which he opened and left on the counter, along with a nippled bottle of foxx-cream. Then he touched her behind the ears. "So long," he said. The door opaqued behind him. He tested its security with an elbow, then peered both ways down the silent corridor; he shivered, feeling watched.

An idea for a destination formed in his thoughts—a drinking and eating hearth—and a pair of psykinetic directional lines appeared, gleaming in mid-air.

The hearth looked dark but warm from the outer corridor. The entrance boundary shimmered as he passed through, and the corridor sounds died, replaced by a clinking of tableware and an undercurrent of string music. He blinked until his eyes adjusted to the gloom. Each of the tables had a closely hooded, colored lightcone; on the far wall, a rusty glow climbed from a hidden source toward the ceiling. A scent of burning herbs and wood drifted in the air.

Panglor crossed the room, feeling a tingle in his skin, a teasing suggestion of arousal. He suddenly felt wary. No one appeared to notice him, however. The next room was a brighter, earthier place, with stone walls and partitions. The burning scent came from a fireplace behind a long S-shaped bar. He took a stool.

The human bartender nodded. "Slaker," Panglor said. "Big one." He settled down into the stool, fiddling with the armrests, and tried to forget his self-consciousness.

The slaker was a lively drink, with a nice green glow. The first sip produced a rush up his spine to the back of his head, followed by a kick to the sternum. The liquor sparkled, as though winking slyly, as it spilled over the edge of the glass to his lips. It was a fine drink for contemplation, with a light taste of absinthe and trake-herb.

He was reminded of a bar in the orbital spaceyards of Eridani Neverlight, one of the rare places he associated with pleasant times. It was a strange association, considering what a bizarre and gloomy world Neverlight itself was, a hot but tilted planet that was habitable only in the half-year perpetual nighttime regions of the poles. His stay in the orbital spaceyards, six years ago, had been unusual; he had enjoyed a vacation from a well-paid job, and in the friendship of Lenia Stahl, a local spacer in the Neverlight system. He wondered why that memory should strike him now; and then he knew. There was a holo-mural above the bar that reminded him of one at that other station. The mural showed a vivid tropical archipelago set in a gemlike sea. As he watched, the image changed: to a supergiant sun, a blood-red eye, with a charred planet in the forefield. The mural's glow drenched the bar with scarlet light, and with it Panglor's thoughts. The memory of Neverlight OrbSpace, Lenia Stahl . . . keep it . . . let it linger . . .

He jerked his thoughts back to the present. For a year he had corresponded with Lenia Stahl; but he had never returned to see her, and it was unlikely he ever would. The memory was riddled with pain.

Panglor tipped the slaker to his mouth again. His hand trembled with the glass. He tightened his grip on the stem and signaled the bartender, thinking to ask for a bowl of barloam stew, something to settle his nerves.

The mural blinked. Now it showed a misted landscape, yellow-orange clouds half obscuring a spaceport on the ground. A tiny ship was caught in the act of descending to a landing pad outlined by blazing red markers; its jets sputtered against the desolate world. This looked like the spaceport at Skyll, in the Boreaum Matrix, the most desperately lonely place Panglor had ever seen—a world that chilled the soul, and turned men into walking shadows of humanity. Panglor had been there once; few men went twice.

"Sir?" said the bartender, peering at him.

Panglor started. He shook his head, closed his eyes, felt the pressure in his skull begin to mount. He opened his eyes and gulped the last of the slaker. The drops twinkled as they ran from the glass and exploded hot and cold and electric in his mouth. He put the glass down, touched the receipt plate on the bar, and turned away, stumbling. A man in red pantaloons watched him curiously. Panglor steeled himself and looked for the way out. There was that tickling at his nerves again, as he went through the hearth, a scratching ghostly touch at his groin, vaguely arousing. Damn hormones, he muttered.

No. Not the hormones. External stimulation; they were trying to sell him a good time.

He left the hearth, and the twinges faded.

The time was 2120, and he was to meet his contacts soon, in the Sky Lore Lounge, wherever that was. Sky Lore Lounge, he thought. He walked along, thumbing and scratching his sides. His thoughts were everywhere, totally incoherent; he walked faster, trying to rearrange them. *Sky Lore Lounge.* Directionals blinked on, and he followed them without another thought.

The lounge was a high-ceilinged place, with platforms and tables supported by slender arms in a multilevel myriad. The walls were illusion-depth black, swirled with nebulas and starclouds. Hovering near the center of the lounge was a slowly evolving art holacrum, at the moment showing the face of a woman in ecstasy. Panglor glanced about uncertainly, then chose a table high in the room. A lift-field glowed faintly beneath it; he stepped into the field and rose to the table.

This time he ordered barloam stew before anything else, and the moment it was delivered, he gulped it furiously. Every few seconds, he peered around with his mouth full, to see if anyone was approaching.

Even so, they surprised him. He looked up as two people slid into the seats facing him. One was a man, slight and pale, with dark, slick hair powdered with silver glitter. The other was a woman, fat and gray-haired, with sharp eyes and small white teeth that gleamed disconcertingly. Panglor choked; he swallowed with difficulty, with one hand on his throat. He sat straight in his seat and looked around. A privacy-shadow surrounded the table.

He shivered and focused on the two visitors. He cleared his throat and released the pressure his fingers were applying to the tabletop. Then he began spooning his stew again, keeping his eyes on the two.

The woman leaned forward, turning her face up at an angle. Panglor hesitated in midbite, his heart beating violently. "Pilot Balef?" the woman asked expressionlessly.

Panglor grunted. He lowered his spoon and pushed the bowl aside, appetite gone.

"I am Secretary Nelisson, of the Barracu Transport and Distributing Company," she said. "With me is Deputy Director Demimoss." The man gazed at Panglor with a cloudy expression. Nelisson opened a small satchel and withdrew a set of documents. "These, Pilot, are a copy of the agreements of lease between Barracu and Grakoff-Garikoff, the owners of your ship."

Panglor blinked.

"And your flight orders." She passed the documents across the table.

He glanced at the leasing agreement, then examined the flight orders. They were simple, but puzzling. He was instructed to fly the ship unladen to Quetzal in the Formi star system; there he would load cargo and receive further orders.

Puzzling, indeed. He grinned, scratching his head,

then frowned. Then he grinned again, shifting his eyes from Demimoss to Nelisson and back. "Well," he said, "no problem here." Certainly there was nothing illegal indicated. But why would anyone send a freighter such a distance empty? Flying a starship through foreshortening was expensive, even for a wreck like *The Fighting Cur*.

He gazed suspiciously at the orders. Though the grin remained on his face, he felt fear creeping up the back of his neck.

Nelisson tapped her fingers on the table and said, "Those are just for the record. That's not actually what you're going to do, of course."

Demimoss stirred, his eyebrows twitching. "No, we have other plans," he said mildly, running his fingers back through his hair. "In fact we—or rather, Grakoff-Garikoff—are going to give you that ship, for your very own, to keep. As soon as you've left this star system." He gestured with his thumb to Nelisson. She produced still another document, but did not pass it across to Panglor. "That's the transfer of title," said Demimoss. "Ready to become effective as soon as you make your foreshortening insertion."

Panglor stared at him, trying not to betray emotion. He had a bad feeling in his gut.

"All you need to do before this document is executed is to perform a certain orbital maneuver in your freighter," Demimoss continued. He stroked his hair back again, his eyes flickering. Panglor was beginning to find the gesture unpleasant, as unpleasant as the implication of his words. "Pilot, are you familiar with a shipper-class freighter, *Deerfield*, owned by Vikken Traders, Limited?"

Panglor shook his head, his nerves pinched with ice. That ship specifically he did not know; but Vikken

Traders, Ltd., he knew very well. Very well, indeed. A major interstellar shipping firm—far greater than Grakoff-Garikoff—they had been his last regular employers. His very last. Vikken was the company that had terminated him, blacklisted him, and left him destitute on Veti IV. If there was a single entity he hated more than Grakoff-Garikoff, it was Vikken Traders, Ltd.

"Well, it doesn't matter if you know the ship," said Demimoss. "*Deerfield* is at this station, and on Thirdday at 0875 it will depart this station, bearing a cargo of some considerable value, which needn't concern you. The ship is scheduled to make foreshortening insertion to Gaston's system." Demimoss peered at him, his eyebrows jittering up and down. "Unfortunately, it will never complete the transit. In fact, no one will know where it has gone, or what has become of it." He fell silent and pressed his lips together. Then he continued, sadly, "And you know what? It will have been a faulty insertion, caused by a near-collision just short of the collapsing-field."

His eyes held Panglor's. "*The Fighting Cur* will be cleared for departure forty minutes after *Deerfield*. The flight plan is already filed. It directs *The Fighting Cur* toward the same collapsing-field that *Deerfield* will use."

Panglor tried to swallow; his throat was full of sand.

"We leave the details to you as to how you program your course. *The Fighting Cur* has been provided with oversized drivers, which are being adjusted right now. Your only obligation to Barracu, and to Grakoff-Garikoff, is to see to it that *Deerfield* is diverted at the last possible moment. You are not to cause her to abort her insertion. You are to make certain that her insertion is faulty. Near-collision, Pilot—that is the report we will be looking for."

"That's suicide," Panglor said hoarsely.

"Not if you're good," answered Demimoss, staring with one eye. "If you plan it correctly, you can divert *Deerfield* with a near-collision and make your own insertion a good one, for your escape. We don't care where you go—hmm? If you make it to another system, you can take care of yourself, I think."

Panglor tried to answer, but the words kept stuttering deep in his throat, never reaching his vocal cords. Finally his protest rumbled up. "Well, then, it's murder. Sending a crew into limbo is no better than murder, is it?" he snarled. Lord, nothing frightened him more than the thought of bad insertion, of never coming out of foreshortening, or of coming out somewhere in the lonely reaches between the stars. He feared it every time he made a transit. Could he knowingly cast another crew to that fate?

Demimoss and Nelisson both smiled tolerantly. "Pilot Balef," said Demimoss, once more stroking his hair back, "I understand that you are held under certain—ah, obligations—to Mr. Grakoff and Mr. Garikoff. Isn't that correct? Of course it is." He sighed slowly. "Now, it's none of Barracu's concern why these obligations exist. But we can repeat to you the assurances that Grakoff-Garikoff gave us when we leased the ship's services—when we asked if you might show reluctance."

Panglor glared.

"May I repeat for you, Pilot? You will be watched on the station. You will be watched in space. Your maneuvers will be watched. If you fail in your assignment, *The Fighting Cur*—the ship you stole—will fail in its escape. In fact, it will fail to make a proper foreshortening insertion at all." Demimoss paused, withdrew a tissue from his inner shirt pocket, and blew his nose delicately. His eyebrows jumped.

Nelisson tilted another document toward Panglor, without giving it to him. "The theft and piracy report on your ship. This document can be executed, or the transfer of ownership. The choice is yours."

For several moments, Panglor could not respond. He was still assimilating the meaning of this grotesque conspiracy. What they were talking about was not a new sort of crime; sometimes it was called piracy, sometimes industrial sabotage. A slight perturbation of a ship's insertion vector could do it. And it *was* done. It was a particularly savage form of corporate warfare.

"You people really work for Grakoff-Garikoff, don't you?" he said finally. He could not quite bring himself to answer their question.

"We told you who we work for, Pilot Balef," Nelisson said, shaking her head reprovingly. "We work for the Barracu Transport and Distributing Company."

Panglor nodded with difficulty. What difference did it make if they were lying or if Barracu was simply a front for Grakoff-Garikoff? "Well, then," he grunted, "why do you want me to do this? What do you have against this *Deerfield*?"

"That, Pilot, is really not your concern," said Demimoss. "But we don't mean to be unkind to you, either. We were given to understand that you might welcome a chance to do the job, after you thought about it."

"It's a hideous idea."

"Think of who will suffer. Vikken. Does that displease you?" Demimoss took a tiny narco pop-bulb from his shirt pocket, bit it, and sucked on it, smiling. "Besides, do you have a choice?"

Panglor fumed. He shrugged twitchily. He had no

doubt that Garikoff could carry out his threats. He could be killed by a Garikoff goon right here on the station if he refused the job.

He refocused his eyes suddenly. Nelisson and Demimoss were both standing, and the veil of the privacy-shadow was gone. Anything he said now was for the entire lounge to hear. Demimoss was the one who spoke, though. "Trust us," he said, stroking his glittering hair back. Then he nodded to Nelisson, and they stepped apart into separate, glowing drop-fields and vanished.

Panglor stared across the empty table, frozen. He felt a great pressure inside his skull, like a wedge of ice. So. No more wondering about the atrocities Garikoff had in mind. No more guessing. No more faint hoping.

His feelings spread like a chill vapor throughout his body. For long minutes, he sat paralyzed. But cracks, eventually, began to split the ice.

It was a Vikken ship he was about to attack, and there could be pleasure in that. But could he ignore the other lives involved? Well, why not? It was his life or theirs, and what did he owe any of them? They were only men, and therefore essentially vicious like all men. Ghosts, phantoms loose in his existence uninvited. Why protect *them*?

And as for Grakoff-Garikoff, well, there would be time enough for them later. They could threaten him with their goons, and they could threaten him with worse things, and for right now he might take it. Right now he might do as they told him. But later he'd make them pay; somehow, he would. Panglor Balef would have his revenge.

The cracks spread through his icy feelings, allowing pain and desperation to leak through. The body of ice groaned, then suddenly shivered apart in his skull, exposing the pulsating nerves within. A hot rivulet ran down his spine, releasing feelings in quick little streams: anger, fear, humiliation, relief. He began to shudder, putting knuckles against his mouth. And then laughter erupted, choking laughter, and suddenly he was breathing again.

2

THE SKY Lore Lounge was filling rapidly for the evening's entertainment. He didn't want to stay here for that, for bejeezus sake—some mutilated holodrama, caterwauling musicians, and who knew what else?—but he didn't want to pick up and move until he had thought this all out.

He had about a day. Escape was impossible; no telling how many goons Garikoff had watching him. Going to the authorities would be like slitting his own throat; if Garikoff's goons even suspected, they'd make mincemeat of him. Not that he'd be losing much if he died, but what about LePiep? She was totally dependent on him. And she was the only creature in the universe who accepted his loyalty and returned it in full. No, he had to keep himself alive, if on no other account than that ou-ralot's.

He had better get back to her right now, and not leave her alone again.

"Sir?" asked a soft voice beside him.

Startled, he looked up. A stunningly attractive woman stepped from the lift-field and stood beside his table. She wore a crimson gown with a high-necked, open collar reaching up under honey-orange hair; her arms were bare and smooth. "Would you care for a refreshment?" she asked with a smile, shaking the hair out of her eyes.

He swallowed hard, breathing with difficulty. This was no holacrum; this was flesh and blood. He could smell her and touch her. His blood rushed and pooled disconcertingly, toward his loins.

She bent toward the table, tilting her head. Her gown shifted slightly, and produced a clear contour of her breast. "Perhaps something else?" she asked quietly, hair falling over her eyes.

Something else? Is that how you do everything in this station? Is that what you're selling now—expensive women? He closed his eyes, trembling, feeling his blood rush upward again, to his temples. Get out of here—*now.*

He lurched away from the table and shoved past the startled waitress. Stumbling, he fell off the edge of the platform. He gasped, tumbling; but a drop-field caught him and brought him gently down to the floor. Conscious of laughter around him, he pushed himself up from the floor and sprang toward the exit. The starry décor swam around him and he staggered dizzily against the wall.

Outside, he ran. A few gasps of fresh air calmed him, finally, and he stopped and crouched in the corridor, looking both ways, getting a leash on his nerves. Calm down, he thought. *Calm down.* A cool sheath slipped over his enraged feelings, and after a few moments he had control again. His anger toward Garikoff was now a cold anger, manageable. The important thing was getting back to his quarters before anything happened to LePiep.

The corridor was empty, except for a small cleaning robot ticking down one side, along the wall. He had no idea where he was, only that the Sky Lore Lounge was around the corner. All he wanted to know was, which way to his quarters?

Directional lines flicked on, winking. "Right," he muttered. He wondered how many of his other desires the psych-monitors could read. It was not a reassuring thought.

When he entered his quarters, he found LePiep snoozing. He looked around carefully for signs of Garikoff mischief, but the only change in the room was a litter of crumbs around the half-eaten packet of wafers. The ou-ralot raised her head sleepily, then groaned and rolled onto her back, stretching. She radiated waves of pleasure. "Whooeeep?" she said, righting herself and blinking at him. She suddenly sensed his disquiet.

"Yah," he said, completing his scrutiny of the room. Grakoff hadn't tried anything, but they still might.

"Peep," he said, picking her up and stroking her, "we have to figure out what to do." He set her down again and paced in front of her, explaining the situation. LePiep responded with a shiver and a plaintive hum; even if she couldn't understand the details, she could sense his fear. She flexed her spine and wing joints and stepped toward him, her eyes dark with empathy. She lowered her nose and pressed her forehead to his cheek.

"Hhrruuu?" she said.

The ou-ralot's courage washed through him like a warming tide, comforting him to the belly. He held her that way for a minute, then lifted her into his arms. "Let's go for a walk, all right?" Maybe if he kept moving, he could make the feeling of courage last.

* * *

They wandered aimlessly, moving upward through the station's levels. Panglor knew he should begin planning, setting up course projections for *The Fighting Cur*, but his mind wasn't on that; he just wanted to keep moving, exploring, finding things of interest or even things *not* of goddamn interest, just anything to distract himself. Gradually they passed out of the section where most of the guest quarters and lounges were located, and into levels intended for both transient spacers and locals.

On Level Nine, he found a room where one could sit and dial images from the station's omnitelescope. Each seat had its own viewscreen and controls. Panglor sat and twiddled the controls for a while; he looked at several planets on this side of the sun—two gas giants and a gaunt cinder—and then he focused on the nearby sights of the waystation itself. He inspected ships and warehouses and field radiators. *The Fighting Cur* appeared in the viewscreen, a battered silver can with a smaller can on the front and a massive driver-ring on the stern, and he was surprised at the affection he felt. Once he'd hated the ship, but she'd brought him alive from Veti IV; she'd done her job well. It wasn't her fault she was owned by Grakoff-Garikoff.

Then he realized that he could probably focus just as easily on *Deerfield*, his prospective victim. The thought instantly gave him the jitters, and produced other thoughts: foreshortening . . . bad insertion . . . limbo. . . . He jumped out of his seat, dumping LePiep to the floor.

"Hyolll!" she cried, scurrying in circles around his feet.

"Hey-y-y, there!" he exclaimed, jolted back to reality. He scooped her up and stroked her nervously. "Didn't mean to do that, old girl," he murmured. Conscious of people staring at him, any one of whom could be a Garikoff spy, he took her out of the room and into the nearest lift-field. He kept rising until he reached Level Seventeen. When he stepped out of the lift-field, a pair of directionals met him, pulsing brightly, pointing to a drop-field. Apparently he was not wanted on this level. He ignored the signal and looked around. Things were different here. The corridor was narrower and dingier and badly illuminated. Exposed conduit and pipe ran along the walls and ceiling. Clearly this was a resident or maintenance section. No one was in sight. "We're as good as the damn locals, right?" he muttered. "Right," he answered and started down the corridor.

The gloom was eerie, and so was the quiet—except for his echoing footsteps. He wondered what this section was really used for. Listening at a door, he heard a faint sound of machinery. That figured. He went to the next door and listened; the door paled at his touch. Surprised, he cautiously peered inside. A single light panel illuminated a dusty storeroom, empty except for several crates in one corner. He inspected them more closely, rubbing dust from one of the crates. Under the dust he found markings of the Elacian National Worlds, whose script he recognized but couldn't read. "Mm," he said. "LePiep—"

He scowled. "Naw." But maybe . . . "Peep, what do you think about hiding up here and just waiting for everyone to leave? Grakoff would get tired of looking, sooner or later, and then we could hop a ship out." LePiep looked at him oddly, twitching her ears. She sat on the crate and thought with him.

"Naw, hell," he growled. It wouldn't work. They'd find him, probably with that damn psych-monitor—in fact, they were probably coming after him right now— and then they'd kill him. And even if he got away, how would he survive without funds? If they didn't deep-space him for piracy, they'd get him for jumping ship.

Oh, he could duck them for a while, but what kind of life was that?

"We've had it, pal," he said. "Let's go. Hup."

LePiep jumped into the crook of his arm. "Hoop!" she cried, muffling her snout against his armpit.

A shadow passed by the door. Panglor froze. Whoever it was did not stop, though, and he waited until he thought it was safe. He looked out cautiously and found the corridor deserted.

Sighing, he continued in his original direction. He planned to take the next drop-field, but didn't want to backtrack. Ahead, a blue-green shimmer screened off the corridor. Assuming that it was just a simple airscreen partition, he went right through. Immediately voices assaulted his ears. There was a doorway up on the left, and from it he heard the sounds of scuffling, a female giggle, and angry shouts. He hugged the wall and listened. The corridor here was paneled and clean; another hall intersected on the right. Get moving down that way before they see you, he thought. But he couldn't move.

A male voice became intelligible. "Day before that she queered the J-scan going up to the department and fed in some kind of—" He was interrupted by the giggle and more scuffling noises. "Hilarious," the voice growled. "Let's take this witch and—"

"Witch?" someone shrieked.

Panglor tensed, listening hard. What was happening here?

A woman said, "Look, let's not—"

"The hell with that! She's a witch, and we ought to just stuff her down a drop-chute and be done with it."

"Try!" A girl burst out of the doorway and yelled back venomously, "You try it and you'll never try anything again!" When she turned toward Panglor, he saw

that her face was twisted with rage. She looked to be about fourteen, perhaps sixteen years old.

His first impulse was to back out of the hellion's way. (Was he going to have to deal with an adolescent girl, for chrissake?) But he couldn't seem to move—despite LePiep's squirming and sputtering in his arms. He hoped the girl wouldn't notice him.

At that moment, her gaze fell upon him. Her rage suddenly wrinkled into harsh gaiety, and he realized that she was laughing at *him*, now. The instant she had seen him, she'd started laughing. What the hell? LePiep was crying in his ear, but he still could not make himself move. The girl's mouth twisted with contempt. Her eyes closed to slits as she studied him, her nostrils arrogantly flared. He could just see her pupils, contracted to black dots.

The face was that of an unusual sort of ghost. A ghost of young hatred. A terribly dangerous ghost.

The ou-ralot, now, was hissing—a soft sound, a whisper. But in her throat was the beginning of a deep, rising grumble.

Panglor trembled and felt his muscles begin to thaw. LePiep erupted with a murderous yowl. *"Yi-i-ip! Yi-i-ip! Yi-i-ip!"*

Panglor swung into motion. His feet moved clumsily, carrying him toward the side corridor. Then he began to run, and once he was running he didn't think of stopping. Why should a goddamn adolescent scare him this way? Never mind, keep running!

Ahead he spotted a pair of lift- and drop-fields, a gateway back to the civilized levels. He slowed, stumbling, as he reached them; his lungs ached, dragging for air.

Psykinetic directionals winked on, pulsing brightly toward the drop-field. He glanced back, thinking he had heard steps. Cheezus. The girl was coming down the corridor fast. "All right!" he snarled, and leaped—not into the drop-field, but into the lift-field.

Now why did you do that? he wondered, rising in the shaft. The next level was the highest one, and he jumped out of the field and glanced around. He was in a deserted foyer, from which several corridors split off. The area looked unused, the walls unfinished. Across the foyer, a ramp curved up against a wall to a high, gloomy exit. Keep moving. He hurried up the ramp and through the exit and into a passageway that continued to ascend. He stopped and listened behind him. At first there was nothing, then light footsteps. He continued up.

At the top he confronted a solid-metal pressure-door. A light beside the signal plate indicated pressure balanced on both sides, so he touched the plate. The door slid open. He stepped through, and it closed again.

He was surrounded by the stars.

The room was a blister on the station's skin, an observatory. With the exception of a com-console on one side, the room was bare. It was a place to look at the stars—and the view was magnificent. The galactic band glittered with a milky profusion of light across one side of the sky; on the other side was the sun, darkened by a polarizer to a dull yellow disk. Numerous bright stars stood out here and there in the night; some were probably planets of this system.

He set LePiep down on a ledge that ran along the circumference of the blister, and he faced the stars, close to the clear bubble. Perhaps the stars could alleviate his pain and his fear, calm him and give him strength. If not, he'd face the future shivering. He walked along the ledge with the ou-ralot at his elbow. Outside, much of the station was lost in shadow, though certain edges and angles were lighted by mirror or direct sun. Overhead, a shuttle twinkled as it passed from shadow into sunlight.

Behind him the door hissed open, startling him. He closed his eyes, hope draining out of him. "Naw, Peep," he said, opening his eyes again but no longer seeing the stars. Perhaps he could feign indifference; perhaps he could pretend to be calm. He turned slowly.

In the doorway stood the girl, gagging with laughter. "Boy, oh boy!" she cried.

He glared at her, his blood quickening furiously. "What do you want?" he growled.

The girl caught her breath, then shrugged, and said with a grin, "Nothing. What do *you* want?" She was about two thirds his height, and skinny. Her hair was clipped short in front, but it hung in a funny curve that made it long in back and on one side only. She wore a man's pocketed pants, and a woman's shirt with a loose and rumpled turtle-neck. She stood with her weight slouched over one hip, thumb hooked over the waistband on the other, fingers drumming cockily against her pelvis. Her eyes were bright and contemptuous.

Obviously the thing to do was to ignore her. Shrugging, he carried LePiep over to the com-console. He activated the screen, scratched his neck self-consciously, thinking hard for a moment, then said, "General information. Display foreshortening departure schedule for the next five days." The console viewer produced a full-tank schedule tree; he studied it with a show of great care.

The girl came over to within a few steps of him and snorted. "You came all the way up here just to do that?" she said. He raised his eyes and found his gaze locked with hers. She stuck out her chin. "What's your name, anyway? Don't you know you're not supposed to be up here? What are you, a derelict?" She shifted her hips and studied him with a mix of puzzled interest and animosity.

He bent back to the console. He didn't know how to answer her, and the fact that she was both female and an obnoxious child made it that much worse. "Go away," he said finally.

"Huh!" she answered, giving no indication that she planned to leave. "My name's Alontelida Castley. You can call me Alo." She pointed at LePiep. "What's your animal? That's a strange one."

Panglor squinted darkly, his thoughts frozen, his anger locked up in splinters of ice. "If you don't—"

"What did you say your name was?"

His breath released enough to grunt, "Panglor."

"Panglor, hey?" She snorted in satisfaction. "What did you say your animal was?" She glanced again at LePiep.

He wanted to squash her like a bug. And yet he couldn't respond, couldn't unlock the fury. "She is an ou-ralot," he said. "And she is not an *animal*."

"What's she, then, a plant?" said Alo. "Or an aphis gel? She sure looks like an animal to me."

"She's worth more than most people I know. Now if you don't—"

"Ho!" Alo crowed. "Gaw-dam, but you're nervous. Ping-lor."

He growled, "Get *away*."

"Pinglor, Punglor. What was it?"

"Pang-lor."

"Yeah. Ponglor. Why are you here? Are you a spacer?" She stared at him in mocking, wide-eyed appraisal.

Are you a spacer? he thought sardonically. And how much more of this are you going to take? Why not kill her, throw her out? Glaring at her, his chest tight, he hissed, "Yes. I am a spacer."

"But probably not a good one."

"If you don't get out of here—"

"Pfffff . . . you won't do anything." She smirked. "You're probably a coward, anyway." Her arms dropped rigidly to her sides, betraying tension. Her eyes narrowed. "What's the matter with you? You don't fight back." She glanced at LePiep again. "What did you say your animal was?"

"Ou-ralot," he said stiffly. Is that the best you can do against a thirteen-year-old? Or sixteen—whatever?

"I've never heard of one of those."

He shrugged and grunted. Touch her and sohelpmejesus I'll kill you. "She's from Faber Eridani. She escaped from a pet merchant on Areax V, and I saved her." LePiep had been starved and terrified when he'd found her about a standard year ago; she'd been his only friend ever since.

Alo studied him noncommittally for a moment, then suddenly moved closer to look at LePiep. The ou-ralot sprang away, whistling, and flapped around to land on Panglor's opposite shoulder. She hissed at Alo, then ducked her head behind Panglor's, grumbling.

"Hey!" protested Alo angrily. "Let me see her!"

Panglor freed her claws from his shoulder, then eased LePiep into a more secure position. He gazed back at Alo through slitted eyes. No way was he going to let her near LePiep. Something clicked in his memory, and he said, "Why did those people back there call you a witch? What did they mean by that?"

Alo's face darkened with fury. "So you're just like them, are you? Only sneakier. I haven't done anything to you, so you just better not make any trouble." Her voice became piercing. "I am a cit-i-zen of the station!" The word *station* seemed laden with bitter sarcasm.

"So what? What did they mean by witch?"

She eyed him with one hostile eye and laughed.

"Nothing. It means I'm smarter than they are. I like to experiment, and I play a few jokes, that's all. And those dull queers always get upset over nothing." She fell silent, but was shaking with emotion.

LePiep muttered quietly in Panglor's ear, communicating suspicion. He stroked her, thinking: The twitch is getting to you now, but she's only a troublemaker. Peep thinks so, and now she admits it herself. Just a ghost like all the rest—a troublemaking ghost.

"I think you're different, though," Alo said.

He felt a spasm. Jesus, was this kid a sorceress? Maybe she was different from the rest, after all—worse. Why the hell did she have to be interested in him?

Alo nodded and said, "You're kind of funny. You don't yell, you don't fight. And here you are pretending to use the computer. You're really doing something a lot weirder, aren't you?"

Words crowded to his throat, but nothing came out.

"Not saying you're any better," she added coldly. "Just different. I've got to go now. It's too bad you're such a coward, I think, because we really could have had a good fight."

She went to the door and, with her back turned, fiddled with something on the wall. He couldn't see what she was doing, and he didn't care; he just wanted her to leave, to end his humiliation. The door hissed open. Alo turned and grinned at him, looking very small and girlish as she rocked on the balls of her feet. Then she whirled and ran out, and the door slid shut.

For a moment, Panglor did not react. Instead of relief, he felt something he couldn't properly focus on, grating at the back of his mind. His heart lurched. Alarmed, he grabbed for LePiep on his shoulder. When his hand met fur, she muttered at his touch, and he relaxed. So there was nothing wrong, after all—nothing, that is, except his impotent rage.

If that was his best against an adolescent girl, how could he hope to match Grakoff-Garikoff and Vikken Traders?

Frustration flooded his body, then relief drained the frustration, then his fear began to poison the relief. Fear that the girl lay in wait for him elsewhere. Fear that he was in danger from Grakoff-Garikoff, that he would be killed if he failed the mission, that he would be executed if he did not.

Quickly he moved to the door. He hesitated, glancing back into the awesome night of the stars; then he turned and listened at the door—not that he could have heard the little bitch out there anyway. He touched the plate.

Nothing happened.

He touched it again, pressing his fingertips to the metal to ensure contact. He felt the metal, cold against his fingertips; but nothing happened, and he pressed harder still, and nothing happened, and the fury rising in his gut grew hotter than ever. The witch had sabotaged the door.

She was not only obnoxious; she was clever. These mechanisms were hard to jam unless you knew precisely what you were doing. He knew that, because with mechanisms, he knew precisely what he was doing.

There were several ways she might have done it. A charge-projector on the plate itself, if she'd been concealing one. Or if she'd gotten up under the service baffle, here—he couldn't remember if she'd reached over this far—ah, *hell*!—he thumbed open the baffle and stared at the power fibers. For a moment he did not even see what he was looking at; a heavy pressure was building in his chest, and his vision was blurred. He could open the door with the manual lever, but that would be accepting the insult. Or he could . . .

The pressure erupted. "Jee*zus*!" he bellowed, whirling around to face the stars, the light and blood of the galaxy. LePiep whistled and flapped away, circling in the air. He whirled again and slammed his palm into the wall. Stinging pain flashed up his arm. Goddamn twelve-year-old lout! Bitch!

And suddenly it was over. He muttered in despair and thought of hitting the wall again. But it was too late—he had vented as much as he could. LePiep landed on the ledge nearby and stared at him with deep, black eyes. "Hhooo-hheeoooop!" she cried, and hopped into the air again. He caught her in his arms and held her, trembling, without speaking. Finally he stroked her, set her down, and went to work on the door.

Taking a unitool from his pocket, he puzzled over the fiber-matrix circuitry, then poked the tool's pin-sized light source into the matrix at several different places and watched the flickering of relays as he modulated the beam. Everything was functioning except the plate, so he simply shorted that circuit with the light. The door whisked open.

Picking up LePiep, he started down the passageway—and heard footsteps ahead of him, running, fading in the distance. The little twitch had been waiting, then. Well, to hell with her. He wouldn't give her the satisfaction of betraying his anger. And anyway, he had to get back to the ship and get to work.

Psykinetic directionals flicked alight, pointing the way down through the foyer and into the drop-field.

When he reached his quarters he went immediately to the com-console. Before he turned it on, though, he had another thought; he went to the service counter and ordered a sting brandy. He waited nervously for it to arrive, and when it did, he drank it down at once and ordered another. The burning in his throat made him feel a little better. He asked the computer for departure schedules and flight plans, and for the first time he began seriously considering the practical implications of the job he was supposed to do. The job he *had* to do.

Aside from general flight parameters, he had to figure in *The Fighting Cur*'s no-cargo mass, her overpowered drivers, and the forty-minute departure lag between *Deerfield* and the *Cur*. The real problem, of course, was not intercepting the other ship but timing the interception to avoid early detection. And then there was the delicate matter of making his final orbit, after the near-collision, lead into a proper escape insertion for the *Cur*.

The consequences of being caught did not bear thinking; but at least one factor in his favor was that they would have to catch him on the run or destroy him, but in a very short time frame. They could not short out the collapsing-field to thwart him, because that could cause a power surge that could vaporize half the field-generating system. Nevertheless, there were patrol craft, and the Garikoff vessels, also, to consider.

But, he wondered—could he bluff the attempt and still escape? There was so much at stake. Not that he minded the thought of a vengeance shot against Vikken—but this idea was a horror. What mattered was whether he could get himself out of it and through foreshortening to a neutral system. There were numerous possible escape destinations: Mastrus via Faber Eridani via Veti; or the Elacian National Worlds via Atruba via Dreznelles 17; or . . .

The brandy was fuzzing his brain. Finally his concentration gave out altogether. He could not stop thinking about that little hoodlum's humiliating him.

And that was trivial compared to the rage that burned in his soul for Grakoff-Garikoff Shippers and Traders

Inc. Veti—the bastards. They may have put him back in space, but for what—sabotage and murder?

It was back on Veti IV that they'd grabbed him. Such a long time ago, such a long time. But it wasn't really, was it? Though four light-years distant in space, Veti IV was less than three weeks behind him.

Hardly enough time to forget.

3

VETI IV was a dreary world right from the beginning. It had only a few million people, most of whom lived in a handful of port and mining cities. The climate was unfriendly, as were the people. Half of two of the cities were built out of the abandoned ruins of the vanished Kili race; Veti IV was just one more world the mysterious Kili had used for a while and then discarded. Panglor figured that the Kili, whoever they were, probably had good sense.

Of all the cities on Veti IV, Nolaran was the first settled, and by reputation the gloomiest and seediest. Derelict emigrants and spacers congregated there, and even menial jobs were at a premium. Nolaran was where Pilot Panglor Balef found himself, nearly penniless, dismissed from piloting by Vikken Traders.

Nighttime in Nolaran was forbidding. Thin clouds swept overhead so fast that the stars were continually changing pricks of light, glimpsed for no more than a moment at a time. On either side, tall mountains loomed somberly over the high-altitude spaceport. The scene matched Panglor's mood well enough. He paused in his work and looked out of the grevik pit, past the freighter's underside drive cluster, and watched a ship across the field lift toward the sky on a pillow of ionized air. The sight only fueled his anger; he jerked his attention back to the job.

Fire him, would they? Give him a bad reference, would they? Write him up for psychiatric incompetence, would they? Just because he'd had an accident last time—because he'd had trouble with the transit? He hadn't lost the ship, had he? No, they'd salvaged both cargo and ship.

With a gauntleted hand he jabbed a switch. The plasma beam glowed, streaming up into the drive-field chamber of one of the freighter's engines. He manipulated the controls, modifying the beam to scour and re-film the field-surfaces inside the drive chamber. The mass of the freighter, looming overhead, was oppressive. How could anyone stand this job? It was hot and dangerous, he had to wear grevik coveralls with a stifling helmet and visor, and the pay was terrible. The plasma haze cooled to pink and then red, and streams of white sparklers began pulsing through it, etching the final random-element patterns on the field-surfaces. Ten seconds later the beam cut off. He blinked, fingering his visor. His eyes hurt, and purple and yellow sparks danced before his face.

With a grunt, he retracted the plasma gun into its stand. He did not move it yet to the next drive chamber; instead, he went to the edge of the pit, away from where the other grevik was laboring on the number-three chamber. He stared across the floodlighted spaceport and scowled. He wanted to rip off his hood and stalk away over the field. He was hot and stinking and tired, and the damn job was fit only for brutes and fools, not qualified men. But it was the only job he could get. He glanced over at the other grevik, his boss, shadowy against the glimmer of the plasma beam. Panglor snorted. Brutes and fools—ghosts, not real to him. Now *there*—out on the field, on the deck of a spaceship— that was where he belonged.

He was not aware that he had made a decision when he walked back to the grevik console, intending to roll the plasma gun over to number four. What he did instead was retract the entire unit, gun and console both, into its coffin at the side of the pit. His boss cut off the other beam and looked at him, face hidden by his visor. "What do you think you're doing?" he shouted, his voice tinny through the visor speaker. "Get that thing back out! You've got number four to do!"

"You do it," Panglor muttered.

"What'd you say?"

"You do it!" Panglor turned away, though he saw the man striding across the pit. A brute *and* a fool.

"Say that again, mister," growled the grevik, face to face with him. "This ship lifts in two hours. Now get busy."

"*You* do it!" Panglor yelled. His fists were knotted at his sides. "I'm leaving." Halfway out of the pit, he looked back; the man was following him slowly. Panglor flipped up his visor and glared, his nostrils twitching in the lingering ozone. The man stopped, startled, then shrugged and went back to work, shaking his head. Panglor left the pit and took the two-man grevik sled back across the field—aware, as he drove, of the ships hunched like giants over the spacefield. The sight pained him terribly, because walking off the grevik job after only eight days was going to end his chances of even working at the spaceport again, much less flying. This was it. Take a last look. No point in ever coming back.

After shucking his pit suit in the locker, he mist-showered—and there he had a bad moment, because he started to choke up from anger and pain, but he controlled himself before any of the emotion was betrayed, and he made no sound—and he dressed in his old spacer jumpsuit, and went to the office, head buzzing and throbbing, and cashed his last wagecard. He left the spaceport by the main gate, without once looking back, and he tried to ignore the jagged sorrow in his heart as he walked toward the town.

A fine, foggy snow had begun to fill the air, and he ducked his neck down into his jacket, trying to keep warm. The bright lights of the spaceport diminished as he followed the mountain road down into the city. He walked—to save money, and also to give himself time to think. His mind was not functioning well; he didn't know what he was going to do except go back to his room, and that wasn't much of a plan.

The road hooked downward from the plateau through a notch in the mountains. Much of the road, as well as the city, especially the Kili sector, was cut directly into the side of the smaller of two mountains. This created a curious splitting of levels in the city, beginning at the outskirts—foundations above road level, buildings delved back into the mountain face and jutting up out of it, and other structures carved downward into the cliffs, beneath the road. Once in the city, he passed alternately along curving precipices and through small canyons cut between towering slabs of stone. In the nighttime gloom and flying haze, he might have been passing by ruins sunk in the depths of a turbid, wintry sea. Nolaran seemed a city mastered by dark thoughts—a disturbing combination of human and alien architectures. Slabs loomed out of the mists of the canyonlike streets, and then disappeared back into the gloom as he moved on.

He was suddenly gripped by a feeling that he had taken leave of reality. The world greeting his eyes could not be the world supporting his feet; it was too strange and cold. There were no real humans there—so why him, why should his life run through this world? There were ghosts, of course—always ghosts—but no real humans anywhere for him to reach, or to touch.

Panglor turned to the right, blinking. The lights in the ravine were the lower city and the railyards, the marshaling area for the transcon tunnels. Slanting up the opposite side of the ravine were the spaceport spurs; freight elements moved up and down them cautiously, to and from the yards. That was life of a sort, human activity, he supposed. But it hardly related to his life. He continued along the border of the main business district, and on into the Naiopean quarter, where most of the bars were located, where he had done most of his wiring and drinking these last weeks.

Five doors past Carmello's Den, he turned into a roofless passageway, at the end of which was Gill's Place, the rooming house. There was no one in the tiny lobby except Franken, the strange man who was always to be found coiled at the entrance to the lift-tube. Franken nodded somberly as Panglor approached. "Time for settling accounts, no?" said Franken, as though to no one in particular. Panglor stopped, startled. He felt a rush of anger at the intrusion. But Franken was always this way, offering obscure words and observations, and Panglor had always thought him a little different from the rest of the ghosts and the fools. Franken, perhaps, was neither.

Panglor had never spoken to him, but he felt tempted to do so now. Their eyes locked, and Panglor suddenly felt that his thoughts and feelings had been read in an instant. Instead of whatever he'd been thinking to say, he just nodded. Then he took the tube immediately to his floor.

Before he had even reached his door, he felt LePiep crying out to him from inside. She had probably sensed him when he entered the lobby. He hurried to unlock the door. The ou-ralot bounded into his arms. Flustered and pleased, he cradled her, smoothing her wings, soothing her; rivulets of joy ran into his thoughts. For a moment he stood holding her, his cares and weariness eased by the ou-ralot's waves of empathy. "Peep," he muttered. "How were you, Peep—okay?" She crooned in response, and he smiled for the first time that day.

When he stepped into the shabby room, though, his problems came back to him in spite of the ou-ralot's comforting presence. He was out of a job, and nearly out of money; he was living in a dive, and couldn't even stay here for long. His employment profile was poison; he'd never get a job in space, not after that accident on his last flight in—when he had gotten just a little upset, being alone too long in foreshortening, and he had unintentionally disconnected the cargo pod before emergence. "Yeah, Peep," he said, putting her down on the cot. "Won't be going back there any more." But where would he go?

One of the two light panels in the wall had failed, so the room looked even gloomier than usual. Lights in the railyard flashed and glimmered through the dirty window. "Hyo-loop?" queried LePiep plaintively. She blinked at him. "Hyoolp?"

He cursed and rubbed his eyes. "I don't know, Peep. We got to eat, don't we?" He scratched the ou-ralot's head and thought. It was a bitch, all right. They could get along for a couple of weeks, maybe, but no more. Vikken had had to pay him a severance bonus, and there was a little of that left, and a little of what he had made in eight days in the spaceport grevik pits. But a month hanging around the Naiopean quarter had drained most of his money. "I tried to stand it, Peep, really I did. I just couldn't take it any more." He sighed and looked at her pityingly. What was it going to be like for her now? She depended on him for everything. Well, she'd eat as long as he did, maybe longer.

Even if she didn't understand, at least she felt for him; she gave him that. And that was quite a lot. If he hadn't made friends with her, back on Areax V, where would he be now? Alone, that was where. Without her empathy touching him and sharing his pain and warming him when he was cold. She was the only companion he'd known in years, and the only one he wanted. They would manage somehow.

Practically the only thing he could see from the window was the railyard down in the ravine, and even that was obscured by the mist and the dark. But he could discern the movement of cars, a string of lights moving down the side of the ravine. That had to be a train emerging from beneath the city, bound for the northwest tunnel that curved away to the left, toward . . . what? Well, it didn't matter. It was one of the passenger trains, bound from here to somewhere else. He wished they were aboard. Any place would be better than here, in sight of the spaceport.

Wishing wouldn't help, though. He couldn't afford a ticket, and even if he could, he'd have no place to go at the other end. Don't think about it. Turning away, he saw LePiep perched at the edge of the cot. She watched him now, humping her folded wings up and down nervously. He stooped to meet her gaze. A pulse of hope touched him, like a physical charge. "Okay," he said. "Let's go out, and if nothing else we can get wired out of our minds. Right?"

"Hoop-lll."

"Right. But you stay straight enough to get us home." He glanced around. Something suggested to him that he not leave everything lying around, so he gathered up his few extra clothes and odds and ends, and stuffed them into his duffel. He patted his wallet and unitool in his pockets, and hefted the duffel thoughtfully. He might as well bring it along—never know what they'd decide to do later on. He whistled to LePiep. She jumped onto his left arm, and together they went out.

The night wasn't getting any warmer, and within minutes he was shivering. Damn this climate, anyway— that, and his worn-out jacket. What he needed was a heatercoat, but the last time he'd had cash for one of those, he'd been on Hubspith II and hadn't needed one. The haze had cleared somewhat, and more people were walking about. With LePiep peering anxiously over his arm, he rounded the corner past Carmello's Den and continued to Fender Way. They'd look around for a while here and perhaps later go down to the rail station, just to check.

Soon, though, the aroma of cooking lured him into a tiny cafe on Fender Way. They took a booth and had fried mock-cheese and moke, with LePiep eating her share out of a saucer on the bench seat. The proprietor looked unenthusiastic about their loitering around afterward, so Panglor paid and out they went. The Naiopean quarter showed more life as the night progressed: lights shining through club blinders and ghost-inhabited bodies walking the streets, entering and leaving clubs, circling by and vanishing in the gloom. When they reached Stet's, Panglor stopped. He pulled on his ear and gritted his teeth. Well, they could walk around freezing or they could go in here and get wired to the eyeballs. Either way, they'd feel rotten tomorrow; but at least one way, he'd enjoy the rest of tonight.

LePiep poked her head up, nuzzling him. She loved

going with him to get wired—the empathy waves must be terrific—but she didn't understand the problem. They couldn't afford to spend the money. Except ... blissful forgetfulness waited in there, available for a price, and not *that* high a price. Oh, hell. He should be doing something positive, taking action. But ... LePiep looked up, purring. Perhaps she sensed his dilemma; after all, whatever made him happy also made her happy. But she obviously wanted to go in. He was torn between dread and desire, and a wish to give happiness to this ou-ralot, who shared without complaint so much of his sorrow. He sighed, closed his eyes, and opened them again, shivering. "Okay, Peep—all right." He walked into Stet's.

Inside he walked around to the drinking bar, where a half-silvered glass cut off the view from the rest of the club. He went past the glass, hitching LePiep up to his shoulder, and faced a barhost. Customers moved past him, some carrying drinks that shimmered with peculiar light refractions. "I want—" Panglor said, thinking first to order a drink but changing his mind, "just a booth."

"For the night?" asked the barhost, not looking up.

Panglor nodded, squinting. "Yeh," he said, when the man looked up questioningly.

"That's thirteen two."

Panglor fished out the money. He patted LePiep and followed the man past several curtained alcoves to an empty one. "Need help?" the host asked. Panglor shook his head and closed the curtain behind him.

He settled LePiep in his lap and picked up the headset pieces. He fitted the two halves together so that they encircled his head around the temples, and then he touched the test control. A wave of pleasure shimmered through him. "Hooeep!" whistled LePiep, pressing her head to his solar plexus.

With a smile, Panglor switched on the set for full cycle.

Ripples of electricity quivered at the edge of his mind, tingled at his extremities, and slowly flushed inward and danced up his spine. His eyelids fell closed, but light—soft colors—flickered inside his skull. There was an itching arousal, stimulating him up and down his spine . . . and the cycles from the wire grew faster, hotter . . . sound and touch washed through him, carrying him toward the bliss of pure fantasy . . . and awareness slipped away, leaving orchestrated pleasure.

When the last tingles faded, he blinked, trying to focus his eyes. The wire set was cold. Somewhere in his mind, echoes of joy diminished to some infinite, internal distance, ebbing . . . ebbing . . . gone.

He tried to remember the wire's pleasures, the sexual stimulation, the hunger satisfaction, the bizarre psychedelic spectrum; but he could no more recapture it now than he could a forgotten dream. Nothing at all of the wire remained.

LePiep stirred, humming, then abruptly shook her head. She was confused; Panglor felt her lingering pleasure subside, displaced by reawakened awareness. She was picking up on his cold afterfeelings. There was no physical hangover, and that was too bad in a way, because he would have liked a blurred, aching head to numb his shame in coming here and squandering time and money. She looked at him, and her eyes turned to pools, as though she thought she had done him wrong. "Ah, Peep, no," he growled. Letting her down, he felt a leaden unhappiness, though, and he struck the countertop futilely with his fist. The feeling did not go away. He snugged his jacket around him, scooped up LePiep and his duffel again, pushed back the curtain, and hurried out into the street.

The air was damp and chilling and misty again. The street was deserted. He set off down Fender Way, the buildings looming over him, dark and enormous. A pale, predawn light showed among the structures and mountains in the east, and the full shapes were gradually beginning to emerge from the darkness. Eventually they left the Naiopean quarter and followed the road downward, looping southeast toward the lower section of Nolaran.

The dawn threw its first rays over the mountains as he crossed a long overpass, from beneath which a transcon rail tunnel emerged. The railyards were a steamy playground, striated by train segments on gleaming inductance rails, single cars moving about like self-willed canisters, shrugging over transfers and switchbacks. Beneath the overpass, the morning passenger train emerged into the yards, one pale light after another in a string, followed by scattered lights on the freight add-on segments. Panglor watched it curve through the yards and disappear into the dim far mountainside, into the northwest tunnel. A longing flickered through his heart, and LePiep stirred with it, too—a longing to leave this city, to sever the past, to ride the rail beneath the mountains.

He turned back the way he had come, looking for the entrance to the rail terminal drop-shaft. The motion brought him face to face with two men—drugged-looking characters, who apparently had been ambling quietly behind him. Panglor started. How had he let two ghosts creep up on him like that?

The taller ghost sidled forward with a conspiratorial air. "Interested in a few grams of trilium sprite, friend?" he asked, not quite meeting Panglor' eyes. "Sixteen quints." He held up a clear vial. In the vial, three tiny tablets tumbled and twinkled in the dawn light. The man grinned slyly.

Panglor stared at the man balefully—but a rush went through his stomach at the sight of the trilium sprite. That was blissful release there, in some ways better than the wire, because when its effects evaporated it didn't leave a black hole of a memory the way the wire did. Strictly contraband, but here it was, at a price he could nearly afford—if he didn't want to eat or sleep under a roof again. God, the release that stuff would give!

This ghost, with long, dusty hair tucked down into his coat collar, watched him with half-lidded eyes; his companion seemed completely glazed. What dope *they* were on, Panglor didn't try to guess. Could he trust these two, even if he wanted the sprite? He closed his eyes for half a moment, then blinked them open anxiously. The smaller man, he thought, was noticing LePiep. "Hrrrl," the ou-ralot muttered, sensing the unpleasant stare.

Panglor drew her close to his breast. "Beat it!" he snapped at the two. They blinked in surprise. Wheeling away, Panglor walked along the bridge railing, fast, trying not to think about the sprite he might have had, trying *very* hard not to think about it. Where the hell was he walking, anyway?

He crossed the bridge and found a footpath that descended into the ravine in a long zigzag. Following it to the bottom, he found himself on a public way that skirted the railyards. He looked back up, but saw no sign of the dealers. The sun was up, judging by the light in the sky, but down here in the ravine the ground fog made it hard to be sure. So what to do now?

Shrugging, he walked along the wall edging the railyard until the wall ended and a fence began. Here he could see into the yards, as far as the fog permitted.

A section of the fence was open, ripped by vandals. He swung his duffel into the opening, then ducked through himself and looked around uneasily. A line of freight cars sat on the nearest track, with steam swirling about their underbodies and lift-carriages. Panglor felt a crazy urge to walk through the railyard—or perhaps it was not such a crazy urge. If he could find an unsealed ventilated freight car being dispatched somewhere worth going, he might manage to snag a ride. But the train on the first track was no good; it was all ore and chemical cars.

He walked along the length of the train, looking for an end. He found a break and stepped cautiously across the track between two cars, taking care not to touch the possibly electrified rails. Once safely on the other side, he looked left and saw several inspectors working some distance down the line, their inspection units glowing eerily in the mist, like lanterns. He walked the other way, conscious of his boots crunching in the gravel, and as soon as he found a break in the next train over, he crossed again.

There was no point in wandering aimlessly. What he needed was to determine where these various trains were bound and when they were departing. Perhaps the cars were marked somehow. He scanned the train on the left. Soon he found an identification plate on one of the cars and stepped closer to read: *Vikken Rail Conglomerate, Division of Vikken Traders, Ltd.* "Damn!" he whispered; he hadn't known Vikken was in the rail business. He inspected several more cars and found the same identification. Could they own the whole yard? "Jeezus." He smacked his thigh with his fist. The last outfit in the world he wanted to get entangled with now was Vikken.

Well, no help for it. But maybe he could get a free ride from the bastards.

He could find no routing information on the tags; it was all electronic. Well, he knew from watching every day that westbounders generally left in the early morning, after being made up somewhere on this side of the yard. If he could find the right one . . .

But how?

Discouraged, he set his duffel down for a moment and shifted LePiep to the other arm. When he stooped to pick up the duffel again, he felt a sudden wave of dizziness. Things were moving around him. But it wasn't his equilibrium; it was the train, moving by electric induction, silent as a breath. He hadn't even noticed it lift off the rails—the undercarriages now floated a couple of centimeters above the guides—but already it was accelerating, the cars and couplings creaking in a soft choir as they moved by. He watched in startled awe.

When the last car disappeared into what was left of the morning fog, he turned to go. And saw two men standing on the opposite side of the track, watching him. "Urrrrl," muttered LePiep. He squeezed her gently, but his own fear began to rise, choking him.

"What are *you* doin', mate?" asked one of the men. They started to cross the track, and they didn't look friendly.

Panglor squinted. He couldn't tell if they were the inspectors he had seen earlier, or guards. Either way, he was in trouble; the question was whether or not they carried weapons. He didn't see any. Clearing his throat, he shrugged and said, "Just moving on my way." He turned and started walking, feeling their eyes on his back. They would follow, of course. But what would they *do*?

"Mate!" the man barked. "I said, what are you doing?"

Panglor glanced back but kept walking. They were following. He was afraid that anything he could say would hurt him—so he ignored them.

"Stop right there, brother," the second man warned. That one had something in his hand, Panglor suddenly realized. The next thing he felt was a tingling numbness expanding from the small of his back down into his legs and straight up his spine. The last thing he was aware of was cradling LePiep and twisting his body to cushion her as he hit the ground.

4

SOMBODY KEPT moving in front of the lights, making them erratic. Dizzying. He was dizzy enough already, and that variation in the light made him dizzier still . . . and nauseous. He rolled suddenly to the edge of the slab he was lying on and was violently, convulsively ill. It was over in a moment—except for the dry heaving, and that lasted an eternity. "For chrissake," someone complained. "Get a bucket. Cheezus, what a smell!" Finally he managed to control his heaving, and he just panted, hanging his head over the floor. The smell brought him to the brink of retching again, and he flopped back, groaning.

"Goddamn," someone else said, poking at the floor with something. There was a humming and sucking noise.

All Panglor could see was a crimson blur, and there was a buzzing of blood between his eyeballs. Gradually, though, he focused on the fact that at least two, and maybe more, persons stood in a room with him. He sensed that they were not friendly; but he felt a wave of caring, empathy. *LePiep*. He squinted, trying to look around, and suddenly he saw her. She whimpered with joy and fear; she was on a table an arm's-length away, caged, her eyes flashing wildly. "Hey, there," Panglor croaked in a whisper. He tried to get up on one elbow, to reach her, but couldn't find the strength.

A hand cut off his reach. "None of that," a man growled. Panglor, with an effort, focused his eyes upward and saw a rough-faced man glaring down at him. What was going on here? Suddenly he remembered: the railyards—he had been stunned with a nervie. "You awake enough to listen?" Panglor stared up at him dumbly. "Cripes," the man muttered, turning away. "You better wake up fast, pal. You're in some big trouble." He returned a moment later with a glass of water.

The glass felt greasy in Panglor's hand, and the water smelled rusty, but Panglor sipped at it greedily. His mouth felt loathsome. He looked back at LePiep and saw her staring at him imploringly. "Why do you have her in that cage?" he croaked harshly. "She didn't do anything."

"Friend, we'll do the talking," the man said, taking away the glass before Panglor had finished. He bent and squinted at Panglor, then turned to another man in the corner of the room. "Okay, Mister Garikoff. I think he's awake."

The man called Garikoff came forward. He was an older man; he was dressed expensively, but his face bore the scars and stains of the cheap cosmetics popular among laborers on Veti IV. Glinting pins held back his hair, and his eyes shone wide and intent. When he spoke, his voice filtered through a layer of gravel. "Pilot Balef, why don't you sit up, so we can talk man to man?"

Panglor slid his legs down off the slab and forced his body upright. He still felt lightheaded; he breathed shallowly, trying not to upset his stomach again.

"That's better," said Garikoff. He stood with his short legs wide apart in a fighter's stance. "Now, Balef, you were apprehended trespassing on the yards of the Vikken Rail Conglomerate."

Panglor grunted.

Garikoff watched him quizzically. "I presume you know that trespassing with intent to steal is a felony here—with criminal and civil penalties."

Panglor remained silent. There was a chill spreading through his gut, but he had nothing to say to the likes of these people. Whatever they were, they were clearly not the law.

"Severe penalties," Garikoff said. "Very severe penalties. And the fact that force was required to stop you—that's resistance."

"Who are you?" Panglor growled.

"I know a lot about you, Balef," said Garikoff. "I suppose it's only fair I should tell you who we are. We're not the law. That's good for you, because the law could be a lot tougher on you than we're going to be." He held Panglor's gaze intently. "I'm Lousa Garikoff. This here's Lid, and that's all you need to know about him, I guess." He was pointing at the man who had spoken first. Now he hooked a thumb at a third man, sitting in the corner. "That's Billijo. Maybe later my partner Grakoff will be in, and then we can have a real party." He laughed contemptuously.

"Okay, Balef. We've got you. Lid here works for the Crompton Security Systems, and they work for the Vikken Railyards, and he can put you under arrest right now. But—he also works for me." Garikoff smiled. "Now me, I don't work for any of them. I work for myself. But I might be able to help you out of this jam you're in. How would you like to fly a ship for me?"

Suddenly the name registered. *Garikoff*. Of Grakoff-Garikoff? That was a shipping firm, relatively small but well known, with one of the lowest reputations in the area. Why would they want him? "No, thanks," he muttered.

Garikoff studied him for a moment. "You're not impressed with my offer, I see."

Feigning courage, Panglor moved as though to stand.

"Sit down!" Garikoff barked.

Panglor sat, feeling cold. Garikoff pulled at his collar and continued. "Balef, you don't stand a chance of getting off this planet. You were canned by Vikken five weeks ago. Psychiatric incompetence." His eyes pierced Panglor. "True, I don't doubt, but that doesn't make you any worse than the rest of the incompetents they've got over there. But that doesn't matter—because you've got that record now, and *you'll never fly again*. Except we're giving you a chance."

He paused to observe Panglor's reaction and seemed disappointed when Panglor displayed none. "All right. You're in trouble with the law—big trouble—and if Vikken prosecutes, you'll wind up in the prison mines. You know about those?" Panglor hesitated, then shook his head. "They're *bad*, Balef. Lots of people don't come out of them alive."

Panglor nodded numbly.

Garikoff gazed at him fiercely, and to avoid the gaze, Panglor looked at LePiep. Garikoff said, "Your animal might miss you."

Panglor looked up angrily.

"Now, don't get upset. I was just pointing out the kind of thing that can happen if you don't use your brains."

Panglor looked back at LePiep and said nothing.

"Aren't you going to ask me why we want you? There's not much in your record to recommend you, especially after that botch of bringing in your last ship." Garikoff chuckled, shaking his head. "Oh, yes, we have your whole record. You'd be a good pilot, probably, if you weren't so unstable. Good performance profiles—but a record from your toes up of bad personality reports. Falling apart between trips and during trips, depression, crew friction—it's all in there." He shook his head again, in mock admiration. "Balef, the hell of it is, you're a good pilot."

"*Damn* good pilot," Panglor snarled.

"But a disaster." Garikoff paused. "Now, if you had the right incentive holding you together, I'll bet you could do a real job. I'll bet you could. And I'm going to give you that chance. Your last chance. What do you say?"

"What's the catch?"

Garikoff shifted so that he was in the way of the light, silhouetted. Then he turned, and his face became visible again, scarred, with those wide eyes. "Why, no catch. Not if you complete the job."

No catch, thought Panglor. That meant there was a very large catch. Probably it was a job no sane pilot would fly—probably dangerous, probably illegal.

"You'll receive a ship and your instructions," said Garikoff. "I wouldn't hide from you that there'll be a certain risk involved, but you did say you were a good pilot. 'Damn good pilot,' I think you said." He looked at Panglor shrewdly, then glanced at LePiep, mewling in her cage. His expression was chilling. "Anyway," said Garikoff, "your alternatives—well, the mines are—well, they're just not a pleasant place to live. Or to die."

Panglor tensed with outrage and fear. It was one thing for this Garikoff to threaten him, but he was threatening LePiep, too, and that was more than an honest man could accept. Well, he wouldn't be pushed this way; he'd do a little pushing back, as soon as he had a better opportunity.

Seemingly reading his thoughts, Garikoff gestured to Lid, who reached for his weapon. They both stared at the cage, at the ou-ralot. Lid fingered the butt of his gun.

"No!" Panglor snarled, halfway to his feet. He was stopped by the sight of the weapon pointed at his chest.

Garikoff nodded. "Do you think you'd rather fly?"

Thinking furiously and getting nowhere, Panglor knew he was defeated—at least for now. Perhaps it wouldn't be so bad; at least he'd be getting back into space and off this damned planet. "All right," he growled. But nothing said he couldn't try to beat them later.

Nodding again, Garikoff said, "Be ready to take tomorrow afternoon's shuttle to the orbital yards. This time tomorrow. You'll get your pass and instructions at the spaceport."

"What time is it now?"

"Seventeen oh five," answered Lid, who seemed disappointed that Panglor had backed down.

"All right. Give me back my ou-ralot, and I'll be there then," Panglor said, standing.

Garikoff scratched his neck. "I think we'll keep your animal here, just as a little guarantee—"

"No." Flatly.

Startled, Garikoff stared at him, then shook his head. "I thought we had an understanding, but I guess we'll have to show—"

"No deal. She comes with me or I don't fly. Period." Panglor squinted at him angrily.

"She'll be returned to you as soon as—"

"No deal."

Garikoff studied him; Panglor crossed his arms and

stared back. He tried to think reassuring thoughts toward LePiep, who was jittering about in her cage.

Relaxing, Garikoff said, "All right. You can take her. But you remember something. You don't have anything—you don't have an ounce of freedom—until this job is done. We've got people in places you wouldn't dream of—and that includes every place you're going. You will only make one mistake, because one will be your last. Am I being clear?"

Panglor glared back, but didn't reply.

The door opened suddenly. A man walked in who looked remarkably like Garikoff, except he was shorter, with fatter features. He looked briefly at Panglor and said, "Well?"

"He's our man," Garikoff said. "He leaves tomorrow."

"Are you sure he can handle it?" The fat man hooked his thumb scornfully at Panglor.

"He can do it. Balef, you ready to leave?"

"You're letting him *go*?" The fat man's eyebrows quivered as he arched them.

"Who is *he*?" Panglor asked belligerently.

"Yeah, I'm letting him go," said Garikoff. "He's Grakoff, my partner. My brother, too, you could say. You can go now. Just remember what I told you."

"Hold it!" Grakoff protested.

Garikoff's annoyance was clearly growing. As he looked at his partner, he said to Panglor, "Tell you what, Balef. Since you may never have the chance again, we'll stand you to a night out—on us. Have yourself a woman if you want; it may be a long time before you see one again—that way, anyhow. There's a place called Jeddle's Nest—go there and have yourself a time, and we'll fix it so you can charge it to us. Okay?" Garikoff's eyes never left his partner as he talked to Panglor. "Now, Balef, get the hell out of here.

Take your bird with you. And be there tomorrow or you're a dead man. Got that?"

Panglor's face was hot as he scooped LePiep out of the cage. His duffel lay on the floor, by the door, by Lid's feet. He picked that up, too, and went out the door without a glance back. Lid slammed the door behind him.

Panglor soothed LePiep and looked around; he was standing in a dingy corridor. He went through a battered door and stepped out onto a landing—and gazed at the spaceport. A flight of stone steps led to the ground. The building was part of a cluster of old buildings in a remote corner of the spaceport grounds. The landing field lay between him and the main entrance. The spaceport lights gleamed coldly on the metal railings in the early-evening darkness.

Somehow the fact that he had been held in an old warehouse made him angrier than ever. Well, he would make things even somehow, sometime. But meanwhile he had better do what they told him.

He hurried down the steps and got away from the spaceport as fast as he could walk.

The first thing he realized was that he was starved, and so was LePiep. There wasn't much money left; but on the other hand, he didn't have much use for cash, beyond a meal and a room for the night. Tomorrow he was off on some deathflight; or if it wasn't, he expected to be paid for it. So there was no reason not to squander what cash he had.

And he had a night at Jeddle's Nest coming, on Garikoff. He didn't much like the idea of taking something from a man who had held him prisoner and threatened him, but he guessed he wouldn't mind having a few stiff bangers, and if there was a stoker he liked, maybe that, too. But he'd pay for his own dinner tonight.

They had dinner in a quiet place he knew. Together, they chewed their way through two main courses and a dessert, then went back to the rooming house. They didn't stay; Panglor simply paid for one more night in the same room and left his bag there. Franken, as usual, sat coiled near the lift tube. "Back tonight, gone tomorrow, eh, sir?" Franken said, startling him. Panglor stared at him uneasily. Franken seemed innocent enough, but his odd remark was too accurate for comfort, as though the man had sources for his insights. Panglor turned away, grunting, "Begone, yourself." Ghost. And he walked out of the lobby and into the street, wondering how soon a report of his actions would reach Garikoff.

After wandering a while, stalling, he gave up and went into Jeddle's Nest. The place set him on edge at once; it was crowded, the music was jarring, and the small holographic figures that danced lewdly in the air both tantalized and annoyed him. He considered leaving—but no, he was here for a few bangers, and maybe more, and he was going to have them. He pushed his way through to the bar, then leaned over toward the bartender and explained that he was on Garikoff's tab. The bartender scrutinized the bartop as he talked, but nodded when he was finished. "Then— I'll have a Feldman," he said. An instant later, he realized that ethanol was really not what he wanted; but it was already in front of him. The bartender was fast.

He shrugged and moved away from the bar, sipping the drink. LePiep was perched nervously on his shoulder. The alcohol spread in a fine mist over the sensory endings of his brain, and he *knew* that this wasn't the right drink for tonight. This would make him groggy; what he needed was a stiff does of jeeric acid to liven him up. LePiep bounced up and down on his shoulder, whistling. "Does that mean I'm right?" he asked her. Or was she just excited by the scandalous things those holographic figures were doing to each other over the tables?

Edging back to the bar, he put the Feldman down and asked for a double jeeric acid (and vaguely wondered how much Garikoff was going to let him spend). He picked his teeth thoughtfully and looked at the glass. The jeeric acid was yellow, with a reddish haze above its surface. He sipped, inhaling the fumes; the effect was like a draft of scented air flowing over his mind, splitting apart the congested lobes, and freeing and re-channeling certain emotional energies.

Feeling faintly exhilarated, he headed for the back room. Normally he wouldn't, not so quickly, anyway— but what was the point in delaying? LePiep murmured excitedly in his ear; *she* wanted him to go ahead. He passed through a shimmer-curtain and looked around. Several stokers were lounging about; he ignored the male and the androgyne and studied the three females. After a moment, he went to the second closest one and asked, "Are you taken? I have credit with the house to-night."

The woman looked up, startled. She had dark-tanned skin and black, shoulder-length hair cut in serrated fash-ion, and wore a silky lounging robe. She glanced at her companions, chuckled, and said, "That wasn't much of a fair-game opening. Don't you want to play? You might win me for free—or Evella, and she's more ex-pensive."

"Are you taken?" Panglor repeated, trying not to let himself become irritated.

"Wouldn't you like to win me for free? The all-night stoke?" she said, blinking slyly.

"No," he said, "I told you, I have house credit." He remembered now: Jeddle's Nest had some ridiculous system of competing for your stokers in a gambling game—the kind of thing he hated.

"You don't—"

"No." He pulled at his jeeric acid. The fumes moved powerfully through his head, and in a few minutes more he might not care; he'd occupy himself for the night with the fabulous mazes being opened in his mind by the jeer. But that wasn't what he wanted. The jeer was just to enhance his mood.

She watched him thoughtfully. "What's your name?" she asked, rising, with a shimmer of cloth.

"Panglor Balef. What's yours?"

"Taleena." She did something behind the railing where she had been sitting, then pointed to a plate on the rail and said, "Print there. You want the night?" Panglor nodded and touched where she had indicated. Satisfied, she straightened up and looked at him. Suddenly she frowned. "Is your animal safe?"

Panglor chuckled. "Sure she's safe. Haven't you ever seen an ou-ralot before? Gentlest animal there is."

Taleena didn't look entirely convinced, but she shrugged. "Seen some girls chewed up by strange pets before, that's all." She motioned for him to follow, and led him back through a dim hallway into a stoking room. The door opaqued behind them. LePiep was purring audibly now, and bunching her wings. Taleena looked at her with a softer expression and cautiously reached out to stroke the ou-ralot. Her hostility toward Panglor seemed to disappear. Either she had decided that she liked him, or she had slipped completely into her professional role. Panglor rather hoped that it was the latter; he could do without the entanglement of genuine liking.

He looked at her and didn't know what to say. The stoking room was comfortable, with a soft mat and wall hangings, and soft lighting; and it was well equipped—

the problem was to choose his favorite stoking enhancement. The truth was, he had little experience in this kind of thing. Taleena gestured along the wall. "We have wire, or lucigenic, or sensamp. And we have some special Kili devices, for something different."

Panglor stared, thinking. He chose the Kili devices.

With the barest of preliminaries, they undressed in silence. They touched, in the Kili field. Soon Panglor was aswarm in the warmth of Taleena's body; his senses rearranged themselves in a sea of electrified darkness. Sight and taste and touch ebbed from his awareness, but hearing and smell expanded and occupied new perceptual pathways in his mind. He heard the sound of his accelerating heartbeat, the rumbling and rushing of blood, and from his ear the huffing and vocalizations of Taleena's quickening breath. Musk penetrated his thoughts, and salt from the organic sea, funneled along live olfactory nerveways. Touch returned, from the *inside*. His skin became hot, and sensitive to the contractions of his own muscles. It quivered at the touch of Taleena's skin, the pressure of her bones, of her muscle and blood. An itching heat sent a runner of sensation up the back of his spine and then sank—a ball of warmth—into his stomach and pelvis. From his pelvis, he felt a stiff, tingling lance culminating in a point of itching fire.

Slowly he moved, aware of his shifting perspective in relation to Taleena; now she surrounded him more, now less, and the angles of touch changed, and with them changed the pressure of the itch that grew from the back of his pelvis forward. Visual awareness expanded. Her gaze bored into him with haunted desire, two eyes with auburn irises, pupils large; they began to revolve, to spin, to spiral into his mind. Electrical fire danced in her eyes, glowed in her cheeks. Musky incense penetrated his skull, stirring him to speed his movements.

Nerves and spine became hollow pathways for energy: tiny orange flames darting and licking their way up and down, and out and back, and expanding into the back of his pelvis, stuttering. A fire was burning in the focal point, feeding forward, flickering out to the muscles, to the base of the skull. Emotions roiled darkly, seeking release, seeking daylight, seeking to be burned clean.

There was a gasping and huffing of air, and dizzily he focused on the sound to realize that it was Taleena panting with mounting ferocity; it was his own breath, too, and the two winds met and split in tongues. The flames danced hotter and flickered yellow and white through his inner space, and leaked out and toasted his skin, and her skin. Hotter still, they smoked of incense, and forged him strong and stiff and hard, glittering at the tip. The focus moved quickly, thrusting, sliding out of rhythm, hard—and erupted from the base of his spine, from the pelvis, firing forward through the lance and out from the tip in two, five, seven shock waves into the surrounding medium. And the medium bucked back, reflecting the shock waves, and across the continuum Taleena gasped and vocalized, her sound waves swarming upon his thoughts. And then the fire was spent, but still the medium rocked with echoes of the eruptions, the waves lifting him and squeezing and dropping suddenly, washing over him like the breath of a hot fan.

Time echoed in its own waves through the continuum, and after certain passages of time, the contact points slid and parted. Electricity leaked away, heat radiated, but the smoke lingered and was the last vestige of the fire to pass away.

Gradually Panglor emerged from the Kili field, his awareness returning to reality. Taleena rolled back from him, her hair tussled, her face glistening. He smiled hesitantly. She returned the smile, and for a moment he was afraid. But the fear danced away. A great charge of emotion had been burned from him, vented in blissful release, and he almost felt sane. He gave her a half-smile and half-frown, and lay back and looked at the Kili field instrument, now dark, its work done, and wondered what the Kili had designed it for.

Be careful now. Keep the thoughts and the wits together.

LePiep touched him gently with her nose. She crouched at the edge of the stoking mat and watched him; she was content from his pleasure, and only at the edge of her peacefulness was there an echo of his uncertainty—bewilderment, in these glowing, fuzzy moments after stoking. Panglor stroked her with a finger, wondering how long he could feel calm.

"She enjoyed it, didn't she?" Taleena asked, pushing herself up on one elbow to watch LePiep.

Panglor nodded. Really, he didn't want to talk about LePiep with a stoker. LePiep was personal to him, and personal matters shouldn't be involved here.

Taleena nodded, as though understanding. She got up. "Come on," she said, tugging at him. "We have ten minutes in the massage." She paled a door in the far corner of the room and went out into a hallway. Panglor watched her rear bouncing, and then hurried after her, stumbling as he tried to pull on his pants. When he caught up with Taleena in a warm, tiled chamber, she chuckled and said, "Throw your pants back in the other room. They'll be all right." Reluctantly he obeyed, tossing them over LePiep's head as she crept in behind him. Taleena did something at the far wall.

A mist issued from the walls, encircling them. Panglor drew back uneasily, but when the mist touched him with a gentle caress, he started to relax. It felt good. The mist deepened quickly, and a moment later he could barely see Taleena—just the outline of her face and arms, the points of her breasts. She stepped closer and put a finger to his chest. "Feel okay?" she asked quietly.

"Hhrruuu," said LePiep, from somewhere in the mist.

Panglor felt a curious pressure against his skin. It was the mist, kneading him with rippling compression waves. He stood silent, blinking; the warm vapors massaged him gently and fluidly. His neck and shoulder and back muscles relaxed, drained of tension. His face softened, and he almost smiled again.

When the mist receded, Taleena watched him with twinkling eyes. She looked down at LePiep and laughed. The ou-ralot was walking in a big circle, grinning, eyes wide, her fur fluffed as though dry cleaned, but glistening with a few droplets of moisture. Panglor was caught by simultaneous feelings: amused by LePiep, awed by the sight of Taleena's unclothed body, and disturbed by her warmth and apparent liking for him. Tension began to reenter his muscles, and he started to get another erection, a funny, twitchy one. Flushing with embarrassment, he turned away from Taleena, scooped up LePiep, and returned to their room.

Taleena seemed puzzled and hurt when she caught up with him. "Didn't you enjoy it?" she asked.

Panglor looked at her again and had trouble breathing. She stood with her legs parted, hands on her hips, her skin and pubic mound still damp, gleaming. "Yes," he said, choking. He tried to pull on his pants, but his erection was growing stronger, and he couldn't manage. He suddenly sat and covered his lap with his shirt. "Yes—yes, fine."

Now she's upset. Why'd you get her upset?

Taleena slipped on her robe, without fastening it. "What's wrong then? You paid the whole night. Are you going to leave?"

"Y-yes," he stuttered. "No." He thought frantically. A chance to stay with a woman, maybe the last ever. "I guess—I'll stay a little while." He couldn't look up at her, though; his feelings were too exposed in his confusion. What is the matter? he wondered. Why can't you just let it go like it was going, and don't make problems?

He looked up, finally. Her robe was partly open, and the frontal view it provided made his nervous system start ringing again.

She noticed his glance and pulled the robe closed, then sat down a few feet from him. "Is that better?"

He nodded and swallowed. Trouble was, he liked her, too. Why did she have to be friendly?

"You want to just talk?" Taleena said, lowering her gaze pointedly to his lap, where his clothes were bunched absurdly. He felt a twinge under his clothes and squinted, shrugging. She was just trying to lighten things. "Hey, it's okay," she said. "Not many spacers I meet in here want to do that, you know? It's kind of nice for a change." He looked at her in puzzlement, and she said, "It's okay to be shy, too." He looked away, red-faced, and reached out to scoop back LePiep, who was wandering away, gurgling in a troubled tone.

"Can I see her?" Taleena asked. Panglor hesitated, then guided LePiep over with his hand. The ou-ralot tiptoed forward and nuzzled Taleena's fingers. Taleena fussed over her for a minute, then said, "She's a honey." She stroked the ou-ralot again, and LePiep crooned with pleasure.

Panglor felt a twinge of jealousy. At once, LePiep hopped out of Taleena's lap and came back to him. "Hrruuu?" she said.

"I can see where her loyalties are," Taleena said good-naturedly. As she spoke, she leaned forward, and the top of her robe fell open, exposing her right breast.

Panglor tensed, torn by confused desires. Taleena pulled her robe together again. "Sorry," she said gently.

"Why? It's your job." He looked away, scowling.

"I wasn't thinking of business. I just didn't want you to feel uncomfortable." She was clearly puzzled.

Panglor shrugged, nodded, shook his head. Sexual desire was dancing above his many other dark thoughts. He could give in to it if it was just business with her. But no—she liked him, she was concerned for his comfort, and any moment she would ask him what was troubling him. That terrified him—the prospect that someone could ask, could care. Perhaps he should get out of here before things got out of control.

"Do you want to talk about anything?" she asked. She peered at him, frowning.

His eyes refused to focus for a moment. This was all wrong. He had come here for a mindless, high-intensity stoking—just flush out the glands, clear the mind, and get out—but look what was happening. She wanted to touch him as a woman, not just a stoker. But he had other worries, he had to get his life in order—no, Grakoff-Garikoff had already done that, hadn't they?— but he still had to do it for himself.

He sat ruminating for some time, before he became aware of Taleena touching his hand, and saying, "Hey. Come on. *Come on.*"

Jerking his head up, he met her gaze. But he couldn't answer. She *liked* him, for God's sake.

"It's nothing," he muttered finally, managing an unhappy smile. He was sweaty, and he felt clumsy, fumbling at his tangled clothing.

"Do you want to get dressed? We can just sit here all night, if you want. Maybe you'll feel like talking later." Her gaze was soft and real, and it was killing him. So warm, so human. Why couldn't she have remained a ghost? Now she was going to be angry because he was failing to respond, and that would be human, too.

LePiep was burrowing nervously into the turned-back coverlet on the mat. He watched her dumbly for a few seconds. "I—" he said. "I—" He looked at his hands, and up at Taleena, and away again, and he blurted, "I—have to go. Now." He struggled to his feet, conscious of his nakedness but no longer caring, and he started putting on his clothes. LePiep whistled unhappily, but he was too busy avoiding Taleena's gaze to worry about LePiep. His left foot caught in the pant leg, and he jammed it through anyway, ripping the fabric. Taleena's expression was narrow and disappointed—he hadn't meant to look; it had just happened—but he couldn't do anything to make her feel better, either. He thumbed down his shirt and pants fastenings, and clipped on his shoes. He looked around. LePiep. "Hup!" he said harshly, and caught her when she jumped. She trembled silently in his arms.

His eyes got blurry as he faced Taleena. She was standing, too, and he thought that she was upset, and maybe crying, but actually he couldn't see clearly to tell. "Uh—" he said.

"Well," said Taleena.

"I—"

"If you have to, then—well, I guess you should if you have to."

"But I—" Blood was rushing so hard through his head that all he could hear was the thunder of falling water, a waterfall drowning thoughts that got swept into the current. Space, tomorrow he'd be in space, and—the waterfall was louder, and a woman who might have touched him was disappearing downstream—rushing water, get away, get clear!

He edged toward the door. Taleena nodded—her disappointment, her humanity stabbing at him. You're a ghost, you can't hurt me, can't.

Closer to the door now, he hesitated one last time, waiting for Taleena to put back on her professional indifference; only she didn't, wouldn't, or couldn't, and he had to walk away from her humanity. He went out quickly, LePiep trembling in his arms. But it was the wrong door. He turned and walked back through, face burning as he walked past Taleena's eyes, and out the correct exit.

The Nest was quiet. He hurried through the parlor and out into the night.

Nolaran fell away beneath him right on schedule the next afternoon. He couldn't see it happen, because all he could see was a scarred green bulkhead in front of his seat, the worst in the shuttle. But he could picture it; and good riddance to the hellhole. The shuttle lurched and banged around, giving him and the rest of the passengers an inexcusably rough ride through Veti IV's atmosphere. He gripped his armrests and thought about getting back into space. That part was okay. What was bad was the worrying about what Grakoff-Garikoff had planned for him.

The shuttle docked late, after a traffic tie-up at the orbital spaceyards. Panglor found his way to the dispatcher's office, where he was given a set of command papers for a foreshortening freighter—Driscoll-class, a dead giveaway that the ship was some damned ancient relic. He studied the flight plan, directing him to jump for Dreznelles 3 and wait for further instructions. According to the schedule dictated here, he had an hour to get over to the ship at her mooring and get her powered up for flight—no time for preflight inspection. That stunk. Panglor Balef never took a ship into deep space, much less foreshortening, without a thorough preflight.

Bastards. He'd see about that; he'd change the flight plan.

He tapped in an opening code for the ship on the com-console. As he did so, he noticed a spacer nearby, a station man, staring at him in a particularly unfriendly manner, clicking his thumbnails together. Callused, strong-looking hands. A Garikoff agent? Probably.

Maybe he wouldn't change the flight plan.

He cleared his throat and looked over the ship's registry. According to the listing here, the ship had no name. He supplied one: *The Fighting Cur*.

Clearing the console, he picked up LePiep in her quarantine bag. Then he went and found a taxi, and hurried out to look over this ship he was going to fly.

5

Panglor eyed the clock grumpily and closed his eyes again. He cared not a damn about these corporations, with their cutthroat rivalries. But they hadn't asked him if he cared.

All of known space was an amoeba seventy light-years long and fifty across the middle, sprinkled with star systems inhabited by man and peppered with systems as yet unexplored. To corporate heads, space was a gameboard in three vast dimensions—and corporate heads were the ones who held the stones and played the game. Not that it was such an inaccurate way of viewing things, or inherently bad—but the games grew extremely fierce. Interstellar business was a strange mixture of courageous enterprise, vain intelligence, trickery and deceit, backstabbing and extortion. None of it made sense to him. With thousands of worlds awaiting exploration, they killed each other for morsels—usually under the guise of peaceful operations and the umbrella of the Foreshortening Trade Coalition. Sabotage and trickery were simply facets of the game. Perhaps the fear of foreshortening hardened corporate hearts; definitely, it increased the stakes.

0358.

Foreshortening—there was the irony. Foreshortening had opened the stars to mankind; it had not been meant as a tool for treachery. Surely it was hard enough to face the uncertainty of transit, frightening in itself, without treachery. And yet, there it was. A capsule of distorted space. A pulled stitch, a kink, a Lang dimensional stress in space—a ten-thousandfold collapse!— and all it took was for the stitch to pop, the kink to straighten, the stress to come undone at the wrong time, and a man was adrift to die, in his own universe if he was lucky or in some limbo if he was not. And here: people deliberately knocking ships into faulty insertions. Was this what foreshortening had been meant for?

0412.

0420.

He came alert with a start. 0425. No putting it off any longer. Time to check out of the waystation and get back to the *Cur*. The flight plan was logged and computed, both the phony and the real, and the *Cur* would leave mooring in four hours, less than one hour behind *Deerfield*.

He had been doing a lot of thinking, all right, but none of it had helped him find a way out of this.

"Hooeep?" whistled LePiep, complaining for attention. She caught his eye and tossed her head insolently.

Panglor rubbed her neck with his knuckles. "Sorry, honey." It had really been more like a brooding stupor than what one would actually call thinking. "Don't see a way out of it, old buddy. We want to still be alive next week, wherever we are, so I guess we're going to bump that ship right into limbo." He hesitated, then shrugged. "They never did anything for us, anyway."

He got up and packed his duffel. There was one loose wafer, which he fed to the ou-ralot. He scratched her, shaking his head.

By 0525, they were back aboard *The Fighting Cur*. LePiep began hopping about, burrowing into the clutter they'd left in the control room. Panglor logged the flight program into the ship's console from his pocket computer, then set about checking the ship. She had been worked over by station techs, and her small cargo of Veti IV metals products off-loaded; but that was all the more reason to check her thoroughly. Panglor never liked leaving a ship in the care of others. He walked through the habitable sections: cabin, galley, airlock, repair cubicle, lifesystems, power room. He sniffed about warily, but found nothing to arouse suspicion.

On second thought, he returned to the power room and checked the remote readings. Internal power and grav-control were fine, but—sure enough—some numbskull tech had failed to tighten an alignment on the neutrino flux. Cursing, he set about making the correction himself; with the overpower circuits G-G had built into the main drivers, he wanted to be damn sure the pile was tuned. No point in blowing himself to kingdom come. That job, by the time he was done, took two hours. He had to hurry the rest of the preflight, then he battened down and went to power up the control room for flight.

By the time he had stashed enough of the clutter to make the bay look like a ship's bridge, the com-console was chirping at him, warning of departure time. "LePiep!" he called, slapping the second couch. The ou-ralot poked her head up, sniffed, and scurried out of sight. He glared. "Peep! Get up here!" he roared. Sighing audibly, the ou-ralot hopped up beside him. He grunted. "Stay there," he said, powering up the board. The viewscreen came alive, and the control bay lights went down. "Waystation Control," he growled into the com. "*The Fighting Cur* to undock and proceed." Control responded and then it became a matter of waiting.

The spidery tugs soon came and latched and pulled the *Cur* out of mooring, and Panglor watched the immense cluster of the D3 Waystation shrink against space like a glittering surrealistic beehive. Then the tugs broke and departed, and he took control over his ship and locked her into the acceleration run in the outbound linear-shift field. For several hours he accelerated under external field power alone; then he engaged the *Cur*'s drivers and used both ship's power and the station's field power to accelerate toward the insertion orbit. They would drive at about four gees for a day, before insertion.

Things would happen fast tomorrow, and he had to be right on the beam to make it work. He would be traveling at one hell of a clip, and so would *Deerfield*. The traffic patrol usually moved fast on regular watch, as well—though not that fast—and if Garikoff was shadowing him, his ship would be doing the same. Quite a party, speeding toward the collapsing-field. Panglor had two main worries. One was having a hole punched in him by the patrol craft if he deviated from flight path, or by Garikoff if he did not. The other was the actual maneuver. *Deerfield* and the *Cur* would be plunging through the collapsing-field at different angles, for different insertions. He had to deviate enough to put him on collision course, count on *Deerfield* to swerve out of his path, and still have his own course set for good insertion.

It was going to be tough.

Once everything was on auto, he frowned at LePiep. "Hungry, bud?" She whistled in the affirmative. He was hungry, too, so they went back into the galley. He had a flatwrap cake and moke, and LePiep had the usual. When they returned to the control room, he brooded on the instruments and the stars for a while, then shrugged and closed his eyes. "Wake me if anything happens, Peep," he muttered, and with that he dozed off.

He woke with thoughts crawling through his mind like termites. It was all he could do to focus his eyes. Was he really going to do what Garikoff wanted? Which was the greater wrath—Garikoff's or the law's? Garikoff would probably be watching him more closely, but still . . . if he was going to risk his neck under the gun either way, why should he do what Garikoff wanted? Maybe they didn't think he would rebel. Maybe they didn't give him enough credit.

Maybe he could bluff.

"Hey, Piglor!" he heard.

His heart nearly seized. He twisted right, then left. Sitting in the corner of the control bay, watching him, was Alontelida Castley—the little twitch who had plagued him back at the station.

He began to choke. He squeezed his eyes closed and forced himself to breathe slowly and regularly. His eyes popped open. The girl was watching him with amusement. "What are you doing here?" he yelled.

Alo chuckled and got up from where she was sitting. "I'm stowing away."

"What do you mean, you're stowing away?" He rose from his couch—and staggered, dizzy with rage.

"I'm here, aren't I?" She shrugged, then backed away slowly. "Now, don't get excited—"

Panglor fumed, staring at her. This was incredible. What the hell? Of all the people in the universe . . . of all the *incredibly* goddamn stupid things for any human being to do . . .

Alo took a deep breath, then blurted: "I know where you're going, and I want to go along. I can help you with the ship—I know a lot about ships." She shut her mouth. Then she shrugged again, eyes glinting.

"You think you know where I'm going," he said sarcastically. He shook his head, trying to clear the cobwebs. This was impossible. "You *think* you know where I'm *going*?" he growled. He snorted.

"Yeah. I checked your flight log. You're going to Quetzal, in the Formi system." She looked at the viewscreen, then at him, then nodded.

"Oh," he said. Christ! he thought. For a moment, he said nothing more, because there was this incredible pressure building in his forehead, right behind the frontal sinuses. "Oh," he said tightly. "It never occurred to you that maybe I was going to Dreznelles 17, then Atruba, then the Elacian National Worlds. That never occurred to you."

"No. Should it have?" She lifted her chin insolently, but her eyes showed confusion. "Are we?"

He cursed silently. His hand stopped LePiep, who was bobbing her head suspiciously toward Alo. Waves of alarm touched him. "What did you do it for?" he demanded.

"To get out of there," said Alo. "I don't care where you're going—I'll go there."

He scowled again.

"I hid in the equipment locker. I needed to escape." She turned toward the viewscreen. Her eyes were dark with emotion; there was something swirling in her gaze, some hatred that he did not want to know about.

"Came to the wrong place," he said sardonically. His head ached fiercely. What was it he had been thinking about? Bluffing Garikoff? "Hope you brought your own food," he added. "Mine isn't for sale."

"As a matter of fact, I brought a whole bagful."

"Good. Go eat it. I have problems to solve, and I don't need you here making them worse." His eyes were watering, and it seemed to be affecting his brain. This bitch—on his ship! Good Christ. But he couldn't worry about her now—he *had* to figure how to beat Garikoff. What was the thread he'd been following? Bluffing . . . how? Start the run on *Deerfield*, then sheer off through the field before any damage was done and hope to escape? At those velocities, G-G would have to be shadowing him pretty tightly to be sure of hitting him.

He stared at Alo, who had returned to the corner. LePiep purred uneasily and padded over to the opposite corner. "I can fly the ship," Alo said. "Just in case you're having trouble doing that."

Panglor grimaced, trying not to be distracted. "No," he muttered. "Too dangerous." It was too dangerous to cross G-G; they were sure to be watching him. They certainly wouldn't trust him.

Any more than he would trust them.

Trust them? They had promised to let him escape with the ship . . . but would they really want a live witness escaping? Suppose they didn't. Suppose they meant for him to be dead afterward. Suppose they had rigged the *Cur*—

With what?

Faulty engines?

Faulty computers?

A bomb?

Bomb. The blood drained from his face. He croaked, "Jesus—a bomb." Of course. The perfect way to guarantee their own safety. Rig the *Cur* to blow apart just before it went through the field—

It was obvious.

"Jesus." He sat back in his couch, feeling dizzy. "A

fucking bomb," he whispered. "But where?" The techs were all over the ship.

Alo looked at him strangely. She squinted. She dug a hand down under her collar to scratch her shoulder. "What are you talking about?" she said nervously. She got up and strode across the control bay and stared at the viewscreen with her hands on her hips. Then she turned. "Did you say there was a bomb on this ship?" she demanded.

He focused with difficulty, cleared his throat, and coughed convulsively. "Might be," he grunted finally. Now think, think, think. Where should you look for a bomb?

"Why?" Alo said.

He lowered his eyebrows. "Are you crazy?" he snarled. "What difference does it make *why*? If there is, there is, and we've got to find it. It could be timed, it could be remote, it could be damn near just about any kind of bomb that there is." Should have been going over the ship instead of wasting time at the waystation. That was probably why they left the neutrino aligner loose—to keep him busy. He pressed the knuckles of both fists to the corners of his forehead.

Suddenly he jumped up. His fingers moved on the console. The viewscreen flickered and showed the outer hull, down one side. "What are you doing?" Alo asked.

"Shut up." He crossed his arms and watched the screen, squinting at every detail; the view switched to another section of the hull, switched again. "Inspection scan. Through the sensor-fringe," he said abruptly. "Look for anything that looks like a bomb."

"What's a bomb look like?"

"How the hell do I know?" He knew he sounded scared, and he wished he didn't. LePiep hopped onto the console, keeping her distance from Alo, and peered along with them, nervously.

The scan ended. "Nothing," he said angrily. He turned to Alo and shouted, *"Nothing!"* He was nearly blind with rage. On the entire hull of the *Cur* they had found nothing but dents. He blinked. "There's a bomb on this ship," he said quietly. "I know there is."

"Probably it's inside," Alo said.

"No kidding. You start down that side, I'll start down this side. Look everywhere—in every compartment, behind every panel. *Jeeez.*"

Together, they began searching the ship, right down to the cargo hold and the interhull spaces; most especially, they searched in places that would normally not be visited. Panglor checked the pile chamber on telescan, and he went down into the hold and poked about in the spooky, echoing chambers. Alo joined him there—but everywhere they looked, they found nothing.

"Why are you so sure there's a bomb?" she asked, her voice reverberating. "What's going on?" Her tone was impatient, as though she suspected him of being fruity, or paranoid.

Stepping toward her, he tipped his head back and looked down his nose. Squash her. Yes, just go ahead and squash her.

Wait—

He had checked the outer hull through the sensor-fringe. Through the computer. Suppose Garikoff had anticipated him, had rigged the computer, had loaded it with recorded inspection images?

"Dear God," he breathed. He stamped out of the hold and hurried back to the bridge. Alo followed. Squinting at the screen, he set the ship into a slow longitudinal roll. "They wouldn't count on just gunners," he muttered. "I know they wouldn't." The stars turned in the screen as the ship rolled. Then he switched to the inspection scan. The image flickered: There was the hull, and behind it were the stars, stone steady. He chewed a knuckle. He wasn't used to this kind of thinking. What the hell could he do now? He worked furiously at the com-console, but couldn't get a real image; Garikoff had set blocks in the programming. *"Damn it!"* he screamed, slamming down his fist.

"They bitched your computer, huh?" said Alo, scratching her cheek. "That probably means there's something out there."

"Got to go outside and look."

"Wait a minute. Maybe I can clear that for you."

"Sure." He started slowing the ship's roll.

Ignoring his sarcasm, she went on, "I mean it. Normally I wouldn't, because you're being such a bitch— but my life's on the line, too."

"Forget it," he growled. "I'm going out, and you keep your *hands off.*"

"You go suit up," she said. "I won't hurt anything. I'll get this program straightened out, and I'll have a search underway before you're even outside. Take you forever to cover the whole ship yourself." Before he could move to stop her, she canceled his de-spin program on the console. He started to protest, but she cut him off. "I still need that spin. Now go."

He gave her a dark look. "Hurt LePiep and I'll kill you," he warned. Then he hurried down to the airlock. Inside, he stripped off his jumpsuit and pulled on the mesh silversuit. Leaving the headpiece in the airlock, he rushed back to the bridge.

Alo had a satisfied look on her face. The screen showed another inspection scan, but this time the stars were moving with the ship's roll. He stared open-mouthed for a moment, then thundered, "How did you do that?"

The girl ignored his question. "Look at these," she said, working the controls. "I'm not sure what they are." The viewscreen split into thirds, showing three different views, three different protrusions on the hull.

Panglor squinted. "Left one's okay—that's sensor gear. The middle one—that's probably a bomb, all right. The right one—no. That's the com-hump."

"I don't mean the hump," Alo said impatiently. "I mean that little thing behind it." She pointed on the screen to a small shape, which looked like a shadow on the back edge of the hump.

"That could be a bomb, too. I gotta get out there." He slapped in the de-spin program and cut off the drivers to kill the acceleration. They would have to make it up afterward. "When I give the word, you zero the g-field."

"Hurry," she said. He glared at her. "I'll keep looking," she added.

He returned to the airlock and put on his headpiece and hardware pack. He energized the field in his spacesuit, and the skintight mesh turned to quicksilver. Thirty seconds passed, while the airlock depressurized. "Okay," he said. "Zero grav."

"Mmpff," he heard, and then he was floating, weightless. He opened the outer port and drifted outside. Had he not been so scared, he would have enjoyed the view: D3, the stars, the galaxy. But he didn't enjoy it. What the hell did he know about bombs? He'd never even seen one—not unless you counted mining charges back in the 82 Eri asteroid belt.

He breathed deeply, then aimed himself and jetted slowly back along the hull, toward the stern. First he stopped over the object he had identified as a bomb. It was a squarish box obviously attached to the hull recently. It was also, he discovered after a few minutes of work, simply a cover over a section of plumbing, probably connected to the modified drivers.

"What'd you find?" That was Alo's voice, loud in his ear.

"This isn't it," he growled. "Have you found anything else?" He pushed himself away from the box, reoriented himself to the ship and the stars, and jetted back toward the com-hump. "Well?"

For several minutes, there was no answer. Then: "Puglor."

"Listen, brat, that's not my—"

"Yeah, well, look behind you, on your right. Something in the shadows, behind that strut."

Muttering, he looked. There was a bracing member that secured the escape pod to the outer hull; he couldn't see a thing behind it until he shined a light. Then he saw it—a box. And this one *was* a bomb. It was a standard blastex rocksplitter, exactly like the ones used in the asteroids, with a remote trigger. "Jesus," he whispered. For God's sake now, be calm! How are you going to be calm with a bomb in front of you? Never mind, just do it! "Kid—I've gotta disarm this bastard. Don't do anything to mess me up." He maneuvered himself into position and drew out a unitool. Suddenly he felt calmer. "Keep looking, though." He reached out with a silvery arm toward the bomb.

Minutes later, the box was in his hand, just one more disassembled mechanism. His heart thundered in his ears. The bastards, the devious fucking bastards. They were going to do this to him.

That clinched one thing. Whatever else he did, he was not carrying out Garikoff's instructions. "I'll kill the bastards first," he growled. Gripping a cleat, he hurled the bomb away from the ship with all of his strength. The box glittered against the black emptiness, then vanished.

He steadied himself from the recoil of his throw, then

started making his way toward the com-hump again. Alo came on, saying, "I don't see anything else." He ignored her and kept moving. The com-hump was forward, partway around the curvature of the hull. "Where are you going?" Alo asked. "Your animal's going crazy in here."

"Touch her and I'll break your neck!" he thundered.

"I won't hurt her," said Alo, annoyed. "Where are you going?"

He squinted, drifting into the ship's shadow; for an instant he could see nothing. "Where was that thing we saw back behind the com-hump?" he asked, revolving slowly to peer along the hull.

"What? Oh, to your—wait, I can't see—okay, to your right and forward about ten meters. Do you think—"

"Just keep searching," he snapped. There it is, there it is—now, *what* is it?

He braked, landing. It was a second bomb, mounted at the base of the hump, like a small mole.

He reached out and quickly began disconnecting the device. He opened its cover, shaking with rage. The bomb was a timed device, probably set to go off after his insertion. So they'd meant to kill him, regardless—no mess, no fuss, no one to talk. The bastards. *The Christin' bastards.*

"Another?" asked Alo.

"I'll *kill* the mothers!" he snarled. Carefully, very carefully, he poked at the fiber circuitry. Could be booby-trapped, though probably they didn't imagine he would find it in the first place. It wasn't; and two minutes later it, like the first bomb, was spinning away into space.

If the sons of bitches thought they'd beat him with gadgetry, they were wrong.

* * *

"Are you sure the hull's clear?" he asked as he strode into the control bay. LePiep hurled herself at him, whistling with joy. He caught her, grunting, and looked around. The room was a disaster; clothes and food packets and papers had gone everywhere in the zero grav.

"I'm sure," said Alo.

He pulled at his lip and studied the screen. Then he tapped new orders into the console, putting the ship back under acceleration and instructing the computer to compensate for the interruption. He had to be on schedule, later.

"What's this all about?" asked Alo, perching in the copilot's couch.

"Shut up." He was trying to think of a way to avoid Garikoff and still make his insertion. Now think, think, think.

"Why can't you tell me—"

"Keep your mouth shut!" he roared. "I can still put you out the airlock." He started tapping furiously at the flight console.

Alo jumped down, glaring.

"Be useful," he snapped. "Scan ahead to the collapsing-field. I want to know what ships are out there."

"But—"

"Do it!"

"Hrrrrl!" cried LePiep, upset by the commotion. She burrowed into the pile of loose clothes. Panglor watched her unhappily, touched by her frustration; but the flight program was more urgent. His hands shook as he worked. Alo grumpily worked at the viewscreen controls.

First he modified the breakaway he'd planned from his legal flightpath. The new plan would not put him on collision course with *Deerfield*, but would leave open a window for a last-minute change to a collision course. G-G's agents could compute; they'd have no way of knowing, until he passed that window, that he was rebelling. But if he took that window, and only later changed to give *Deerfield* a safe berth—that could buy him time, make time so short that he'd have a fighting chance of making insertion even if G-G started shooting. Still, there would be the traffic patrol yelling, and possibly firing . . . and maybe G-G wouldn't be fooled long enough . . . maybe there was a third bomb, yet undiscovered . . .

But it was the only chance he could think of.

They worked for nearly an hour. Alo looked at him several times, opening her mouth to speak; but each time she remained silent, giving him a dark look. Finally, she blurted, "What's the matter? Why am I looking for these ships?"

"They might start shooting at us," he said.

She digested that, while he kept working. Then she returned to the scanners. Some time later, she reported, "There are two ships accelerating toward insertion, one ahead and one behind, both in normal traffic patterns. Two other ships are on parallel courses ahead, but slower, and not aiming for insertion. What are they— patrol?"

Panglor picked his teeth, studying his flight projection. "One of them, maybe. Feed me the figures on all of them." The figures came onto his board, and he grunted. It was going to be a delicate course to thread.

Going to be a busy time.

Hours later, he rubbed his eyes, waking. Couldn't remember when he'd dozed off—but it was just an hour now to insertion. His stomach hurt.

"Want some moke?" he asked in a gravelly voice. Alo eyed him and nodded.

He turned on the brewer in the galley, then went to the head and freshened himself. When he came back, the moke was steaming, and he poured two mugs and carried them to the bridge. "What's going to happen when we go through?" Alo asked, accepting one of the mugs. She seemed subdued.

"Find out soon," he said, manipulating the viewscreen. Alo had kept a track on all the ships she'd spotted earlier; that made it easy. He put a high magnification on *Deerfield* and found a tiny silver bug swimming through space. "Mmmmp," he said. His stomach crawled, in presentiment of the danger ahead. Feeling a wave of fear, he turned and saw LePiep rolled up, trembling, her eyes wide. "Easy, babe. Easy," he whispered, touching her. He wished somebody would say the same to him.

Precisely on schedule, *The Fighting Cur*'s drivers kicked up to eight gees, nearly full power. Panglor swayed and steadied himself against the vacillation of internal grav, until the field compensated. They were now boosting out of the legal flightpath toward a near-interception of *Deerfield*. Control would start yelling soon.

"Are you going to tell me what's going on?" complained Alo.

"Keep watching that screen and tell me if anyone else changes course." He glanced up and saw her displaying an uncooperative expression. "Listen—later you're going to tell me what you're doing here, but right now you're under the gun with me. So the less trouble you cause, the better your chances of being alive to talk later. Right?" His stomach still hurt. Having the girl aboard was even worse than being alone. Concentrate, now.

Alo pinched her nose. "Well, since you were right about the bombs, I guess maybe . . ."

The Fighting Cur was already hundreds of kilometers closer to *Deerfield*, and was closing faster every second. Panglor had to watch the console closely; the *Cur*'s control system was not quite adequate for keeping these oversized drivers precisely on the beam, and without his override, the ship tended to shake from oversteering by the automatic system. If I were going to send some loser out on a job, he thought, sweating, I'd at least give him the right machinery.

On the other hand, they knew he was good. They knew, too, that he'd be panicking if he didn't have to concentrate so hard on flying. He knew they knew that, and it made him madder still.

"What are those other ships doing?" The sweat began popping faster on his forehead.

"Not much—wait." Alo fiddled with the screen. "The patrol ship seems to be doing something—changing orbit." She licked her lips. "Yep. Moving in."

"Don't sound so happy," he growled.

The com started warbling with an incoming call. Every muscle in his body tensed; he tried to ignore the sound, but couldn't. "All right," he said. "Put it on."

A harsh voice roared into the control room, until Alo cut the volume. "—*is Patrol A Seventy-three. State at once reason for departure from flight plan. You are warned that you are in violation of Traffic Code ten-beta-fifteen. Police action will commence at once if you do not respond.*" The message began repeating.

Then Alo said, "There's another call coming in—on a tight beam from that other ship."

"Great." The demands of piloting were mounting rapidly; he had to make a course change in one minute, and he had to hold his present course right on line. The drivers were running hot but holding stable.

"*Balef, we are monitoring your orbit. So far so good.*

You are within range of our weapons, and there is a remote charge aboard your ship which we control on this beam. If you do the job right, we won't have to use the charge. Keep that in mind, and good luck."

Gee, Panglor thought, watching the computer feeds like mad, funny they didn't mention that time fuse they had on the other bomb.

"You going to talk?" Alo asked brusquely. "Who are those guys?"

Panglor cleared his throat and snapped several relays. A loud feedback hum from the com filled the room until he yelled, "Turn the damn thing off!" She obeyed, and the hum went off. "Goddamn junk they give me," he complained, turning off several other unnecessary systems. There was a surge as the drivers changed thrust, and the ship pitched several degrees. Damn com was probably defective, he fumed. Like Garikoff's soul.

The *Cur* accelerated on a course now that would take them within a dozen kilometers of *Deerfield*, if he made no further changes. But he was going to make another change. In half a minute, he would swerve to give *Deerfield* more room and line up for his own insertion. It would take everything his drivers had, for a minute and a half.

The collapsing-field was visible in the screen now, a bluish–white dot glowing fuzzily against space. *Deerfield* was still a silver bug, but growing. There was no sign that its crew had heeded them; both ships were accelerating at converging angles toward the collapsing-field. Two other slivers moved visibly: Garikoff and the patrol.

Panglor wanted to switch on the com again, but didn't dare; he needed all his concentration. The next maneuver was coming up now: the ship lurched and pitched nineteen degrees. They continued to accelerate toward the field, but started killing some of their sideways vector. Drivers went to full power, running smooth but hot.

"Give me center view again."

Alo readjusted the screen. "I wish you'd tell me—*uh*!"

He looked. A bit of light streaked across the screen and flared, more or less where the *Cur* would have been but for the course change. He suddenly had trouble breathing. LePiep jumped into his lap, crying. "Christ!" he whispered, nudging her aside. He kept his eyes on the controls.

"That came from the patrol ship," Alo murmured. "Hey, maybe you should talk to them and—"

The viewer went white. Alo fiddled for a moment and produced a picture again, but a slash of discolored fuzziness cut diagonally across the view. "Laser cannon," Panglor said, swallowing hard. "Warning shot." He was surprised that they were good enough to pick off his sensor-fringe that way. They were *good*.

Alo switched on the com.

"*—last warning. Veer outward—*"

The sound broke up, and a static-filled voice came through, on Garikoff's channel: "*You are off course. We are opening fire, and will fire until you have—*"

That broke up, too, but a hull sensor lighted. Hot spot on the hull. A laser was grazing them, but unsteadily; Garikoff was a poorer shot than the patrol. Panglor's fingers danced at the console. The drivers began to stutter, varying in thrust around the correct value. "Kid! Pipe that last message over to the patrol and tell them we're under fire and have to go through the field."

The *Cur* shook dangerously from the pulsating thrust; it wasn't built to accelerate that way. Judging from the hull sensors, though, the maneuver was succeeding. The computer was varying their acceleration randomly, and

Garikoff couldn't keep a laser on them. Now he worked furiously at the program, trying to make their final velocity come out right.

"NO!" he roared, hammering on the console. They could no longer make the angle he needed.

The collapsing-field was growing, and he had lost his track on *Deerfield*. "We've lost the window! We've lost D17!" He worked frantically, thinking. Was there another insertion window they could still hit?

The collapsing-field grew fast, blue and terrible, filling a third of the screen.

Alo and LePiep were both yelling as he tried desperately to remember the insertion windows available. There *was* another, nearly at the same angle . . . could he make it? Throttling the drivers to full, stable, he pitched twenty degrees back toward *Deerfield*'s course. They were far enough apart by now that a collision was impossible, for sure.

The hull sensors flickered. The viewscreen fluttered and went dim, but not out. The guidance-lock sensors went dead. Garikoff was burning him; their control system was blind. "Bastards!" he screamed. In a fury, he took the controls completely on manual.

The collapsing-field filled the screen. Warning lights blinked. Panglor grunted and held his breath and cut the drivers.

A silver ship slid into view from the upper side and hurtled down off the screen. It was *big*. Alo shrieked.

The field blazed, the ship shuddered, and the screen went blank.

Panglor sat shaking, staring dumbly at the screen, a great emptiness in his chest. Alo was still shrieking. LePiep clung by her claws to the front of his shirt, trembling.

That was *Deerfield* they had nearly hit. And an instant later they had plunged through the collapsing-field—off course—and they were now coasting between the stars, encapsulated in a flowing cell of stressed, foreshortened space. They were free of Garikoff, and they had escaped the D3 system alive. Where they were going, he couldn't say. But he thought he knew. And he would rather have died.

6

EVENTUALLY ALO stopped shrieking.

It was a while longer before the voice in his own head quieted down. Then he pried LePiep's claws loose from the front of his shirt, and calmed himself enough to stop gasping; and he squinted at the console, as though in calm, scholarly curiosity, rather than the crippling anxiety he actually felt. The computer log produced a record of the preceding minutes, and what he had actually done in those blind, frantic seconds. The record was bewildering, especially with the loss of the guidance sensors. He was more numb than frightened. Almost certainly he had sent them on a no-return journey into limbo; he just had to confirm it, that was all.

"Where are we going?" asked Alo in a subdued voice.

Panglor grunted. "Don't tell me you're worried, suddenly."

She stared at him. "I'm not scared. I just want to know where we're going."

"Well, now, if you'd bought a ticket for this trip, I might feel like telling you. But you know, stowaways don't have the same rights as passengers." He was muttering words, not even listening to himself. He needed to babble to calm his nerves, because he couldn't make heads or tails of the information on the screen. LePiep crooned, nuzzling him.

Limbo.

That was where. That was the answer.

"Anyway," he said, trying to ignore the buzzing in his head, "I'm still mapping out the course."

Alo crossed her arms impatiently. Panglor went back to figuring. He knew he had come close to putting the *Cur* into another foreshortening window, but he couldn't remember what the destination star was. That he could check later; what he needed to know now was whether he had hit *any* window, because if he hadn't nothing else mattered.

"You don't know, do you?" Alo said.

"I *will* know. Except our sensors got burned, so there's no way to be sure. I'm doing inertial right now." The computer could figure it based on internal measurements of acceleration—assuming that the instruments were accurate.

"Why were they shooting at us, anyway?"

Panglor felt his temper slip close to the edge. He said nothing, but replied with a silent expression.

Her face darkened. "We've had it, haven't we?"

He bristled. "Not necessarily." Do you know anything about foreshortening piloting?" He rolled his eyeballs toward her.

"Some," she said. She shrugged. "Well, I know more straight space stuff, but foreshortening I know theory and mechanics. I've never actually piloted it."

Panglor nodded. Maybe she knew something, maybe she didn't. He returned his gaze to the console and worked for a moment. The program ran and gave him the answer.

The answer was, if the internals were correct, they were finished. He had missed the window.

He sagged in despair.

LePiep shoved her face up to his, peering. Waves of reassurance cascaded from the ou-ralot, washed over him like a soothing rain, like a mistmassage. He breathed deeply, and found his voice and it was filled with fighting anger. "There's something you ought to know, and that's that you don't always have to be *exactly* on the beam in your insertion. Sometimes you can be pulled along from one field to that other one lightyears away—pulled right on into line as if you were on a string."

"Yeah, but—"

"As though there's something in that stressed space, something that we don't know anything about, that nobody, not even the big brains, understands—that wants things in foreshortening to move from one point to the other. Like a big strand of taffy. Hell, we'd probably miss half the time if there wasn't something like that to keep the trajectories honest."

"Yeah, but you have to be *close*," Alo objected.

"We *are* close. We're just a little off." And it was true, nearly enough. "So. Sometimes ships get pulled *off* course, and we never see them again, and sometimes they get drawn in the right way." He looked up at the screen, a dark blue blank. His heart beat fast again. There was nothing any instrument could show him about their trajectory. Only the scoopscope functioned in foreshortening, and that only just prior to emergence.

Alo thought about it for a while and finally said,

"What about that other ship that missed us? It followed us right in."

Panglor stared at her, dumbfounded. He had totally forgotten the Vikken ship. "Well," he said slowly, "it could be right here with us, actually. Or right behind us. Even if they were on a diverging course." He rubbed his temples hard, thinking. Now that was a real possibility, though it involved some unknowns. It made him nervous as hell. On top of everything else, they might have *Deerfield* in transit with them . . .

Alo frowned in puzzlement.

"Field effect," he said. "Two bodies go through a field close enough together, and they can be entrained in the same foreshortening distortion. Even if their tracks are different. The lines of space bend to convergence by the time the field is captured and undistorted."

Alo looked skeptical. She sat in silence for a few moments, then said, "How about some food?"

"What?" he said, startled. "I don't even know what you're doing here or why I haven't tossed you out, and here you are, asking—"

"You didn't toss me out because I was helping you," she huffed. "Anyway, I told you, I brought extra food."

"Huh? Go ahead, then—and bring me something." Her nerviness gave him the jitters, but he had to admit she had been helpful.

While she was in the galley, he fed LePiep from a packet he found under his seat, and snapped hot a moke for himself. Alo returned, eating an enormous flatwrap sandwich. She handed him a smaller one. "What happens," she said, "if the two ships are flying too far apart, and they don't converge in the field?"

Panglor stared at her, his mouth halfway around his first bite. He grunted and chewed slowly. He swallowed and drank from his brewed moke. "What happens if they don't converge?" He shut his eyes, opened them again. "Probably they rupture the field, and then it's all over. The field disappears, and both ships—" He shook his head, unable to complete the statement.

Alo studied her sandwich. They ate in silence.

An empty mug toppled from the armrest and clunked to the deck. Panglor blinked out of a brooding reverie and glanced at Alo. She plucked at her shirt and returned his glance. He sat upright. "I think it's time for you to talk," he said. "Who let you on the ship, anyway?"

She rolled her eyes. "Ye gods, no one *let* me on. I just came." She smoothed her shirt down, then stretched and sighed.

Panglor remembered the observatory door. "Yeah? What for? You must have known you'd never get back home."

She snorted. "*Home?* You kidding? That place was a prison."

"What'd you do wrong?"

"Who said I did anything wrong?" Her eyes flashed. She reached under her hair to scratch.

"What'd you do wrong?"

Her mouth scowled, but her eyes moved from side to side.

Panglor felt the familiar pressure in his forehead. "What kind of trouble were you in?"

She jerked her gaze away. "They were going to come after me. I don't know if they knew yet."

"What?"

"I fixed a girl's shuttle scooter. They had to go out and rescue her. She had it coming."

"A spacecraft? You sabotaged a *spacecraft*?"

"Well, why not?" she answered hotly. "It was no big thing. And what were *you* doing? Looked like you were pulling something funny back there, with them shooting at you and you doing crazy maneuvers. What are you yelling at me—?"

"So you came on my ship?" he demanded.

She stopped talking, mouth open. "Yah," she said. "You seemed different. I thought it had possibilities. And I couldn't stay there—they'd have run me in, and the way those people are they'd have put me in confinement and forgotten about me." She shrugged and turned to face the lifeless viewscreen.

"Yeah, well, you haven't said why you sabotaged a spacecraft," he said. "You try something like that on my ship, and I'm going to break both your arms and both your legs, and after that I'm going to break your neck." He gripped the arms of his seat, his tendons bulging.

Alo faced the screen silently.

"Well?"

She shrugged. "Well, *what*?"

Panglor growled to himself and shook his head.

Half an hour later, he told her to go bunk out in the cabin. "We're going to stand shifts. When you're on, you're going to do nothing with those controls but *watch*, and you're going to wake me if anything happens that I need to be awake for." Alo squinted uncooperatively, but when he reached for her arm, she yelped and scuttled out of the control bay. "Witch," he muttered. And he meant it. But he wasn't so sure anymore that she was a ghost.

Though physically and mentally exhausted, he kept working at the console. He wanted to find out what star system he had, maybe, flung them toward. The answer, when it came, made him sweat—and made him check the library files for confirmation of what he thought he remembered hearing once, sometime, somewhere. When that answer came back, he stared at it, trembling so hard that he woke up LePiep with his unhappy feelings, and she leaped up onto the console and peered questioningly at him.

Dreznelles 1. That was where they were going, if anywhere. Dreznelles 1. A nearby star, in the same group as D3. It was the site of a relay waystation rather like the one at D3—but with a difference. "It's empty, Peep," he whispered. "Abandoned. There's no one there. Do you know what that means?" He gazed into her moist eyes and tried to keep himself steady. It's okay to shudder, but don't let it go too far, don't let yourself slide, don't let yourself come apart, *don't*. LePiep crooned to him—but what could she do?

The waystation at D1 had been closed down and abandoned half a century ago, when D3 had taken over its functions. The foreshortening field generators, if they still existed, were defunct. It did not matter if he had made the insertion or not, because he might as well have been aiming straight into limbo.

He shuddered harder. He had done to himself what he had always feared, and not even LePiep could reassure him now. Thank God the witch was in the cabin and not here to see this. *Jesus!* He was making grunting noises, almost sobbing, and there were tears in his eyes.

LePiep twitched, startled by something. He looked up, eyes blurred, and saw Alo standing just inside the control bay. No, he thought, *no*. Jesus Christ, not her, not now.

"What are you doing here?" he croaked.

"I wasn't tired, and I wanted to find out something."

His voice cracked. "What?" His patience was gone. His world was gone.

"You sure are upset about something," she said. "Maybe you should go to sleep."

"What do you want?" he shouted. LePiep flew off the console and batted about the control room in terror. "Peep!" he cried. "Come here." She landed, trembling.

"Well," said Alo, "I just wanted to find out where we were going. Optimistically speaking."

Panglor sank back into silence. LePiep sat with him, radiating misery.

Alo found out what she wanted to know, though. It was right there on the console screen, and after she read it she blanched, then pursed her lips and sat with her chin in her hands, staring at LePiep.

There was only one practical thing they could do, and that was to start whatever repair work on the ship was possible. Alo proved surprisingly skilled at working with the technics, and though Panglor would never had admitted it, he could not have done the work without her. They checked the hull integrity and adjusted the drive-converters, and then started working on the guidance sensors. Though it was impossible to go outside the ship while they were in the foreshortening field, the external sensor probes were designed to be removed from inside the ship, first into a space between inner and outer hull sections, and then through a service lock into the repair section of the power deck. They worked over the probes for some time. The damage was considerable, but they managed to restore most of the visible light and radar sections. The guidance computer would still be missing half its input, but they would not be blind. That was assuming that they would emerge somewhere, with somewhere else to go—and that they were not in a tin coffin bound for limbo.

They lunched in silence, until Panglor said, "So what was wrong with the station? You grew up there, didn't you?"

Alo sat in the corner of the galley, ignoring him while she ate. Finally she said, "Nothing wrong with the station. Just with the people."

He shrugged.

A few moments later, she added, "Of *course* I didn't grow up there. I grew up on Earth. They're too stupid to realize that people from somewhere else might have something. They're too dumb to know that they're provincial, closed-minded jerks." Her lunch was disappearing in ferocious gulps.

Panglor watched her silently. Whatever had happened to her, she certainly was bitter about it. The point was well taken, of course—people everywhere were stupid, provincial jerks. But it surprised him that she recognized the fact.

"Jerks," she repeated, making mincemeat of her weyso-leaf steak. She stabbed at it with her fork and waved a piece; it flew from the fork to the deck, and LePiep scampered to gobble it.

"Yah," said Panglor, and he got up and went to the control bay to see if anything was happening.

It was. The EMERGENCE light was on, blue. The fore-shortening field was changing. The light blinked to amber. LePiep whistled.

Panglor yelled, "Hey!" He peered into the scoop-scope. "Yeah, here we go," he said, when Alo came in. He adjusted the scope. "We got the points starting to converge, here. The field's distorting, all right." The warning light did not necessarily mean they were emerging successfully; it simply warned of gross distortions in the foreshortening field.

"Well?" said Alo.

The clusters of dots in the scope danced toward convergence. He peered, squinted. "Get ready—any second."

He heard the tone and felt the twinge in his gut, and he looked up. The viewscreen came alive again, dark, with stars. He shifted the view and was rewarded with the sight of a capture-field shrinking, a dull red glow against space. "Ho-ho!" he crowed.

Then he stopped, bewildered. "What's that doing here?" And there was something else, too, a flash of silver—*Deerfield*. He put a track on it with the sensor-fringe.

"Of course there's a field here," Alo said. "They left it on so they'd have a way to get back if they wanted to. Naturally they'd leave a gateway open"

Panglor was trying to get a scan on *Deerfield*. He didn't know whether they would be armed or not, but he was sure they'd be pretty sore. "Where the devil—" he fumed. "There they are!" He snapped a fix on their position and velocity for the computer to work on; and he queried, also, for a base map of this system. The screen showed confirmation that they were, indeed, in the D1 system.

"The real question now," Alo was saying, "is whether there is a *collapsing*-field working. That's not such a sure thing, because they might have programmed it to shut off, and they figured if they ever came back they could turn it on themselves when they wanted to leave."

"What the hell are you talking about?" Panglor said irritably. He was trying to coordinate some readings on the *Cur*'s trajectory, and he was having trouble making sense of it.

"I was just wondering if we'd be able to get out of this system again," said Alo. "We don't want to stay here forever, do we?"

Panglor scowled at her. Then his gaze fell on the viewscreen. "Mother of God!" he whispered. There was a planet on the screen, and it was no farther than a few hundred thousand kilometers away. No wonder the readings had seemed strange. Why would a capture-field be located so close to a planet?

"That's not right," said Alo.

He turned. "What do you know about it?"

"Quite a lot, actually," she said. "History, you know. Dreznelles 3 was built to replace the D1 station. They were having troubles here—weird stuff, superstitious crap—and the capture-field was not located in planetary orbit."

"It *is* in planetary orbit!"

"I can see that, yes, thank you, Captain Pangy. But it was not there before. It was in Trojan orbit, just like at D3. And there was a waystation, but no planetary colony. Everything was just like D3, only not so big."

He studied her suspiciously. "You seem awfully sure."

"Yes. I am." Sitting back in the mate's seat, she crossed her legs.

"Well, if you know so bloody much, would you please tell me why the field is here now if it wasn't before, and where the bloody station is, and for God's sake where the collapsing-field is?" he roared.

Alo shrugged. "I can't tell you all that. We'll just have to find out. But if there's a field working, we should be able to find it."

"Terrific. Start looking."

She settled at the viewscreen controls. Panglor, meanwhile, went back to tracking *Deerfield* and evaluating their position and velocity with respect to the planet. It was a terrestrial body in terms of size and mass; and it had an atmosphere, though there were no glaring indications of life in the spectrum. He instructed the computer to work up a picture of the planet, based on sensor-scan and library data, for later; right now he was worried about where he was flying, and where *Deerfield* was flying.

The com started crackling just then, and after a few seconds he heard a human voice: "*Other ship, other ship, this is Vikken Limited ship* Deerfield. *This is* Deerfield." The voice repeated the ID several times.

Then it said, "*Other ship, what the fucking hell do you think you are doing? Please fucking respond.*"

Panglor stared at the com, trembling.

"Aren't you going to answer?" asked Alo. "I was kind of wondering what you were doing, too."

"*This is* Deerfield, *other ship. We are armed, and we are going to burn you into little pieces if you don't answer.*" The voice sounded angry, he thought. And Panglor was starting to become angry, too. Goddamn Vikken ship. He'd tried to avoid diverting them; he'd tried to give them a berth. And what did they do to deserve even that? He should have rammed them, sent them to real limbo. They were from Vikken. Why the hell had he risked his life for them?

Suddenly he shouted, "Vikken, this is the goddamn *Fighting Cur*—that's who! It was all an accident, you morons—but maybe it was too good an accident for you! Maybe we should have dumped you into a goddamn star, but maybe *that* would have been too good for you, too!" He was fuming, years of anger boiling up.

Alo opened her mouth in astonishment. Awe filled her eyes—a combination of terror and admiration.

Panglor glared at the computer readouts. *Deerfield* was indeed changing course to intercept the *Cur*. But their emergence velocities had been different, reflecting the difference in their insertion velocities and *Deerfield* would have to go some to catch them. And if he decelerated the *Cur* into a corkscrewing orbit around this planet, they'd have an even tougher time. Good. He worked at the board; the ship turned over, and the drivers kicked on full.

He studied what he had done, making sure he had got it right. Then he sat back, picking his teeth. By God, he wasn't about to apologize to Vikken, not by a long shot.

"Pingly," said Alo. "What's with them? Do you hate them on general principle, or for something special?"

He twitched. "Didn't I tell you to look for a collapsing-field to get us out of here?"

"Yah, I did," she answered, scratching her side. "Didn't find any. But I found the station, in orbit around the planet. Still don't know why." She displayed the station's track on the screen.

Panglor nodded grudgingly. Even if she was a witch, she was an astonishingly good spacehand, too. He would have preferred thinking he could deep-space her without loss. But she was too good; she was the best assistant he'd ever had.

"Are you going to tell me what's going on between you and them?" she asked.

He tapped his teeth. Checking *Deerfield*'s track, he muttered quietly to himself. The other ship was aiming to intercept, but the *Cur* had a good lead. "You haven't told me why *you* did what you did. All I know is that you're a juvenile delinquent who stowed away on my ship." He met her gaze, hard.

"I am not a juvenile—"

"That's not answering the question."

"I asked you first."

"I'm the captain. And I asked you hours ago. Are you afraid to tell me?"

"Why should I be afraid?" Her eyes burned. She pulled at her disheveled hair, then shrugged. "You know what it's like to have everyone thinking you're weird or something, and you know they're the ones who are weird? Just because I didn't come from there." She stood and talked to the viewscreen. "They've never *been* to Earth, and they think they know all about it, think there's something better about being born in a huge can in a star system that doesn't even have a decent planet. I think they're jealous. They never left me alone—always picking at this or that, and when I did better in training, and when I was a better spacer than they were, they just did it more."

She turned from the viewscreen and back, and then began to pace. Her eyes smoldered. "That's when they started in about my parents and how they were *afraid* of something, and that's why they were immigrating, and that's why I was there." Her voice was steel. Panglor swallowed, but she wasn't finished. "The bloody bitching bastards, talking about people who aren't even there to defend themselves. They're cowards—they know they aren't half the people we were."

LePiep crouched nervously, watching Alo, sending out waves of alarm. For a moment, Alo appeared to soften, and she reached toward the ou-ralot. LePeip backed away.

"Where are your parents, then?" Immediately he wanted to take it back; he didn't want to know.

Alo turned toward him, looking right through him, and answered in a strangely light tone of voice, "They're dead. The stupid bastards killed them. They let our ship crash at the station, because they couldn't keep the traffic straight. And still they think they're smarter than anyone in the universe. I'm glad we don't have to go back." Her eyes were unfocused, and her lips were set in a childlike, icy smile.

Panglor started to clear his throat, but stopped, afraid to make the sound. A cry of sympathy was trying to escape from his windpipe, and he grunted to keep it down. He sat rigid, elbows at his sides. Jittery waves of fear came from LePiep; it was too much pain coming from too many directions. But it's just coincidence, he thought. And not even true coincidence: her parents were killed in a spaceship crash—and that's not what happened to both *his* parents. Just his father. And then his mother left him, but that's no big deal, not in the 82 Eri belt, with community parentage.

"So," he choked. "They gave you a hard time, and you got them back. That it?"

Alo's eyes narrowed, and she began to show consciousness of her surroundings again. "The bitch. Marney. I should have rigged it to kill her—she didn't deserve to be rescued. Should have put a flag on the wreckage: 'The Earthwoman did it.' What I should have done." She turned and busied herself with the viewscreen, sweeping space.

Panglor, his heart thundering, pumping blood against the backs of his eyeballs, forced himself to study the planet they were orbiting.

"So when are you going to tell me?" Alo demanded.

"What?" He glanced up nervously. The silence had been comforting. They were decelerating smoothly in a loop around the planet. He had been puzzling over the presence of the foreshortening station in planetary orbit. Could some alien race, perhaps the mysterious Kili, have come here and moved it, for their own purposes? And the planet—it didn't correlate with *any* of the library data.

"You know frinking well what," Alo said. "Why is someone out to kill us?"

"They're not out to kill *you*," he said sardonically.

She snorted. Panglor sighed, finally, and told her about the orders from Grakoff-Garikoff, and why he had been trapped in such a bind. He explained, also, about Vikken—how they had fired him for "psychiatric incompetence."

"They were probably right," Alo said, clucking evaluatingly. "But they're bastards, and you ought to get them.

Panglor hooked a finger at the scanner-tracking of *Deerfield*. "Vikken ship," he said.

Alo thought a moment and nodded.

Panglor, however—spurred by the memory—was feeling greater hatred at the moment for Grakoff-Garikoff. If he could avenge himself against them . . .

"What about you?" she said suddenly. "I'll bet people where you lived didn't like you either."

He blinked, then growled, "You listen here—"

"Isn't that right?" Alo said. "We're just alike."

"No, it's not right," he answered, but his voice betrayed him. What she had said was true; he had never been liked. There was Lenia Stahl, of course; and Edor, a boyhood friend, but he'd moved to another part of the 82 Eri belt. But . . . "Well, not like you're trying to say. Of course there are all those goons you meet in the shipping business, and most spacers aren't fit company for dogs. But there have been people here and there, in different places, who—" He stopped.

"Who—?" she prompted.

"What?"

"People who *what*?"

Panglor shook his head dumbly. He'd said enough.

LePiep hopped across the console at that moment, chasing a ball of dust. Panglor watched her, then noticed the viewscreen. "Hey!" There was a ship in the screen. It was *Deerfield*—too large and too close—and there was a flickering of laser light on its hull. "How?" Panglor demanded. "They shouldn't be there!"

Alo stared, mystified.

"How?" screamed Panglor.

A hull sensor hooted. Panglor scrambled and hit the variable thrust program to dodge the laser. "Get me a new track on that station!" he commanded. Alo darted to work, and Panglor began blocking out a course change.

"We can't reach the station this way," Alo reported. "The orbits are all wrong."

Panglor gargled and shouted, "*Our* orbit's all wrong! What's happening here?" His head was starting to swim. Something very strange—was he losing his sanity? Orbits don't play tricks. "Scan that planet. There must be something . . . explainable." The planet was twice the size it should have been on the viewscreen; it was a misty, ochre-and-white ball, much lighter in hue than he remembered it being earlier.

A blast of static interrupted her answer. "Fighting Cur, *this is Captain Thaddeus Drak of the freighter* Deerfield. *Cease your evasive actions and respond on open channel at once.*"

"Turn that thing off!" Panglor snapped. What, what, what? The navigational computer was spewing nonsense. He checked the hull sensors; good, the laser was missing them.

Alo shook her head. "We shouldn't be this close for hours yet."

"*Deerfield* shouldn't be in range, either. Orbital configuration's all wrong." Panglor muttered. He looked up. "What are you scanning with?"

"Huh? Radar and dopplering."

"Check angular size and use this for comparison." He punched up the planet's physical data from the previous sighting and transferred it to Alo's screen.

"No," she said, a moment later.

"What do you mean, 'no'? Just do it."

"I mean, no, it's not right. That's odd."

"You mean you did the correlation already?"

"Yes, of course." She pulled on her tangled hair. "Something must be wrong with the instruments. I'd better do it the long way and take star sightings."

Strange feelings were running up and down inside

Panglor. "Why?" he asked, though he knew the answer. Wouldn't anything stop this thundering in his ears?

"None of this is making sense," Alo said. "I check our velocity and distance one way and get one answer, and I check it another way and get another answer."

"I don't have to listen to this," Panglor warned, startled by the almost hysterical edge in his own voice.

She looked at him in confusion, and he returned her stare, trembling. The pressure behind his eyes was terrible, and there was a large constriction in his throat. He turned to check on *Deerfield* and was surprised to see that the Vikken freighter had fallen behind, so much so that it was about to be eclipsed by the planet's horizon.

The planet's horizon?

"Hey, uh," he started, but stopped when he saw the look in Alo's eyes. She had seen the planet, too. There was no way this could happen; but the planet was close enough to swallow them. The horizon was a gently curving rim of golden brown against black space; a tissue-thin hazing of atmosphere was visible, as though brushed on as an afterthought.

They were impossibly close. They were in a *low* orbit—no more than a few hundred kilometers up.

Panglor made a sound of distress, then deliberately stopped his hand from shaking. Well, he could deal with impossibilities with the best of them. He reached out calmly and cut the drive engines. "What's our distance from the planet's surface?" he demanded.

Flaring her nostrils, Alo said, "Three hundred thirty-two on radar—or one eighty-seven on laser. Take your pick."

"Wrong." he said. "It's two eighteen from here. You know how to read those instruments?"

She shot him a corrosive look. He shrugged and said, "Okay, figure me a periapsis, and when do we hit it?"

That took her a couple of seconds. She bit her nails

and said, "A hundred and three kilometers in seventeen minutes, or—" her voice became hoarse"—minus three in twelve."

He met her gaze. "I get one seventy-three in thirteen." There was a bad buzzing in his skull, and his lips felt numb. If her last estimate was right, if the lowest point in their projected orbit was *minus three kilometers* . . . then that meant they were about to . . . crash.

"Christ!" he howled, slamming the console. "Nothing means anything!" Shaking, he prepared to start the drivers to raise the orbit. But what sense could he trust? Direction? He couldn't trust anything else; could he trust *backward* and *forward* to mean anything? He kicked the drivers on again, muttering to himself. The direction and attitude seemed correct.

"Think we'll crash?" asked Alo, squinting. She seemed unafraid, except for a twitch in her mouth.

The planet grew in the screen. The horizon flattened, and now they could see the planet's surface crawling beneath them. It looked rocky and lifeless. But the atmosphere was terrestrial: nitrogen, oxygen, trace gases. "Give me a readout on the atmosphere," he demanded, keeping his voice tight.

"You being funny? There's no atmosphere."

Panglor chuckled desperately. "No atmosphere? Okay, we'll—*ohh!*" His stomach dropped, and he suddenly began crying, with real tears.

"What?" Alo demanded. "What?"

He pointed. "Auh!" said Alo. The hull sensors showed the nose heating, rapidly. They were entering the atmosphere that didn't exist, and they were going to burn up, because the *Cur* was not an atmospheric craft. Panglor tilted the nose up and throttled the drivers to full, trying to climb out. Tears broke from his eyes and ran down his cheeks.

"It's not going to work," Alo said, and she was

right—it wasn't working. The planet continued to grow in the screen, until it was nothing but a blur of speeding landscape.

"Why?" Panglor was having trouble seeing, because of the goddamn tears, and because of LePiep climbing his chest again, pushing her trembling nose against his cheekbone. But he could see well enough to see every instrument on the console fluctuating wildly. "Ah, hell," he cried, and reached out to cut the drivers.

The *Cur* fell, uncontrolled.

Butchered your last mission, he thought, holding LePiep to his breast. And then the waves of terror and despair that LePiep couldn't hold in any longer washed over him and obliterated all other thought.

7

"PANGLY, WHAT'S going on here?" was the first thing he heard. He brought his eyes back into focus and saw Alo standing, hands on hips, staring at the viewscreen.

"Don't call me that," he muttered. He held his head in his hands for a moment, then got up, with some difficulty. Gravity was about one gee, perhaps a little more. It occurred to him that he ought to be dead; but he was not—LePiep's confused chirping assured him of that—and he ought to go see what Alo was looking at.

If he'd thought he was coming unhinged before, now he was sure of it. *The Fighting Cur* had landed safely on the surface of the planet—which was impossible. Ridiculous. He could not remember any sensation whatever when they had landed. Now, how could that be?

The view in the screen was of an apparently lifeless plain outside the ship, under a night sky filled with stars. They had been on the dayside when they had entered the atmosphere. The plain was illuminated by the starlight and by wispy auroras above the horizon. He massaged his eyebrows; he did not want to admit that he was bewildered, but LePiep was chittering in confusion, betraying him. Self-consciously, he switched the screen to a full sweep around the ship's perimeter.

"Huh?" said Alo.

The view on the other side was quite different. The ship sat at the edge of a rugged expanse of bluffs and ridges, carved and sculpted rock laid out like a maze as far as the eye could see. The terrain gleamed as though in bright moonlight, but there was no moon in the sky. The light appeared to be coming from the stars, from the auroras toward the north—as indicated by the nav—and from a faint golden airglow low in the west, over the ridges. The twisted landscape, glowing in the curved front wall of the control bay, looked like some incredibly surrealistic work of art. Nothing moved.

"Do *you* see anything moving?" Panglor said.

Not answering, Alo squinted and moved one way and then the other, studying the entire panorama. With her attention focused on the screen, she stumbled and lurched into Panglor. "Uff!" he grunted, startled. He caught her by the shoulders and lifted her—then, embarrassed, pushed her out to arm's length. "All right?" he said, dropping his hands to his sides. His fingers tingled strangely.

She gave him a puzzled glance. "Yah," she said, and looked back at the screen. Panglor lifted LePiep from the console. The ou-ralot was crooning in response to his embarrassment; he shushed her nervously, which seemed only to confuse her. "There!" Alo said, pointing at the viewscreen.

Something very small—a faintly silvery object of some sort, perhaps a bird—was moving in the air at a distance of perhaps fifty meters from the ship. It drifted out from between two outcroppings of rock. Another spot emerged, trailing the first. They converged, approaching the ship; then a third appeared from a cleft in a ridge, and the first two sailed into shadow and did not reappear. The ghostly illumination in the sky seemed to be failing; but glimmerings of light now shone from among the rocks themselves—a series of scintillations in the eye, like the light of jewelry.

"Huh," said Alo. LePiep purred appreciatively.

Panglor checked readings. If the instruments could be trusted, the atmosphere outside would sustain human life. In fact, conditions were not only adequate, they were like a summer evening in Eden. That made no sense; but what did? He scratched the stubble on his cheek. "We'll have to sample with the suit airborne biodetectors."

Alo lit up. "We're going out?"

"Don't be so eager," he said sourly. "You've got the rest of your life to spend here. Of course, that may not be long. Come on—let's eat, then we'll go out."

They prepared a meal in silence. When Panglor was halfway through his leafloaf and brew, Alo tossed her tray into the disposal and announced, "I'm going now."

"The hell you are!" he roared. But the girl was already out of the galley and halfway to the airlock. He smacked the counter with his fist, then sat back with a sigh. To hell with her. She wants to get killed? Let her.

He finished his meal and then went to the airlock. Alo spoke through the com. "It tests safe. I'm taking off the suit and going out."

"Leave the suit on!"

"There's only one suit," squawked the com. "I'm leaving it for you."

He flushed. "Listen, you," he growled. But he was helpless to do anything to stop her, and he knew it.

"My name's Alo," she answered. "Not 'you.' "

He cursed and looked in through the airlock window.

She had the suit off and was only half dressed, picking up her clothes. She was slender and pale, with small hips and breasts, but more mature in body than he had thought. He jerked his gaze away—to the com—and strained to think of a reply. He had trouble taking a breath. "I know your name," he said finally.

"Good. See you outside." Before he could think of anything else to say, the outer hatch light signaled OPEN.

For a moment, he stood dumbfounded. He realized that he was committed. The airlock was flooded with outside air, and there was no way to decontaminate it; and he couldn't very well leave her out there alone. Like it or not, they were in this together. "Peep!" he called. With a scrambling sound, the ou-ralot popped out of the galley. She trotted down the passageway and grinned up at him. Suddenly Panglor changed his mind. "No, you stay here," he murmured. "There might be something out there that would hurt you even it it doesn't hurt us." Disappointment touched him, but slowly subsided, leaving loyalty and acceptance. "Right," he said.

Turning, he cycled the lock closed and gave it a flush with ship's air. Then he entered the lock, sealed the inner door, and checked the readings on the suit monitors. They registered clear, for what it was worth; Alo had done the test correctly. Hanging the suit in its locker, he took a breath and opened the outer hatch. He let out his breath and inhaled again. The air was perfect. So far.

He stepped outside onto the top of the cargo hull. The ship sat upright on the plain. The landscape below was spooky but beautiful in the night: rock features against a pale airglow. He looked for Alo but couldn't see her. "Where are you?" he called.

"Right here."

He saw only a dark, empty plain. "Where?"

"Here."

He scowled and peered over the edge of the cargo hull. *"Right here,"* he heard, in an exasperated tone. "On the ground. Looking right at you." Her voice seemed to be coming from directly below. He swung himself around and climbed down, using the service rungs on the side of the cargo hull. When he dropped to the ground beside the ring-shaped main drive unit, he looked around. Then he circled a third of the way around the ship, and found her standing, hands on hips, watching him. Her expression was quite sober. "You okay?" she asked.

"What are you trying to pull?" he growled. "Why didn't you move to where I could see you?"

She looked puzzled. "I could see you perfectly," she said, pointing above him at the ship. He turned. The hatch was in full view, high in the air at the base of the cabin hull. That was impossible. He had circled a third of the way around the ship. He scowled.

"Let's look around," Alo said, nudging him.

"All right." They turned and moved away from the ship, over a rise. The ground was uneven underfoot, and the air was breezy, with a scent of clay. Many of the rocks along the way shone with a peculiar light, as though impregnated with a fine powdering of luminous material. They walked past a shoulder-high ridge, rounded its end, and stopped.

Before them lay a flat, glistening mist. It was a marvelous pool, filled not with water but with vapor, which convected slowly and glistened white under the stars, between sparkling banks. Above the vapor, in the air, floated several . . . creatures.

Fish?

Panglor stared in amazement at half a dozen large, rather sluggish fish, silvery and blue and green—all of them floating in the air. Several of the fish turned and stared at him with dark, unblinking eyes. They swam languorously, moving freely above the vapor-pond; but they seemed bounded by its banks, as completely as if submerged in liquid water.

Panglor blinked hard.

Several glittering objects appeared at the far side of the pond, drifting toward the airfish and toward Alo and Panglor. They seemed to float directionlessly among the fish.

"What's that?" Alo murmured, cocking her head. Panglor turned questioningly; then he heard it, too. Musical tones rang faintly across the pond—chimes or small crystalline bells, ringing irregularly, like harbor buoys. He moved his head, trying to localize the sound. "They're singing," Alo said. She pointed at the new objects; and, in fact, the sounds grew louder and clearer as the objects approached. Their features became visible in the gloom. They were floating crystalline arrays, with tops that looked like flowers or fans, and with gnarled stems pointing downward toward the vapor-pool. Two of them drifted close to the bank. One had a top that resembled rose quartz, a bladed horizontal dish that vibrated up and down, producing a beautiful alto tone. The other bore a silvery blue, vertical sail, which sang in a quavering soprano. One of the fish turned, drawn perhaps by the music, and glided slowly past the two aerial crystals.

Alo reached out to the rose-quartz crystal, which was now little more than an arm's length away. The crystal's singing grew louder and strained as her fingers closed toward it; it trembled with off-key harmonics. "Listen," she said, awed.

"Careful," Panglor warned. Alo gave no sign of hearing; she stretched farther, leaning out over the mist. The crystal wailed. "Wait!" Panglor cried. Alo's fingertips touched the crystal, and the dish shrieked. *Bang!* It exploded. Fragments of pink glass rained onto the bank and into the vapor-pool. The unadorned, gnarled stem of the crystal slowly tipped and wobbled, touched the mist, and sank from sight.

Panglor growled in disapproval, until a stinging sensation in his right hand distracted him. He was bleeding, cut by a shard of crystal. He sucked on the cut. The other crystals continued to sing, in a disquieting minor key. "Why did you do that?" he complained. Alo ignored him and surveyed the wreckage, hands on her hips. She looked dazed. Two airfish hovered nearby, one of them fat and lumpy, and the other narrow as a barracuda, with forward-hooking fins on its sides. Their eyes moved somberly, as though they were assessing these destructive intruders.

Alo made an unhappy sound and said, "Why did it do that? Why did it die when I looked at it?" She stared vacantly. "I just looked at it."

"You tried to grab it," Panglor corrected her.

"I just looked at it. Look—each one is different. That one's gone now. There will probably never be another like it."

Indeed, each crystal appeared distinctive. The one with the blue sail had drifted away, and the others were clustering at the far side of the pond. There was a channel of some sort leading away, a channel carpeted by mist. Several of the fish swam that way until they were out of sight.

The landscape was growing darker. The airglow in the sky was waning and so, too, was the light from the rocks. "Let's go back to the ship," Panglor said. He had seen too much to think about already.

Alo nodded, and together they returned the way they had come. Panglor thought the path looked different on the return, with that ridge on the left now a little higher, and a huge boulder where he thought there had been a low spot. He cocked his head, then shrugged.

The ship, at least, was unchanged. Panglor was greeted by waves of joy from inside. The ou-ralot met him, bounding, as he opened the inner door. "Hey, Peep!" he cried, with enormous relief.

"Hoolyoop! Hweeloruu!" echoed LePiep, leaping into his arms.

"Right!" he cried, hugging her. "I'm hungry." He turned to Alo. "Let's see what there is to eat around here."

They were both famished, though it seemed they could hardly have been outside for more than an hour. Panglor roasted a pan of fish-fingers and seed muffins, and they attacked the meal ferociously, sitting cross-legged on the galley deck. Afterward, Panglor brewed a pot of moke.

"That was good," Alo remarked. Then she became somber. "You know, I really wish that crystal hadn't broken."

"'So why'd you grab it, then?"

"I told you. I didn't do *anything*!"

"I watched you. This isn't doing anything?" He mimicked reaching out. He noticed with a start that the cut was gone from the back of his hand.

"That's ridiculous," Alo retorted. "I did nothing of the kind. I might have lifted my hand up, but I didn't reach." She raised her hand, but kept it close to her breast.

Panglor snorted. "I quite clearly saw your hand go out."

Alo shrugged, shook her head.

"Well," he said. "Well . . ." He brought two mugs of brew and sat down on the deck again.

Alo yawned, then smacked her lips and blew on her moke. "This is a strange place, huh?"

He looked away for a moment, toying with his earlobe. For some reason, he had just remembered how she had looked in the airlock, with most of her clothes off. LePiep raised her head, purring.

"Where do you think that other ship is, Pangly?" she asked, edging forward, with her arms clasped around her knees.

He blinked uncomfortably and backed up an inch or two. His gaze went to his ankles, crossed in front of him. The deck suddenly felt extremely hard. "Don't know," he said.

"I think they're up there in orbit. They probably have us spotted by now."

He tensed; LePiep sent a silent wave of concern. Easy now. Don't pay attention to her. Relax. He tried to relax, concentrating on each muscle, staring in his toes and working up. But each time he relaxed one muscle and moved on to the next, the previous one tensed again. "I think," he said, "It's time we got some sleep."

"Of course, they might not be able to see us."

"We both need sleep," he said.

"They might see an iceberg here."

"What are you talking about?"

"Or a dinosaur."

He stared at her in irritation. "I *think*," he said, "we had better get some sleep."

Alo stared right back at him. "Okay." She nudged his toe before rising. "You can pretend to be mad all you want. But you don't fool me." Then she hopped to her feet and went off into the cabin, across the passageway. A moment later she called back, "Are you coming in here with me?"

He stiffened, and saw LePiep arch her back. Getting slowly to his feet, he said, raising his voice, "I'll be in the control bay." The only trouble, he realized a moment later, was that the cabin was where the only head on the ship was located. He weaved with indecision for a minute, then went to the cabin door. "Hey," he said, knocking.

"Hey, who?" came Alo's voice.

"Who do you think? I have to come in a minute." He made a fist and opened it.

"So come in."

Cautiously, he opened the door and stepped inside. He flushed hot, but controlled his emotions carefully. Alo was undressed again, except for skimpy panties. She was half turned away from him, but she was bent over the sleep bay, with her rear sticking out and those breasts, not looking quite so small, hanging down from her chest. He cleared his throat, not quite knowing what to say. She didn't respond; she was preparing the sleep bay. "Listen," he said finally.

She stood up and faced him unselfconsciously. "What?" she said.

God—this girl was how old? This nonsense couldn't go on. "Listen—put something on, will you?" he kept his gaze averted.

"What's the matter?" she taunted. "Afraid of a little girl— a 'juvenile delinquent,' didn't you call me?" Her eyes sparkled.

He jerked his gaze to stare her full in the face. She grinned; he trembled. He refused to lower his eyes. "Put . . . something . . . on," he growled, and then he angled past her and went into the head, and shut the sliding panel behind him. Jesus Christ, he muttered silently, quaking, refusing to look into the mirror until he had controlled himself . . . and refusing to ask himself, Do I really like that kid?

When he was finished in the can and couldn't put it off any longer, he drew a breath and came out. Alo was sitting in the sleep bay, wearing a shirt, watching him reproachfully. "All right?" she said coldly, as he edged by to pull clean clothes out of a compartment on the other side of the cabin.

He faced her from the door. "How old—?" he started; then he cut himself off and said abruptly, "Good night." He shut the cabin door, went into the galley and got a beer, and took it to the control room. There he calmed himself, muttering, sipping his beer, and stroking LePiep. "Not twelve, that's for sure," he mumbled. "Or fourteen, either."

"Hrruuu," LePiep said, radiating appreciative and soothing feelings, coming down slowly from a state of excitement. Panglor nodded and stroked her, glad for the reassuring company. But his heart still beat quickly, and for the next hour he brooded in silence.

What woke him was Alo banging things about in the galley. He turned halfway over in the pilot-couch, aching in every joint, and rubbed his eyes, wondering where LePiep was. Not in the control bay. So where? He grumbled and blinked, orienting himself. Turning on the viewscreen, he inspected a rocky vista, with one gas-pond visible and a few moving spots that were probably airfish. It was nighttime still, or again. Rats only knew how long a night was on this planet.

He heard a purring from the passageway. A moment later, LePiep sailed into the control bay, airborne, flapping her wings furiously. She landed with a thump on the control panel in front of him, and gazed at him with pulsing eyes. "Peep. Where have you been, girl?" She hunched her wings and folded them into place. He was touched by subdued confusion, and by echoes of warmth.

Alo shuffled in and halted just inside the compartment. She was dressed in a long pink skirt and gray bunch-cuffed pants. Her manner was shy—almost contrite. "LePiep was watching me fix breakfast," she said, her voice trembling slightly. "We talked. We got to be better friends."

"Oh?" he managed. What was this, an apology for last night? He cleared his throat thoughtfully. He spent a good ten seconds doing that, and by then Alo had disappeared again.

She was back a minute later, with two mugs. "Do you want coffee?" she asked. "I found some real coffee in the stores, and thought I'd make some."

Panglor nodded grudgingly. He did love real coffee and had been saving it for either celebration or cheering up. It seemed to fit the occasion. Alo watched anxiously as he blew on it. "Don't stare!" he complained. She nodded and continued watching him surreptitiously. He sipped and suppressed a choke. It was gritty and tasted like charred toast. Swallowing with difficulty, he looked up to see her staring. He made a bold effort to smile; then his will collapsed. "Oh, hell!" he said, grimacing. "It's awful! Don't you know how to make coffee?" he worked his tongue, trying to get rid of the taste.

Her eyes darkened. For an instant he thought she was going to cry. Her face twisted, she stomped angrily out of the control bay.

"Oh—" he grumbled. He went after her and stopped, amazed, at the galley entrance. Instead of crying, she was bent over the counter, concentrating furiously on the outmoded brewer that was part of the *Cur*'s galley equipment. He quietly poured his coffee into the disposal and then leaned on the counter. "You figure *Deerfield* won't see us?" he said. "You think maybe we'll look like something else to them?"

"Shh!" she said. She frowned at the brewer, tracing the mechanisms with one finger.

"Look," said Panglor. "That thing is so obsolete you'll never get it figured out. Especially not if you use logic. I don't even know if it works right."

Alo didn't look up.

Panglor sighed. He found an instant-pack of moke, added water, and snapped it hot. He poured it into a clean mug. "Okay. But would you do it later?" Alo made no reply. He rested the side of his head on his knuckles, in exasperation. After watching a few moments later he said, "How old are you?"

That time she looked up—but only for a moment. Then she stared at the machine again. "Hard to say." She put a finger to her lip thoughtfully.

"I know. How about if you make it easier for me to say, by telling me."

"Well," she said. And she stopped and pursed her lips. "Think I've got it. The water runs through *here*, to the roast coffee *there*, and—"

"*Age.*"

She glanced up. "Well, if you need to know exactly, I can't tell you." She hesitated, licking her lips. He arched his eyebrows. Finally she said, "It would be several people's best guess. One of them is mine, but my best guess is no better than anyone else's."

He turned his palms upward in exasperation.

She peered at the brewer. "Somewhere between seventeen and twenty-two standard, we figure."

"*We* figure?"

"Yes, Captain Panglor, Pinglor sir," she said, trembling. "Yes, Captain Puglor. *We* figure. Me, Urula, and the meds. Based on tentative adjustments due to relativism in space travel, time inaccurately recorded in locations of nonstandard local year, and the hypothetical contents of destroyed documentation. Also on physiological measurements by the meds—rendered uncertain by the factors mentioned above—as well as by unknown environmental exposures to radiation, gravitation, and respiratory and dietary chemistries."

"But—"

"And based upon my own memories, which are not accurate because of—because of, b-blocks caused by unresol-unresolved—" She stopped and focused very hard on some point behind Panglor. "Un—" she started again. Then she hit the counter. Then her thigh. She grimaced, and got control. "You can read my report on D3, if it's so important to you," she snapped.

Panglor struggled with an obstruction in his throat. LePiep ran into the galley and hopped up onto the counter, and looked back and forth between the two. She rumbled, radiating bewilderment and fear, caught between them and unable to help. Panglor thought desperately. Say something useful. "So," he tried, "since you're not sure ... is that why ... you were ... the way you were ... last night?"

Alo's head jerked up. Her eyes smoldered with rage. Wrong. Said it all wrong! "What I mean is—"

"Sure," she said, her voice icy steel. She opened the storage compartment and took out a wrapped lunch.

"I think—" he stammered.

"No, you *don't* think," she snapped, and she stormed out of the galley.

"Wait!" he yelled. She didn't stop. She went straight to the airlock and slammed the port behind her. "Hey!" he shouted. There was no answer. He dithered in the passageway and finally went back to the galley, furious. The damn witch—grown woman or not. Neurotic little twit. He'd be better off without her.

A man can't make a mistake—can't choose his words wrong?

Grabbing his cooling mug of brew, he said, "Come on, Peep," and stumped back to the control bay. The viewscreen was still on, but there was no sign of Alo. He gulped his moke grimly. LePiep radiated alarm, and he tried to soothe her. Finally he started fiddling with the viewscreen controls. Might as well find her and see that she stayed out of trouble.

There was no sign of her. Probably she was already in trouble. Well, to hell with her.

He went and mistshowered hurriedly, put on a clean jumpsuit, and returned to the bridge with a flatcake and a fresh mug of brew. Immediately he saw Alo in the screen, walking away from the *Cur* in the same direction they had taken earlier. He watched tensely. LePiep perched on the console, staring at him, wide-eyed and nervous. Alo disappeared behind a limb of rock. Panglor took a sip and waited for her to emerge. He strained his eyes. A curious twilight still lay over the land, making visibility uncertain, but he did not see how she could have moved off in either direction without crossing his line of sight. Probably hiding, he thought. Sulking. Or looking at the pond.

LePiep hopped onto his shoulder and began sniffing unhappily at his hair. "Hey, bud, you figure she'll be all right out there?" he asked, patting the ou-ralot uneasily. "Sure she will. What could hurt her?"

LePiep muttered, radiating anxiety.

When *was* that girl going to show up?

8

SETTING OUT in search of her, Panglor picked his way among the boulders, LePiep on his shoulder. He noted that certain features of the landscape seemed altered. It was more a feeling than a specific observation, but the angles and dimensions of the ridges jarred with his memory. Daylight was approaching. The sky behind the ship glowed with a lemon-orange light, which somehow imbued the landscape with ghostly illumination without actually chasing away the darkness.

He intended to return to the gas-pond, figuring that it was probably what Alo had done. Following essentially the same route they had taken last night, he looked for the pond—and instead found himself standing on unfamiliar ground, where he thought the pond should have been. The ridges behind him were familiar, but the land ahead was not; it was all carved channels and ravines. An anxious feeling crept through him, and LePiep murmured nervously in his ear. Frowning, he turned to look back at the ship, to doublecheck his bearings.

What he saw was an empty plain, beyond the ridges, and in the far distance a rocky-rimmed horizon—and above the horizon, a pale, yellow sun. The ship was no longer visible. He stared at the sun with wide eyes. LePiep grumbled throatily; his own heart-rate surged. Cradling the ou-ralot, he scrambled up onto one of the ridges for a higher view. The plain was still empty. No spaceship. He swallowed tightly, controlling his emotions. LePiep, though, squirmed and whimpered softly. "Easy, babe," he muttered, unnerved by her waves of fear. He turned carefully, and saw a tumbled and confusing terrain, glinting here and there with what appeared to be crystals—or perhaps water—but no signs of the vaper-pool.

Something was dreadfully wrong here.

Taking a deep breath, he yelled: "Heyyyy!"

There was no answer, not even an echo. He squinted. His forehead buzzed. His heart raced.

He climbed down from the ridge and continued walking in his original direction, away from where the ship had been. Well ... where did it say that things had to make sense? Perhaps the ship would be there when he turned back. But what about Alo?

Pausing in his tracks, he hazarded another glance back—and was startled badly. The sun had changed; it was now a smoky disk, rimmed with fire, giving the appearance of a yellow sun being perfectly eclipsed by a darkly translucent body. The sun flamed coolly against a dark sky, lighting the landscape but not the heavens.

Panglor blinked hard and moved on, but he was aware of waves of increasing anxiety, and for a moment was unsure whether he was radiating or receiving from LePiep. Or being amplified by LePiep. The ou-ralot peered to and fro nervously, and looked up into his eyes in fear. She was worried; but was she worried about Alo? Panglor's insides twisted just a little as he realized that *he* was afraid for her. And afraid of being left alone. *Where was that girl?*

He yelled again, with more lungpower: *"Hey!"* As he walked, he called repeatedly. Finally it occurred to him that Alo probably would not answer to *hey* even if she heard him, and he began calling, "Alo! Hey—Alo!" But there was still no answer.

The terrain gradually changed, becoming even more confusing. Though the ground seemed level enough, his feet carried him into deepening ravines among the ridges. He realized that he was in danger of becoming lost in a labyrinth; and by the time he realized it, he was already lost. Turning back, he could not even say which of several pathways he had just stepped out of; none of them looked right to him. The steeply chiseled walls of all three passages were partially lost in shadow; but the angles of the shadows were bizarre and contradictory. Sweating, Panglor tried to decide on a course of action and found that he could not. Nothing he had done so far had produced a logical consequence.

Where logic failed, then, guesswork would have to take over. Intuition. "What do you think, Peep?" he said softly, turning to look all around the tricky landscape, unsure of his directional sense, unsure of what he would do even if he knew which way he was facing. He was here to find the girl, but of what use would that be if he was hopelessly lost himself?

"Hwup," murmured LePiep disconsolately.

"Yah," he said, feeling his fear begin to creep out of control. He shivered involuntarily, and for an instant loosened his hold on the ou-ralot.

A sudden wave of joy flooded him. "Hrruu!" LePiep cried, and as he started in surprise, she leaped from his arms and scampered across an open flat. She vanished into shadow at the foot of another ridge.

"Peep!" he screamed in horror and lunged after her. By the time he reached the spot where she had disappeared, she had scampered on. He spotted her darting down a narrow ravine, visible for a moment in a beam of sunlight, then gone. What was she doing? He realized dizzily that the ou-ralot was running as though to greet someone she knew. Could she have seen Alo? "Wait, Peep! Come back!" He heard LePiep's whistle echo back through the convoluted rocks, but she was gone, through the ravine and off in heaven knew what direction.

Frantic, knowing it was probably no use, he stumbled down the length of the ravine; when he reached the end he peered about and sagged in despair. He faced a choice of at least five paths through the labyrinthine terrain, with no sign of which LePiep had taken. He called the ou-ralot, called again . . . and finally chose a path at random. Fear weighed heavily on him as he walked. He tried not to think about aloneness, because when he thought about it he began to tremble. His companions gone; his ship gone. Alone and lost.

After a time, he emerged into a large hollow among the intertwining ridges. The light of the sun fell strangely across the basin; the far side was in deep, inky shadow. He stared nervously at the area of shadow. It seemed unnatural: too dark, too absolute. He raised his eyes, and was startled to see LePiep running across the top of a ridge beyond the shadowy area. He caught faintly echoing waves of confusion.

Shouting, he dashed across the basin to intercept her. One moment he was in sunlight, the next in shadow, and then . . . he was somewhere else. He saw pale light in darkness, gleaming ghostly walls like stone but not stone. There were too many walls; they intersected and

crossed around him, and he blinked until he realized
that he could see through one to another, and if they
were truly walls, he could not see which way it was
possible to walk. Edging sideways, he tripped and fell
down a sloping pathway, and regained his balance as he
stumbled out between two quite solid boulders onto an
open ledge. He jerked to a stop, facing a body of water,
and shook his head. What the *hell* was going on?
LePiep . . . where was she? . . . what was this?

The water before him was turquoise-green, under an
invisible sun. Its surface was wisped with mist, but
when he cocked his head he caught a glimpse into the
depths. He was standing at the edge of what appeared to
be a small inlet on a large bay; but the horizon was
blocked by low-lying clouds, and it was impossible to
see far from shore.

"This is crazy," he muttered, other thoughts driven
momentarily from his mind. The sight before him was
compellingly, stunningly beautiful. He stepped to the
edge of the bank. He looked into the water and up into
the sky, which was blue—the first blue sky he had seen
on this world—and gazed along the shore. A breeze
stirred the mist, but nothing else moved.

This planet was playing tricks on him, and doing a
damn good job of it. "Well, why not?" he muttered,
rubbing his chin. "Every other goddamn thing is crazy."
Strangely, he felt sure that what he was seeing was really there; he did not think he was hallucinating, or suffering illusions. Which was, itself, crazy. An intuition.

He cocked his head and peered again into the water.
Had he seen something moving? The surface shined and
danced with mirrors for several moments, then cleared
suddenly. He found himself staring down through many
meters of water to the shadowy seafloor. What he saw
made his face twitch. Sitting upright on the bottom, its
image shimmering with the distortion of the water, was

a spaceship, all silver and shadow. It was *The Fighting Cur.* It looked rather like a large toy in the misty gloom, suggesting that the water was far deeper than he had thought. He stood dumbly, his stomach kinking like twisted rope. The *Cur*, sunk? He'd been wrong, then; he *was* hallucinating.

But no. He couldn't believe that.

Several tiny-looking fish moved in the gloomy depths, and he watched them maneuver around the structure of the ship. The *Cur* really was there, on the seafloor. But how? He felt his chest and arm muscles lock against one another with tension; he felt sweat form on his forehead. Okay, he thought grimly, as though someone might be listening—sink my ship. Take my friends. Go ahead and do what you want.

He blinked. The water rippled, and the angle of visibility changed. He saw something else on the bottom— another spaceship, not the *Cur*. And not *Deerfield*. A wrecked ship, broken in half, its insides exposed to the green depths. Panglor trembled, feeling excited and confused and more fearful than ever. Other people had crashed here, then. This planet had already taken lives.

He wrenched his gaze from the water and looked around frantically. His heart pounded. "LePiep!" he bawled. "Alo!" His voice rang out across the water and returned. The echoes died.

Grimly he turned to his left—and saw Alo.

Some distance off, a natural stone bridge arched out over the water, extending from the bank at an impossibly shallow angle and then curving back to the same bank. What supported its weight, Panglor couldn't imagine. But at its outermost point, Alo stood looking across the water. She seemed not to have noticed him. He shouted at the top of his lungs: *"Alo! Over here!"* His heart beat mercilessly as he skirted along the bank, looking for a clear path to the bridge. Alo, meanwhile, turned and began walking away from him, toward the far end of the bridge. She gave no sign of having heard his shout.

Panglor broke into a headlong dash to catch her. Several massive obstacles of stone forced him to jog inland from the bank; he ran in and out among rocks and ledges and gullies, trying to keep close to the water. He jumped up onto an elevated slab to search anxiously for Alo—and he clenched his fists in excitement. Alo was walking *toward* him on the bridge, and trotting at her feet was LePiep. Panglor yelled joyfully.

Alo still showed no reaction. But he caught a wave of emotion from LePiep—satisfaction, determination. (Why couldn't they hear him? It didn't matter; they would soon be reunited.) He leaped down and dashed the final fifty meters. Rounding a precariously balanced boulder, he trotted out onto the foot of the curious stone bridge. And cursed miserably.

The bridge was empty. The full sky covered it like a luminous bowl, and the water below glowed emerald. But Alo and LePiep were gone. He shouted. He ran out to the extremity of the bridge's curved midsection. He called and turned in every direction—to no avail. There was no sign that either the girl or the ou-ralot had ever stood here.

God no, he thought, and then all of his thoughts were lost in a rush of dizziness. Numbly, he walked the entire arch of the stone bridge, looking forward, looking down, staring at the mistily mirrored water. Sighing leadenly, he turned and walked back along the bridge, scanning the shore with half-focused eyes.

He sat down, letting his feet hang over the water, and gazed into the depths. He saw shadows and slanting rays of light, but no spaceships. Only deepening color, hinting at the hidden seafloor. Despair and bewilderment were all bound up in his chest, and he found it impossible to think in a linear fashion.

The sky overhead took on a warmer hue, with a blazing white sun in the center of a growing orange aura.

Clearing his throat, and blinking at tears that were not quite yet in his eyes, he struggled to get to his feet. A wave of hysterical desperation washed over him, almost knocking him back down. It was an instant before he recognized that the emotion was not coming from him, but from LePiep. He gasped weakly, turning.

The ou-ralot was running along the bridge, whistling mournfully and radiating waves of lonely desperation. "Peep!" he cried hoarsely. The ou-ralot sped up, scampering toward him. Waves of hope cascaded from her. She approached—leaped. "Here, babe!" he called with a stunning rush of happiness, and reached to catch her.

And she leaped *past* him as if he were not there, as if he were a ghost. He whirled in dismay to catch her, to grab her.

And she was gone.

Panglor's knees trembled, his eyesight wavered, his lungs had trouble holding air. His mind reeled drunkenly; thoughts and emotions fired like a thousand sparks, sputtering and short-circuiting his nervous system. *"Peep!"* he wailed. He began to sway, began to lose his balance. He swayed backward, forward, backward . . . and then tumbling, toward the sea.

The water never touched him. Sunlight whirled around him like an enormous wheel, and then it went out, and he was submerged in blackness. That lasted for several heartbeats, and then into the blackness came a reddish glow that at first only brushed at his senses, then slowly grew stronger. There were sounds, as of rushing water, rushing air, rushing particles . . . He felt that he was still tumbling, twirling slowly, and he perceived that he was falling into a vast, crimson-glowing halo in the darkness. He was frightened and dazed, and for a terrifying moment he thought that he was finished and that this was the limbo he had always feared. And then he heard voices.

Voices?

Yes—at least three separate voices echoed faintly around him. Each one came from a different quarter; none sounded human. One was high and whiny; another was thick as gravel and faint as a whisper; the third was a thrumming of strings. And now there was a fourth ... and it was ... LePiep.

He tried to localize LePiep's whistle, but a sudden cacophony of winds and voices assaulted his ears, confusing him. He strained dizzily to recapture LePiep's voice, but it was lost in the darkness. He was still falling, falling endlessly toward the cozy gloom of a fire-lighted cavern, which he could never quite reach. He felt a rush of *curiosity* ... and he squinted to peer around in this strange *non*place, and what he saw was LePiep looking up at a strange, gangling creature dressed in a robe. It was LePiep's curiosity that he felt.

Frustration exploded in his mind. He tried to reach out to her, to move toward her, to do *something*, but all that he could manage was to struggle futilely against an unyielding emptiness. He was invisible to LePiep and this other creature. He shouted for their attention, and when that failed, screamed. His vision of the two darkened, and he cried and pounded his fists in fury.

And suddenly he fell silent. Awestruck, he quit worrying for a moment about LePiep, or about himself. Clarity came to his thoughts. None of this made sense, at least not as he usually thought of it. But did that matter? No. What mattered was that certain things were happening; and whether he understood them or not, whether it was the planet playing tricks on him or someone else playing tricks, it would do no good to yell and become frantic—because look how much good that had done him so far.

So. He should keep watch and be ready to move when the tricks turned his way. Maybe he would awaken, and things would be different.

But in the meantime, he should accept.

Strangely, he found that not so hard to do—to remain calm, open, and understanding. But his head felt large and a little spacey, and he felt a heightened sense of geometry, of perspective, though visually there was little for him to see. LePiep and the other were gone; there was a reddish haze in the darkness, and a sensation of walls surrounding him, and then a pale outline in scarlet light. He walked, and after a time the outline resolved itself into a cave opening, and he passed through and found himself standing on high, solid ground, staring across a curiously jumbled-looking garden under a lemon-lime sky. See? he thought dazedly—you just be patient and everything works out. He set out along a narrow path leading down into the garden.

What he found was even more unusual than he expected. The "garden" was set in a basinlike formation, and it consisted of oddly shaped and textured shrubs that looked very much like carved stone. Approaching, he saw that the tallest were chin high, and the shortest, knee high. They looked rather like enormous mushrooms, carved out of stone by waters or winds of vanished ages. Each was distinctive, and most were so thoroughly and delicately chiseled that they seemed to have actual branches and leaves that bobbed and twisted as he passed. Frowning, he brushed one of the larger shrubs with his fingertips. A branch almost imperceptibly tilted to meet his touch. It was greenish-brown stone to his eye, but to his fingertips it felt cool, moist, and resilient. For an instant, he swore that it was whispering to him. "Rock-plants, huh?" he muttered. He shook his head and moved on. The rock-plants quivered as he passed, responding to his presence with gentle, rippling movements.

The garden was large, and the path wound through it with many twists and turns. The air was sweet and the sun bright, and despite his concern about his companions and his ship, Panglor gradually relaxed. If one could summon forth such peaceful surroundings, perhaps it was worth a certain amount of bewilderment. Farther ahead, the path hooked sharply to the right, around a queer twin-peaked muffin of a bush, and he followed it, sighing.

He stopped. The blood drained from his face. The next bush was a smooth-capped polyp a meter high. Stretched out across the top, limp and still, was LePiep. Her wings were partially unfolded, her eyes open but vacant. She did not stir at his presence. For a moment Panglor could not move, could not speak, could not breathe . . . could not tell if she was alive or dead. She was so still, so limp, he could not see even the tiny undulation of her breath.

The paralysis left him and he choked and moved forward, fighting anger and tears. She was dead—he had lost his only friend. On his third step, as though he had passed an invisible barrier, he met a wave of misery, of despair.

His heart trembled with uncertainty—then soared. "Peep!" he cried and rushed forward.

LePiep lifted her head listlessly, radiating a new wave of despair. Suddenly Panglor understood. She had given him up for lost and lain down in surrender, to die—just as once before, on Areax V, he had found her near death from loneliness, after her escape and flight from the pet dealer who had owned her.

Panglor halted beside the stone bush and reached for the ou-ralot. His hand passed through her, as through a mirage. LePiep looked about in confusion, glancing directly at him, but though she obviously sensed *something*, still she did not see him. His heart pounding, Panglor edged sideways around the rock-plant and LePiep. Suddenly she scrambled to her feet, radiating recognition and tormented excitement. Panglor circled farther around.

"Hiiieee! Hyolll!" she shrieked, spotting him. She sprang at him with such force that she knocked him backward into the next plant. *"Hruuuuu!"* she cried, squirming in his arms with anguished pleasure. Joy and love flooded Panglor's heart, shimmering back and forth between the two, like a small sun.

"Peep . . . babe . . . Peep . . ." he mumbled, hugging her desperately. The ou-ralot clung to him, quaking with exhaustion. He stroked her over and over, soothing her, calming his own ragged nerves. Eventually they settled down and regarded each other silently, gratefully. They were both exhausted, but they would make it—together. "Never let you go again, babe," Panglor muttered, and LePiep warbled in reply. Cradling her carefully in his arms, Panglor set off again along the path. The change in his heart was enormous—the warmth, the renewed care, the hope for the future. Concern for Alo.

Alo! And where was the ship?

"Kroool," said LePiep soberly, reflecting his feelings, even as he cut off the thoughts to keep them from muddying his mind. LePiep emoted hopeful worry. He scratched her head and walked silently on through the rock-garden.

On the far side of the basin the path angled upward into torturously ridged terrain. The path remained visible through the desolation, though, and Panglor shrugged and followed it. For perhaps an hour he trudged up one ridge and down another, muttering to LePiep, sometimes enjoying a wide view of the land of carved rock, and sometimes having no view at all except looming stone walls.

From the peak of a ridge he spotted—far to one side, half buried in a gully—something that glittered and that appeared to be the wreckage of an unfamiliar spacecraft. He continued along the trail, hoping to get a better view from further on, but he did not see it again. LePiep clucked as he considered the puzzle, walking on. Could it have been a human ship? *Deerfield?* He thought not; it had appeared too odd. Further on, he encountered pieces of actual hardware scattered along the path. He noted a guidance vernier, an acceleration recorder (of different vintage from the vernier), and a sensor scope of entirely unfamiliar design. He inspected each object closely and slipped one of the pieces, a small valve, into his pocket. Then he moved on, wondering, Is this some elaborate hoax?

The next object he encountered startled him somewhat more; it was an upright canister, with odd plumbing attachments on its sides, perched atop a rock. It was the coffee brewer from *The Fighting Cur*'s galley. Panglor stared at it without comprehension, but with carefully restrained emotion. It hardly seemed likely that anyone had dismantled the *Cur* in his absence, so . . . just accept, Balef . . . nothing was beyond belief now, though a great deal remained beyond understanding.

He thought of Alo. Where did she fit into all this? And what was she doing?

LePiep became agitated and fretful when he thought of Alo. He stroked the ou-ralot between the wings, calming her, and kept moving. Fifty meters further on, he rounded a bluff. *The Fighting Cur* stood just beyond a promontory of rock, bold against the sky. "I'll be damned," he whispered.

Then he saw Alo. The girl was pacing to and fro atop

the promontory. "There she is, Peep!" he hissed, feeling a rush of confused emotions, some of them more than a little scary. But damn, it was good to see that girl—his passenger, his crew.

The ou-ralot peered up at him, reflecting his joy and adding puzzlement. Didn't she see Alo?

As they drew closer to the *Cur*, Panglor saw that the promontory was not just an oddity of the landscape; it was a long incline, a ramp that ended precisely flush with the top of the ship's cargo hull, near the hatch. Someone—the planet?—had built them a gangway.

Panglor hurried up the ramp with LePiep. Now where had Alo gotten to? He called . . . no answer. He entered the ship. She wasn't inside either; but everything else looked normal enough—including the brewer, which was in its usual place in the galley. "Okay, buddy," he said to LePiep, after searching the ship. "Let's go look outside—but you're staying with me, you hear?" His anxiety was rising again. If strange things were going to keep happening, he wanted above all not to lose LePiep again.

From the cargo hull, he gazed in all directions. The terrain appeared much as it had originally, except for the promontory and the fact that the sun, pale green now, was in the sky. He yelled, but got no answer. Time passed. LePiep remained quiet, attentive at first, and then dozing in his lap. A cluster of pastel-orange clouds moved across the sky.

Yawning, LePiep raised her head and peered about. Panglor stroked her unhappily, keeping a watchful eye around him. Suddenly the ou-ralot hooted, jumped up joyfully, and bounded out of his lap. "LePiep!" he bellowed. "No!" She was already halfway down the promontory. He started running, but was already left far behind.

LePiep streaked to the foot of the promontory and

darted behind a massive boulder. Panglor stopped, gasping, hoping she would appear on the other side. She did not. "Peep!" he cried in anguish, smacking his fist into his open hand. Agonized moments went by.

"Hoop . . . hoop . . ." he heard distantly.

"LePiep!" he yelled.

Alo appeared from behind the boulder—carrying Lepiep. Panting, Panglor ran to meet them. "There you are!" Alo cried. She was trudging wearily, and she looked angry. Her eyes were puffy, as though she had been crying. LePiep whistled tentatively, blinking back and forth between the two, radiating a hopeful warmth. "Where have you been?" Alo snapped.

Panglor stared at her in astonishment. "Looking for you!" he roared. "I've been looking all over this goddamn planet for you!" With an effort, he caught his breath and looked at Alo appraisingly. She was disheveled, and obviously tired, but appeared unharmed. "You okay?" he asked gruffly. He hated to admit it, but she really was a welcome sight.

"I'm all right," she said irritably. "Here—so's LePiep. You want to take her? I've been carrying her for a couple of hours." She hoisted the ou-ralot into Panglor's arms and continued plodding up the promontory toward the ship.

"Couple of hours?" Panglor said, keeping pace. "You couldn't have had her for a couple of hours. She was here with me, and she just ran off a minute ago to meet you—she spotted you before I did."

Alo snorted, not meeting his eyes. As they stepped onto the cargo hull, she said reproachfully, "You were gone all night. I've been back here twice, and I waited for you all night. When you didn't come back, I went looking. Found LePiep near a big vapor-pool, like the one we saw before—she was all upset—and I came back with her. But I had trouble finding my way."

Panglor stared at her, squinting. "This is a very strange place, Captain Puglor," she said. Panglor nodded and looked around. The sun was moving, edging along the horizon. How was anyone supposed to measure a day here—or anything else, for that matter?

Alo entered the ship and he followed. Only after sealing the hatch did he let LePiep down again. He was ravenous. "Want to eat?" he said. He opened a food compartment in the galley and blinked. "You took enough food."

"You were gone a long time!" Alo retorted hotly. She really was angry and he couldn't understand why.

"I told you—I was looking for you. I got lost myself, and so did LePiep. I saw the two of you together—long time ago, before I found LePiep—near some big ocean. But you didn't hear me when I called."

Alo frowned at him, her forehead wrinkling. She shook her head in disagreement, in bewilderment. Their eyes met.

"Gah!" Panglor said abruptly. He dug into his food, and when he had finished eating, he leaned back against the counter. Alo regarded him carefully and made herself a mug of brew. Panglor puckered his lips thoughtfully and made his own mug of brew.

LePiep, curled up on the counter, watched them both with sleepy eyes and reflected mingled feelings of wounded pride, bewilderment, and puzzled hope.

Once they had gone over both of their stories, it was clear that they were hopelessly inconsistent. Alo's time sense of their separation was far different from Panglor's, and although she reported spending a good deal of time near a gas-pond, watching the singing aerial crystals, she insisted that she had never seen any body of water. And the only time she had seen LePiep was just before her final return to the ship. She had been at the gas-pond then.

Panglor recalled his near-misses with LePiep—the times he had seen her at a distance, emoting joy or distress for no obvious reasons, and the way she had lain in utter despair atop the rock-plant, not seeing him until he was at just the correct angle. Strange images. But some of them tied together, if you didn't mind a few distortions of reality. He could almost discern a kind of logic to what was happening. "I think I see what we've got here." He hoisted LePiep up to gaze at her eyeball to eyeball. The ou-ralot hummed warmly. She made him feel confident; she even almost made him feel warmly toward Alo.

"Sure," Alo said sardonically. "Everything's clear."

"Sure, it's clear," he said. He lowered the ou-ralot and studied Alo thoughtfully. "What we've got here is a kind of system of mirages. You see from one direction, and I see from another—and we don't see the same things at all. I see you, standing by some lake or ocean, and you say you were somewhere else at the time, and anyway you never saw water, you only saw the gas-pond. LePiep is lost, looking for me, and she runs right by me, looking overjoyed. The ship—the *ship*, for chrissakes, vanishes when we turn our backs on it."

"Wait a minute—"

"Wait what—can't you see it?" he said impatiently. "That's it, it's got to be! Something is distorting time and space—like a continuous mirage, only instead of bending light it bends all of reality." He closed his eyes and envisioned an enormously complex system of refractions, twists in reality, convolutions in the structure of space itself, perhaps. What a thought—but why not? If manmade foreshortening generators could stress space in a single dimension, couldn't natural forces create even stranger and more complex effects?

"Pangly, maybe we hallucinated—"

"Nah," he said, shaking his head. He knew he had seen what he had described. Besides . . .

He remembered something and groped in his pocket. His fingers found a small metal object, and he pulled it out for Alo to see. She squinted. "Valve component from a spaceship," he said. "I picked it up near the place where I saw the brewer."

Alo examined it skeptically, turning it over in her hand; but her eyes were wide. She jumped up, went into the control cabin, and returned a moment later with a sparkling violet crystal the size of an orange. "I picked that off a bush," she said. "No mirage."

Panglor studied it, thinking. "True, mirages can't account for all of it," he admitted. "But assuming that there are real objects here—like this, and like us— what's happening among us all is being affected by—by—"

He stopped to scratch his head. "Okay. Look. It's nothing to get upset about—it's just that the physical laws have been discontinued here, at least the laws as we know them."

"Revoked, huh?"

"Well, suspended, anyway. Remember the way we landed? And did you see that sun?"

"Ho! Red, with yellow stripes," Alo said. "It was kind of nice."

Panglor was startled for a moment, not remembering any striped sun, but he shrugged. "Right. But the question is, can we get *out* of this place?"

"Mmmm," said Alo thoughtfully. Suddenly, catching Panglor by surprise, she crossed over to him, hooked an arm around his neck, and kissed him on the mouth. Then she jumped back, grinning.

Panglor grunted, dazed. His mind fogged, cleared, and fogged again. Why had she done that; why was she grinning like that? And why was LePiep up and prancing on the countertop, whistling and emoting happy thrills? What the hell was going on? He felt his face glowing red.

"Pangly," said Alo. "Let's go out and see if the sun is setting yet. I saw a terrific sunset last night."

He blinked as though seeing her for the first time, and opened his mouth. Alo turned to go to the airlock before he could think of anything to say, so he cleared his throat and followed. LePiep yelped; he turned to catch her. Then, with Alo, he went outside.

The sun appeared to be coming up over the horizon. "Nuts," Alo said. The sun was pale yellow again, and the sky surrounding it was pitch-black, with a sprinkling of stars. "Hey, look at that," she said, pointing out over the plain. What had been vast desolation was now grassland, rolling lazily into the distance. Panglor looked on the other side, to the tumbled land. There, too, life had sprung into being—grasses and shrubs and small trees inlaying and changing the entire visual character of the terrain. The air was scented with chlorophyll.

Panglor breathed deeply and stood silent a minute, letting the sight saturate his senses. He turned back toward the plain. "Uh-oh," he said. "Look at *that*."

Half a kilometer out on the plain, a silver spaceship was materializing, like a ghost ship appearing out of the ether. It was the *Deerfield*.

9

"UM," SAID Alo, moving closer to him. "That's them, huh? They're gonna be awfully mad."

"More than just mad, I think," he said, shading his eyes and squinting. *Deerfield* lay on its side, a giant silver cylinder gleaming in the sun. A dark spot appeared as a hatch was opened, and a man came out. He went back in, and soon half a dozen men spilled out. They milled around, agitated, and several of them pointed in the direction of *The Fighting Cur.* "Something else I think," Panglor said, "is that they're going to get here in about two minutes, and we'd better get the hell out of here before they do." He glanced at Alo, expecting to see fear. But she set her face determinedly and nodded.

"Better play for time, until we can get an advantage," she said. "Wait a sec." She dashed into the ship. A minute later she came running out, with a totebag. "Food," she said, breathing hard. "Might get hungry."

Panglor gave her a look of admiration. Then they ran down the ramp and into the rocky maze.

"Slow—down—" he gasped, after trotting for several minutes.

She fell back as he caught his breath. "I think they'll have trouble following us," she said, grabbing for his hand. That felt strange to him, and apparently it showed, because she let go of his hand and snagged a tool loop at the waist of his tunic. "Just keeping us together," she said cheerfully.

The greenery that crowned the twisty path made the situation seem somehow less desperate—unthinkable that men could follow this way with assault or murder in mind. Panglor, in fact, believed they were safe as long as they kept moving. He did not feel so safe about *where* they were going. A course straight away from the ship might bring them right back to it, as far as he knew, but right now the terrain ahead looked deep and labyrinthine. Perhaps he should worry more about finding their way back when they wanted to return.

Alo hummed as they walked. He glanced sideways at her and wondered at the change in her personality. "I think the planet's letting us get away with this," Alo murmured, looking around contentedly. They were skirting a pond of real water with several airfish gliding over it. The sun was zigzagging its way to the zenith.

"Could be," he agreed, feeling mellow. "What's the matter, Peep?" The ou-ralot was squirming in his arms.

"Hyol-hoop," said LePiep, and she leaped from his grasp and ran along the bank, radiating excitement.

"Hey! Damn—*LePiep*!"

Alo touched his arm reassuringly. "It's okay, I think. She won't stray. She knows."

Panglor clenched his hands nervously. "Stay close," he called unhappily.

LePiep looked back, ruffling her furry wings. "Hy-

oop!" she cried agreeably. Then she turned and marched
forward, leading the way. Alo chuckled and clenched
the bottom of Panglor's tunic.

They halted, facing a low escarpment. The easiest-
looking path was to the right, along the base of the escarpment. But the ou-ralot, heedless, scampered directly
up the cracked and layered face. "LePiep—don't!" But
the command was in vain. The ou-ralot went straight
to the top, and there was nothing to do but follow her
up. They made the climb cautiously, and from the top
they followed level ground for a distance. The path
ended at a low drop-off.

"Pangly!" cried Alo. Before them was a wide, shallow basin. Along the right was tumbled landscape, and
to the left was a glinting vapor-lagoon. On the lagoon's
banks rested a grounded spaceship—a huge, rhomboidal
oblong, greatly enlarged at both ends. Its hull was emerald silver in color. One end of the ship was partially
submerged in the pond.

"Is it alien?" Alo said, awed.

"Jeez." Panglor scratched his head. "Looks like it."
He saw no sign of life. No reason to expect to. The ship
looked as though it had made a hard landing; the hull
had buckled and split on the underside. There was no
telling if its inhabitants had survived—and no telling
how long the wreck had lain there. "No one home,
looks like, but we'd better be careful anyhow."

"There goes LePiep," Alo cried, grabbing his arm.
The ou-ralot capered down the slope toward the lagoon
and the wrecked spaceship.

Panglor leaped after her, scrambling on rocky foot-
ing. LePiep looked back, grinning, and with a toss of
her head ran on.

The dash ended abruptly at the foot of the slope.
LePiep was poised by the lagoon, sticking her nose out,

and within moments several large airfish drifted into sight and came over to regard her silently. She poked and sniffed, not quite touching noses with them, and then she peered up at Panglor in satisfaction. "Okay?" he said, bending to scoop her up, carefully, so that she could still face the airfish.

"Hrruuu."

The fish departed, moving their fins gently. "Lots of them over there," Alo said, pointing toward the ship. At least a dozen or more of the airfish hovered near the submerged end of the craft, and they were not the only sort of creature present. Someone or something resembling a man separated from the cluster of airfish.

"What's this?" said Alo.

Panglor made no immediate reply. He recognized the creature as the one he had glimpsed with LePiep, when she was lost. From a distance it looked like a man, but he soon realized that, although it was humanoid in appearance, the creature was no human. Perhaps this was the owner of the spaceship. The alien walked toward them—or perhaps floated; its movements were exceedingly graceful, and its robe nearly brushed the ground, so that its feet were invisible—and met them along the lagoon's bank.

The being was as tall as a man, thin and spry, with facial features resembling a man's, though sharper. Its nose was a beaklike affair, and its square-pupiled eyes peered out from beneath large-boned brows. The alien bent right, from the waist, and then left, in a swishing movement—as though bowing, side to side.

"Hwell-wee-trwullyoo-k-k-zhuum," the creature said.

Panglor heard that, but also understood, "Greetings. I welcome you to my ruins, humble though they be. I trust they will suffice to provide hospitality to two ship-wrecked, and perhaps forlorn, humans."

Panglor met the creature's gaze warily. How could it

know who they were? he wondered in astonishment. LePiep, however, emoted reassurance as she squirmed in his arms; apparently she trusted the alien. Well, she had met it before, and she had a good sense for whom to trust and whom not to trust—so, Panglor thought, he might as well follow her lead. He bowed forward in human fashion. "Greetings to you, too," he mumbled.

Alo nodded. "Hi."

The alien spoke again in its own tongue, which Panglor heard as, "Would you care to accompany me to my ship?"

Panglor gazed curiously at the alien. He looked male to Panglor, at least by human analogy, and Panglor thought something else, too; he thought the creature was a Kili. Panglor had never seen a Kili—no human had—but he had seen artists' renderings, based upon artifacts found in Kili ruins, and this alien looked a lot like those renderings. That would be something— finding the first Kili ever to be seen by humanity!

"Sure," he said, answering the invitation. He nudged the ou-ralot in his arms and added, "This is LePiep."

The alien again bowed sideways with a swish. "LePiep. Yes—we met earlier. My name is Tiki. May I ask yours?"

"Oh—I'm Panglor," said Panglor. "And this is Alo."

Alo smiled with surprising charm, and the alien bowed and swished again. Then he turned and led the way toward the wrecked spaceship.

Alo whispered to Panglor, "I like him. I wonder what he is."

Panglor grinned, nudged her, and hurried after the alien. "Say—ah—Tiki."

The alien turned and looked at him serenely.

Panglor squinted and said, gesturing self-consciously, "Ahm—say, aren't you a Kili?" He cleared his throat and flushed.

Tiki stared at him for a moment. "I see what you mean," he said. His eyes lost focus.

"What?"

Tiki's gaze cleared. "Yes. I am. At least in the sense that you use the word. Kili." He bowed. Then he turned and started walking again.

Panglor squinted, trying to figure out what that meant.

"Hurry," said Alo, prodding him. "Keep up. Maybe he'll hide us in his ship."

Oh, right. There was still *Deerfield* to worry about, wasn't there? "Good idea," he whispered back. "But I don't know what to expect from a Kili." Alo shrugged and tugged him by the arm.

They approached the ruined spaceship beside the vapor-lagoon. With a flourish, Tiki ushered them to the entrance, the nearest of two large gashes in the angled underside of the hull, behind the enlarged front end. Tiki remarked, "The original entrance port has disappeared. The hull will no longer change structure to let us pass through." He sounded sad, as though a friend had left him. Panglor glanced curiously at him, and at the torn, yet smooth, edge in the ruptured hull.

They entered a storage hold cluttered with boxes and machinery, then a short passageway. Panglor and Alo ran their fingers along the walls, touching the subdued metallic finish inquisitively, and briefly inspecting every object they passed. Tiki led them to the enlarged front end of the ship, and here the passageway dipped and opened into an enormous spherical chamber. Panglor stared up and turned around in astonishment. The entire inner surface of the sphere was studded with what looked like seats, oddly shaped tables, and instruments. "Damnedest thing I've ever seen," Panglor said. "What kind of gravity control do you have?"

"None, anymore," said Tiki.

"It's crazy," Alo said. "Is it for zero gravity?" She darted up the curved incline and ran down in a big arc testing the shape.

"Before," Tiki said gravely, "we had selectable gravity against the inner surface, and we chose what we wished. And the shape, of course, changed as we wished." His neck twitched. "But none of that now. We had a rather difficult crash." He blinked somberly.

"We crashed, too," said Alo.

"Of course," Tiki said. "Many do. Would you like to sit? Can I bring you anything for refreshment?"

"We have food," Alo said, holding up her totebag. She sat on an odd-shaped couch that was nearly level, glanced at Panglor, and patted the seat beside her. Panglor released LePiep to nose about and sat beside Alo. He took a sandwich and a bulb of juice and faced Tiki, who was drawing something for himself out of a small panel. A long stick, apparently food.

"You mean other ships have crashed here?" Panglor said.

"Oh my, yes," answered Tiki. "Did you imagine you were the first? I can take you to see other shipwrecks, if you like. Some of the finest ones are just a short walk from here."

"You're joking," Alo said, munching.

"Why would I joke with a guest? I don't have guests often—it's been a while since my last ones disappeared."

Panglor scowled. "Disappeared?"

"Just vanished, most of them. I've tried to organize shipwrecks into groups to work for the social betterment, and so forth, but it never works. Most of the people go crazy and just fade out or wander off, and that's the last you see of them. Usually it's the sane ones. That's why I'm here, still, and my poor fellows and keepers aren't."

"What do you mean, that's why you're here?" asked Panglor.

"Sorry, I thought you knew. I am considered unwell, almost not *Kili*. Mad. Never could follow it myself, though." Tiki turned his two eyes inward, crossing them for a moment, and then relaxed and bit off a piece of his stick. "I hope you don't mind my digesting while we talk. My fellows would not have approved, but then, they're not here anymore." He looked cross-eyed again, then gazed back at the humans.

"You are humans. I have met some of your race-fellows. Actually a number of them have crashed here through the years, but the crews never were able to adapt. The place just didn't coincide with their conceptions about how things ought to be."

Panglor cleared his throat uncomfortably. He waved his sandwich in the air, then took a bite and started to talk with his mouth full. Alo interrupted him. "How'd they get here?" she said. "How'd *you* get here?"

"Why, the same way we all did, I imagine," said Tiki, brushing his sleeves. "Pulled right out of stressed space."

"Stressed space?" said Panglor, wonderingly. He jerked his thumb upward. "We were brought down from orbit."

"Were you, now? How interesting! Does that mean your people are exploring here again?"

"Uh-uh. We got here by—well—never mind that. What about this planet. It acts just like, I don't know, a—"

"Discontinuity," said Alo. "Like there's a discontinuity in the physical laws here, or surrounding the whole planet."

"Well, really," said Tiki, spreading his hands and arms, "I think we can be more precise than that. After all, we're all here together, aren't we?" Panglor could have sworn that the Kili was manifesting embarrassment. How strange. "I think we can describe it," Tiki continued, "as a locus of many smaller discontinuities that naturally occur in the behavioral fabric of space, or, if you prefer, as an interference fringe of many aberrations in the wavefronts of spatial reality. You could define it as a zone surrounding the planet, or perhaps you could define the planet as an artifact of the zone itself. To be honest, I'm not sure that this planet exists at all, except as an interference effect."

Panglor plucked at his teeth with a fingernail. "Yah?" He glanced at Alo, who had her eyes half closed, thinking. "So—" he said to Tiki, "how do all these ships happen to wind up here? They just pop in out of space?"

"Like a big, natural capture-field," murmured Alo, blinking.

"It seems to attract ships the way a gravity well attracts objects in unstressed space," Tiki said. "Or a counter-collapsing field in stressed space." He bit from his stick and chewed delicately.

"So . . . so ships get caught like flies. Right out of foreshortening." Panglor felt a series of hot and cold flashes of fear—the uncertainty he felt in foreshortening, the terror that his ship would fail, would lose itself in limbo. "Maybe," he said, his voice trembling, "maybe space is full of planets—discontinuities—like this."

"Loci. Interference patterns. No doubt you are correct. My sane fellows of the Kili have lost ships without explanation, and I have met others with similar problems. Still, I would hardly say that space is *full* of them. Rather, I think they are scattered about, and perhaps they cause eddies and undercurrents that draw straying ships to them in the stressed space."

"Right!" Panglor said. "Of course!" He started to become excited; the fear was changing to an adrenaline rush. These loci, these interference patterns, could be like shoals in an uncharted sea. Perhaps they were irregular, perhaps they shifted; but if they could be known, they could be avoided. "Yeah! Yeah—hey, we ought to be able to detect these things and stay away from them." He jumped up and faced a startled Alo, then turned to a serene-looking Kili. He was bubbling with enthusiasm. He heard a whistle and turned to catch an excited LePiep in his arms.

"What a discovery! This is where the lost ships are going!" He chuckled wildly; he could not believe his fortune. "Wait till we report this! They'll have to listen to us!" he exclaimed. "They'll have to! My God, this could be the most important discovery in—"

Alo interrupted him, tapping his arm. "Pangly," she said. "Pangly—have you forgotten? That's great, knowing all about this—this discovery. But how do we get back to brag about it? We're stranded here."

"Why, we—" Panglor said, and his spirits sagged. She was absolutely right, of course. *And it wasn't fair.* "Ho-loo, ho-loo," mourned LePiep. Panglor sat down, utterly deflated.

Alo sighed. "Don't worry, Pangly, we'll think of something," she said, patting him on the knee. She tickled LePiep under the chin, and LePiep's pleasure touched Panglor, relaxing him a little. Alo turned to Tiki. "How long have you been here? What's it like?"

"Ah," said Tiki. "How long? Who knows? My friends the fish out there experience time more slowly than I, and I more slowly than many other folk. Why, there was one other madman I saw, who was neither of your race nor mine—who was mad enough to stay but too mad to enjoy it—and I saw him grow old and die, finally, poor soul." He crossed his eyes and became still.

"What do you mean, he was 'mad enough to stay'?" Panglor asked, scowling.

Tiki remained still, apparently not hearing Panglor's question. Finally Alo cleared her throat and Tiki suddenly stirred and said, "Madness, of course, makes it easier. My good but new friends—I have been here long, even by my own reckoning. I have seen ships appear, and sometimes disappear. And I have traveled, of course, but I have always come back."

"Where?" said Panglor, startled.

"Here, of course."

"No, where have you traveled *to*? Around the planet, you mean?"

"Oh, that. It's hard to say, of course. But I believe there is very little more to see in this world than I have seen already. If you travel far, you always return to your beginning. I think there is really not so much area here. Which makes me think it is not quite so much the real planet as it would seem." He rocked his head back and spoke as though his listeners were above him. "No, I have traveled to other discontinuity zones—elsewhere. I do not know where. Perhaps they are all linked. Sometimes there are voices . . ." He gazed wistfully upward.

"Bah!" said Panglor, looking away. "Voices! *I* hear voices, but that doesn't mean I'm connected with the rest of the universe." He fumed. But he wasn't really angry with Tiki; he was angry with his helplessness. He was angry because they were stranded here, and because he didn't like being reminded of the voices *he* had heard and hadn't understood. And because it was all so damned frustrating!

Dismay touched him invisibly. Then Alo said, "Pangly, turn around."

Sighing, he faced them. Tiki was staring into space, eyes skewed. He seemed paralyzed—hurt by Panglor's doubt? Panglor felt shamed, but was too embarrassed to speak, until LePiep scrambled up into his lap and lent gentle support. The ou-ralot peered at the robed creature and radiated concern and sympathy, and she peered back up at Panglor. "Well—" he said. "Well. Tiki—hey, I didn't mean to be insulting or anything. I was just upset about what's been happening. Kind of got me off edge, you know?" He held his breath, waiting for a sign that the Kili would come around. LePiep stretched her neck toward the alien, purring.

Tiki hissed sputteringly. Slowly, his eyes realigned themselves and he focused on Alo and Panglor. His lips wrinkled, and he swayed. "Yes," he said. "Well, the place—the planet—the locus—the interference fringe— responds to thought and to state of mind. Maybe the *place* doesn't, but what happens here does." His eyes crossed again. "My poor shipmates. Poor shipmates ..." He began making creaking noises, and his face turned shades of red and brown. His creaking became a high keening. LePiep cried and curled herself into a quivering ball, radiating sorrow and pain.

A tremble passed through them, through the ship. Panglor heard a distant rumbling, as of a thunderstorm or an earthquake. His weight increased; his arms grew leaden. With difficulty, he held LePiep protectively and looked around nervously, as Tiki wailed. My God, he thought, is the ship taking off? Please, no!

Alo couldn't stand it any longer. "Tiki!" she cried. "Tiki!"

The Kili's eyes popped straight, and the colors drained from his face. The vibrations in the ship ceased, and Panglor felt his weight return to normal. "My manners!" Tiki whispered. "Forgive me! I failed to seek your approval before my emotional display. But I thought of my shipmates—they couldn't make the adjustment." His square pupils opened wide. "They were too rational, too stable. And so they went truly mad.

They broke. While I, who was thought unKili mad, remain here."

Tiki's eyes narrowed and he rose. He turned around, then back. "Why, I believe we have more guests coming," he said, blinking rapidly. "Are there other people with you? Should we go meet them?"

Panglor's limbs went cold. For a moment, he could neither move his eyes nor speak. Finally he asked, "Are there humans out there?"

"Indeed," said Tiki.

"Wait. Don't go out yet." He chewed his lip, thinking.

Tiki obviously sensed Panglor's alarm. The ou-ralot was up now, chirruping and radiating dismay. Tiki gazed at Panglor, canting his eyes inward just enough to indicate his concern. "Is something wrong?" he asked. "How may I help, friends Panglor and Alo and Le-Piep?"

"They—" started Panglor, and he shook his head, trying to think how to say this. "If they are the people we think, then they followed us, and their intentions will *not* be friendly."

"What may I do to help?" Tiki asked, swaying. "Are they evil or violent men?"

"They're angry," said Panglor, gesturing futilely.

Alo said, "Can you—?"

"Will you talk to them?" interrupted Panglor. "Find out what they want, but don't let them know we're here?"

"Of course I can do this," said Tiki, patting down his robe. "Can you doubt it? Is it so difficult?" He seemed almost to be chuckling.

Panglor gazed at him uncertainly. Doubt? Certainly he did; this was a self-confessed insane Kili. What did he know of murder and mayhem, and of lying and making sense to bloodthirsty men? Perhaps much; perhaps nothing. But what choice did they have? "No, no," he answered.

"But be careful," said Alo. "Please."

Tiki bowed so far left, and then right, that it looked as though he would topple over. Then he straightened and said, "Careful is all a matter of viewpoint." And he glided out through the passageway.

10

PANGLOR AND Alo joined glances for a moment. "You know what?" Alo said. "He reminds me of Urula."

"Who?"

"Tiki."

"Who's Urula? What do I care who Urula is? I'm worried about those men out there. They could kill us."

"Urula's my teacher," said Alo. "Only teacher I had at the station who was any good. He had a little robot. Never took me, himself, or the robot too seriously. I liked that."

Panglor let out his breath like a steam explosion. "What the hell do I care about some teacher when there are men out there ready to kill us?" He glared at her, until she furrowed her brow, gave him a crinkled smile, and shrugged.

"Okay, okay," she said, standing. "Let's go see what's happening. We can spy."

He grabbed LePiep, and they went out, following Tikki.

They peered into the outer storage compartment. Nothing stirred; Tiki must have gone outside. Alo nudged him, and they moved closer to the opening in the hull, where sunlight spilled into the compartment. There they took up a position behind some crates, in relative darkness, where they could listen and peer cautiously outside.

Tiki had walked some distance along the lagoon, and he was now greeting two men. The men were dressed in uniforms—probably Vikken, though it was impossible to be sure—and they seemed to be holding sidearms. Alo hunkered down beside Panglor and whispered, "I wish we could hear them." Panglor shushed her and strained his ears. He edged one way and then the other, behind the crates, and suddenly found a spot where he could hear the voices of the men and Tiki, distantly.

"We're looking for a human like us," said one of the men. His voice sounded unnatural; perhaps it was a trick of distance. "We have to find him."

"Whatever for?" asked Tiki. "Don't you have enough?"

The man replied, in confusion, "Have you seen this human, is what I'm asking. We're trying to find him because—we're just trying to find him. We think he came this way."

"Yah. We think he came this way," echoed the second man.

"I don't know what to say. It's been simply ages since anyone like yourselves came by here," said Tiki. "I've seen all sorts of people, of course, human and—" his words became unintelligible "—and—" unintelligible "—and—"

"Yeah, yeah—right," interrupted the first man. "Look, we'd be interested in all that, except for the fact—the fact is, we're shipwrecked here, and we—we—"

"Of course you are. Everyone here is shipwrecked," Tiki said.

"—we've got to get this guy, because, well, he's the one put us here. And Jeeb sent us out to find him and told us not to bother coming back unless we did." The crewman broke off, coughing. He looked terribly upset.

Panglor trembled, absorbing what the man had said.

The second man added in a wounded tone, "That just wasn't like Jeeb. Cap'n Drak, maybe, or some of those others we were lucky enough not to get—they're bastards, they are, some of them—but not Jeeb. Why, Tal, he'd as soon tell the cap'n himself not to come back as he would talk that way to his crew."

A sudden, terrible heat made Panglor sweat.

"Pangly, what's the matter?" whispered Alo, crowding close. LePiep peered up, emanating concern.

Jeeb. Tal Jeebering? Panglor swallowed, clamping down a rush of emotions. Steady, Balef, steady. Tal Jeebering was a Vikken officer he had worked under, briefly—the only Vikken officer who was not a rat-buggering dog, the only officer who had treated him with a semblance of human dignity.

"Pangly!" Alo hissed. "What's *wrong*?"

He shut his eyes, trembling. Now Jeeb was on this planet. Marooned, with the rest of the *Deerfield* crew. He had done that—Panglor Balef had done that, to the only decent man in the Vikken fleet. And now that man wanted Panglor's head. And who could blame him?

An elbow caught him in the ribs, jolting him from the depths of guilt. He met Alo's eyes, dark hazel and intent. She gestured, palms up, trying to make him speak.

"I know that guy they're talking about," he whispered, finally. "One of the *Deerfield* officers. The guy who told them not to come back without me." Alo stared back, uncomprehending. He realized, then, that she hadn't heard the men's voices; she had no idea what he was talking about.

"Listen," he said, pointing into the sunlight. He blinked and squinted. Tiki and the two men were closer now; Tiki kept moving in front of them as though to halt their progress, but the men just kept walking by him.

Panglor shifted slightly and heard the first man say, "We've got to search your ship." The man rushed past Tiki in an exaggerated movement. Tiki hopped back, startled. The man jumped, startled by Tiki's movement, and pointed his weapon at the Kili. "Going to search your ship. You don't mind, I don't mind. Right?" Tiki blinked and trilled. The man grunted and waved his partner along. With Tiki following, they approached and surveyed the ship.

"What do you think?" hissed Alo. "Can we ambush them?"

Panglor squinted sideways. His thigh muscles were cramped from squatting behind these crates; his knees, his ankles, and his back all hurt. His left foot was jammed against some kind of machinery, and something else was poking into his side. He did not feel quite up to jumping out at armed men. "Let's get inside," he hissed back.

Alo raised her eyebrows, but looked relieved. "All right, let's go," she whispered. Panglor grunted. His muscles didn't want to coordinate. He edged back toward the inner passage, then hesitated, still squatting, and tried to figure a concealed route across the compartment. Alo jarred him from behind, and he tumbled forward, knocking cartons over with a clatter.

"Hey!" a man yelled. Panglor scrambled to his feet, still holding LePiep—and saw a *Deerfield* crewman blocking the sunlight. The man squinted into the gloom, brandishing a nervie.

Panglor jumped back for cover—then saw Alo standing, exposed. "Get down!" he hissed.

The crewman started and yelled, "Stop, you!" He fired the nervie. The gun belched a bright-blue fireball, which zigzagged slowly through the air. The ball hovered in the center of the compartment and then exploded into a whizzing display of fireworks: streamers and fire-flowers and stroboscopic images of wildcats chasing each others' tails. The fireworks ended with a *pop*.

Panglor and Alo blinked at each other, and at the crewman. The crewman blinked, baffled. Then his partner entered the ship and the spell broke. "How did you do that?" the first man shouted. He pointed the nervie with both hands.

Panglor laughed. "I didn't," he cackled, shaking his head. Then he fell silent. Nervie or no nervie, they were caught.

"Okay, you," the crewman ordered. "You're coming with—" His voice dropped. Alo was bristling indignantly, and he had just noticed her. "Who are *you*?" he growled.

"Alo," she said. "Who are you?"

The second crewman squinted and brought his weapon to bear. Tiki slipped in behind both, watching. "Alo, huh?" said the first man. "And you?" He waved his gun at Panglor.

"That's Panglor Balef. *Captain* Panglor Balef, of *The Fighting Cur*," Alo said sharply. Panglor stood mute, trying to analyze the situation. It analyzed badly, so he tried it again another way. Alo said, "You haven't told us who *you* are."

The two men exchanged scowls, and the first said, "We're from *Deerfield*, as if you didn't know. Spacer

Godspey"—he hooked a thumb at his partner—"and I'm Spacer Turret. We've been looking for you for days. Now you two are taking a walk with us. Back to face the music. And boy, are you—"

"Is Tal Jeebering an officer on your ship?" interrupted Panglor.

Turret glared and said, "Yeah, and he's going to chew you so bad you'll wish—"

"He's a good man," said Panglor abruptly, and taking Alo by the arm, he stalked past Turret and Godspey and out of the ship. He nodded to Tiki, who fell in beside them. LePiep muttered in his arms.

The two crewmen charged after them.

"You hold it right there!" Godspey shouted. Panglor stopped, looked back, and dug at the bank with his toe while he waited for the men to catch up.

"Get on the com," Turret ordered his partner. "Tell Jeeb we've found them, and ask him what we should do about this alien." He silently guarded his captives, while Godspey attempted to contact *Deerfield* on his personal com. The sputter of static was audible to everyone.

"Can't get anything," Godspey said.

"All right. We start walking, then. You, there— alien—you can come if you want, but we won't force you." Turret waved his weapon at Tiki.

"Why, that is most generous of you," replied Tiki.

"You being sarcastic?" Turret squinted. "Never mind. Balef, you and the girl start walking. That animal—you can't bring it. Leave it here."

Panglor eyed him, then said, "Let's go, Alo." Together they set off in the direction they had originally come from. Panglor stroked LePiep as he walked, and she crooned unperturbedly.

"You hear me?" growled Turret. "Leave the animal."

Sighing, Panglor turned. "Shoot me," he suggested.

LePiep whistled in delight, encouraging him. He shushed her.

Turret and Godspey advanced threateningly. "That's enough of that!" shouted Godspey. Suddenly he whirled, gaping. Tiki had vanished. He had been walking alongside Panglor, and now he was gone. Godspey made gurgling noises.

Alo nudged Panglor and grinned. Panglor shrugged in bewilderment, but chuckled. The crewmen were looking around furiously.

"What's the matter?" said Tiki, standing beside Panglor. He stretched and contracted his mouth oddly.

Panglor choked. "Where'd you go?" he whispered. LePiep chittered, enjoying what she obviously took to be a game.

Turret swung around and caught sight of Tiki. He glared indignantly. "Are you planning to cause trouble?" he snapped.

"Why, what are you all talking about?" Tiki asked. He started to fade, becoming partly transparent. "Oh. Oh, I see," he said hollowly and became solid again. "Yes, yes. No trouble. I don't have guests often. Why would I cause trouble?" His eyes skewed, and he started to fade, but then became solid again. "I'm not sure if I'll be staying here with you just now," he added hastily. "I'll let you know."

Turret started to reply, but another voice interrupted—neither a human voice nor the Kili's. It was a tenor sort of voice, and it muttered sonorously for perhaps five or six seconds. A deeper voice took its place, speaking in an altogether different tongue. Panglor cocked his head, trying to recognize the sounds. "What's that?" cried Turret, swinging his weapon wildly.

"Voices," Tiki said.

Turret went red in the face and for a moment looked

apoplectic. But finally he spoke through gritted teeth. *"What voices?"* There was a distinct crack to his own voice.

"Oh, well, I couldn't tell you specifically," answered Tiki. "Not anyone around here, I'm sure. Possibly they're from another discontinuity, from across space."

Turret and Godspey stared at each other. Godspey was making quiet, funny noises, and that worried Panglor a little; the man might be on the verge of some kind of breakdown. Panglor cleared his throat and said, "Uh, maybe we should keep on moving—"

A new sound interrupted him, a melodic tone like the voice of a whale. It, too, came out of thin air, but its source sounded very close by.

Tiki beamed, obviously recognizing this voice. "Why, that's ... [unintelligible]. I haven't spoken with her in so long! How I would love to see her again!" he cried. He wavered, almost disappearing, then solidified long enough to say, "Do have a pleasant time, all of you. I'll speak with you again." Then he vanished. LePiep chirruped curiously and continued peering toward the spot where the Kili had been standing.

"Oh no!" cried Alo.

"All right!" Turret snarled—fed up, and obviously shaken. "Let's get going!"

"We were going," Panglor said mildly, "until you stopped us. So let's go."

Turret gestured silently with the gun. They started walking.

The terrain had turned oddly lush. Exotic bushes and trees lined the path, glistening waxily under a billowing red sun. The tree leaves and stems resembled plastic, yet felt alive, venting moisture and breath. Panglor felt an illogical sense of ease, walking with LePiep perched on his shoulder radiating contentment, humming and purring as though all were going exactly as planned.

After a time, at Alo's request, he passed the ou-ralot over to her. It occurred to Panglor that compared to these two Vikken men he was staying sane, keeping his equilibrium very well indeed. Now, that was a reversal from the usual state of affairs, and he rather relished it.

None of them knew where they were going, of course. Turret and Godspey followed, guns drawn, as Panglor and Alo picked their own direction. But after about an hour, it seemed, they sighted *The Fighting Cur* over an outcropping—her hull gleaming dustily in the sun. As they circled past the intervening ridge, the ship shifted in perspective disconcertingly, but did not disappear.

They emerged onto the grassy plain. *Deerfield* was about a kilometer off in the distance, but several of its crew stood guard at the base of *The Fighting Cur*. The sloping promontory to the *Cur*'s hatch was gone.

"Hey!" Turret yelled. "Call Jeeb! We got them!"

The guards jumped to attention. One of them darted off toward *Deerfield*. The others met the party.

Out of the group, a wiry little man strode aggressively up to Panglor and squinted. "So!" he growled. His slitted eyes flickered menacingly. Then he blinked in confusion and stepped back without another word, his eyes dazed. Another man said threateningly, "No way you're getting back in your ship." He hefted a co-beam gun large enough to crater the side of a spaceship. Panglor grunted noncommittally and edged closer to Alo. He hoped that the man wasn't crazed enough to actually use that weapon.

LePiep peered at the men and muttered curiously. She was scarcely fazed by their bullying postures. "Hrrrl," she rumbled, hanging over Alo's arm.

Turret waved them all on toward *Deerfield*.

Alo set LePiep back up on Panglor's shoulder and took his arm. "We'll show them, Pangly," she murmured. Panglor nodded, but he wasn't nearly so confident.

The Vikken ship was farther away and larger than he had thought. As they drew close, he realized that *Deerfield* must have carried at least a dozen crewmen and a sizable cargo. And he had brought them all to this forsaken place. He stole a glance or two at the guards, expecting to see grim faces; but actually, two were grinning, one looked frightened, and another looked ready to kill. Panglor shivered.

More crewmen met them from *Deerfield*. These new arrivals were angry-looking men, and probably only Alo's presence deterred them from immediate violence. She seemed to unnerve them. First one man and then another looked askance at her; none seemed to know how to respond to the presence of a female in this situation. But toward Panglor their mood was clearly ugly, and he half-expected at any moment to feel blows thundering about his head and shoulders. He lowered LePiep and held her protectively in his arms. He felt a wave of perplexed sympathy and warmth as the ou-ralot squirmed in his arms, looking around. Several of the crewmen noticed the creature and suddenly looked abashed and confused. LePiep's emanations of friendliness rippled through the crowd, causing more than one pair of eyes to blink and soften.

"Hold it!" ordered a familiar, deep voice. The crewmen mumbled uneasily and jostled about to make room. "Balef! Panglor Balef?"

Panglor's breath caught. He could not answer.

At tall, red-haired, orange-eyed man strode through the group and halted before Panglor. It was Tal Jeebering, exactly as Panglor remembered him—but with eyes afire. "Balef—it *is* you. I was ready to have you hung and your throat slit. What are you doing, mixed up in this business? Was that you who deflected us off course?" Clamping his mouth shut suddenly, Jeebering rocked his weight back, crossed his arms, and scrutinized Panglor grimly.

Panglor flushed with shame. He was still unable to speak. LePiep whistled once in fear and tucked her head into his arms.

"All right!" Jeebering bawled suddenly. "You men, return to your duties. Godspey and Turret, you stay here." He glared at Panglor. LePiep trembled and peeked out at him. Jeebering noticed her after a moment, and he scowled, then said, "Okay, I'm going to give you a chance to explain, although I'm damned if I know why I should." He turned and strode toward the ship, to a spot near the hatch where several crates had been arranged to make seats. Panglor and the others followed; two of the guards sat on crates along with Jeebering, and everyone else sat on the grass.

"You don't look as though you're starving," Jeebering observed. "Did you carry off enough food to hide out for two weeks, or did you grub?"

"Huh?" Panglor said, finding his voice at last. He looked at Jeebering in confusion. "We were only gone a day. I can explàin about the deflection. Listen—I tried not to—"

One of the *Deerfield* crewmen suddenly erupted with a gargling sound and lunged forward, reaching for Panglor's neck, fingers twitching. "Genslick—none of that!" Jeebering bawled. Alo growled. One of the other men slapped Genslick's arm away, then beamed at Jeebering like a child who had just diverted a smaller child from the cookie jar. Jeebering touched his forehead with the fingertips of both hands. "Balef," he said softly, staring at the ground. "Do you have any idea what's been happening to my men? Why did you do this?"

"Didn't mean to," Panglor mumbled sorrowfully.

How could he explain? He noticed that just as many crewmen surrounded them now as before, despite Jeebering's orders. Their expressions reminded him of disturbed children. These men were not holding up well, and he had an uneasy feeling that their condition would get worse before it got better. He wondered what bizarre experiences these men had been suffering.

"The Old Man—" Jeebering said, shaking his head and hooking a thumb over his shoulder. He failed to finish the sentence, though, and appeared to have forgotten what he was going to say. LePiep lifted her head, warbling encouragingly, and that appeared to draw Jeebering back to the present. "Balef," he said, "did you or did you not put us all here by pulling some harebrained maneuver back there at—" He waved a hand vaguely, evidently referring to D3.

This is bad, Panglor thought. If Jeebering is losing touch with reality, what hope do any of us have?

"Well, Balef?"

"Yah," he answered abruptly. "But I was trying to *avoid* doing it. Grakoff-Garikoff had me by the—"

"Garikoff—are they behind this?" Jeebering growled. Panglor nodded, and explained the situation and how he had tried to circumvent it. Jeebering shook his head grimly. "Garikoff," he muttered darkly. "Christ, no wonder. You know what we're carrying in this hull?"

Panglor shook his head.

"Well, besides a load of tech products, we've got a hold full of superheavy-doped semicrystals. Very valuable neutronics stuff. Don't know how those Garikoff bastards found out about it, but this load is worth a mint. The Old Man damn near had a stroke after what you did. He's in his cabin flat on his back now." Jeebering ran his fingers through his moppish red hair. His eyes flamed. He glanced around at the circle of crewmen and shook his head. "Balef, where have you been hiding out for the last two weeks? Things here aren't right. My men aren't well. Two of them claimed that they were attacked by dragons the other day. Another man said they were vultures, not dragons. And three men have said that they almost fell off the edge of the world!" Pain crossed his face. He appeared more confused than angry.

Panglor hesitated, surprised. Weren't they going to try him, convict him, and execute him? No one here looked capable of that much concentration.

"Two weeks, Balef. Where have you been?"

"Jeeb, I told you."

Alo interrupted impatiently. "It's the time discontinuity. Haven't you even figured out what's going on here yet?"

Jeebering suddenly noticed her. "Who are *you*?" His eyebrows danced in astonishment. Evidently he had not seen her before.

"Alontelida Castley. Who are you?" She stirred, as though to rise in her own defense.

Anger surfaced in Jeebering's eyes. "Young lady," he said crossly—

—and the world abruptly went dark, then light. Panglor swallowed, held LePiep tightly, and felt his stomach lurch. The ground dropped away beneath him and his weight left him—but he did not fall. The landscape began turning, as though he and the others were revolving on a carousel; their faces blurred, making him dizzy, and then jumped back into sharp focus against the moving background—Alo, Jeebering, the others, all with fear in their eyes. Panglor smelled the fear, felt it prickle on his skin, felt it ripple like an electric current around the ring of people.

Only LePiep was unaffected. She perked her ears. "Hyolp!" she cried, radiating joy. Instantly Panglor felt his own fear lessen; the carousel gradually slowed, the ground became solid again, and his weight returned. The sky shivered with yellow and green and black bursts, as though lightning had flashed up from beyond the horizon. Thunder rolled distantly. And suddenly all was still, normal—and the sky turned pale and the world was as before. Except that Tiki stood in their midst.

Mutters of bewilderment rose from the circle. LePiep beamed happily. "What's going on here?" Jeebering demanded harshly, jumping to his feet. He glared at Tiki with hands on his hips.

Tiki swayed solemnly before Panglor and Alo, then turned and repeated the motion before Jeebering and the others. "Greetings," he said brightly. Though the words were in his own tongue, everyone seemed to understand him. He said to Jeebering, "You must be the chief choker of this group, aren't you?"

Jeebering started. "Chief choker?" he said. "I haven't heard that expression in years! Who are you? Where did *you* come from?"

"Ah—Jeeb," Panglor said uncomfortably, "this is Tiki. We were over at his shipwreck when your men found us. He's a *Kili*, Jeeb. He was marooned here with a Kili ship—been shipwrecked here a long time, I guess."

"True, true," said Tiki.

Jeebering frowned at both of them. But Panglor continued, "Tiki, this is Tal Jeebering. He's—he's—" Words failed him; the pounding of blood in his head obliterated whatever he had meant to say.

"Mate," grunted Jeebering. "Balef, you served with me—when? Eight years ago? On the *Randolph P.P. Lupollof*?" He shook his head unhappily, as though trying in vain to link the past with the present.

Panglor nodded dizzily. Lord—how was he going to straighten this out? He forced himself to speak. "Tiki,

Jeeb is First Mate on *Deerfield*." Calm, Balef—calm, he thought. LePiep muttered, bolstering his spirits; she looked up at Tiki and hooted her welcome. Jeebering observed this without comment, but LePiep's waves of enthusiasm appeared to ease the tension in his eyes.

"Pleased," Tiki said, beaming. He spoke to Jeebering. "Were my good friends Panglor and Alo and LePiep explaining to you about the discontinuity locus that's responsible for your ship being here and your crew losing their minds?" He swayed politely left and right.

Jeebering blinked in bewilderment, ignoring Tiki's question. "You're a Kili?" he asked skeptically. He scratched his ear. "Huh. I guess maybe you are." He looked around at the perplexed faces of his crew. "What do you think of that, men?"

"Nobody's ever seen a real Kili," said one of the men, gazing intently at Tiki. "Chee."

"Jeeb," said Panglor insistently. "About this discontinuity zone—"

"A Kili. Think of that!" crowed another crewman.

Jeebering drew himself up formally before the Kili. "I am First Mate, and these are crewmen of *Deerfield*, freighter of the Vikken Traders, Limited, shipping line," he said. "Our Captain is Thaddeus Drak. He is in the ship, and is not well."

Tiki bobbed. "You are of the Vikken line?" he said. "Indeed! I have seen several of your ships, in times gone by—and many men of the Vikken line, of course. How nice to see more of you!"

Jeebering's eyes bulged. His lips twitched and went up at the corners, crookedly. "You've seen other Vikken ships? Vikken men?" His eyes narrowed and turned grim.

"Yes, indeed," said Tiki. "Ovid ships, too, and Sloane Lines. I never could understand why those men were so vain about loyalty to their shipping lines. But I've seen quite a number of them here, from time to time."

Nostrils flaring, Jeebering turned a burning gaze onto Panglor.

"Hey, wait!" Panglor protested. "I had nothing to do with any other—"

"What's going on here, Balef?" Jeebering said. He grabbed Panglor's upper arm, hard. "What's happening? What's all this talk about ships, about men?"

"Oh God," Alo said. "Don't you get it yet?"

Jeebering was actually trembling now. The men stirred in confusion and muttered in an ugly tone. Panglor was very nervous about the mental state of those men. "Hey Jeeb—" he said urgently, stroking LePiep as he talked, hoping that she would radiate soothing feelings. "It's not that terrible a thing. Now, we'll explain it to you—why don't we all just spread out here on the grass, and maybe someone can go get refreshments, because I don't know about all of you, but we're kind of thirsty and . . ."

As he talked, the others quieted somewhat, and Jeebering released Panglor's arm and focused his eyes more clearly; and eventually everyone did exactly as Panglor had suggested. Then Panglor explained the discontinuity locus that apparently surrounded, or defined, this world. He described the sequence of events that had brought the *Cur* down to the planet—which, he learned, was roughly the way that *Deerfield* had arrived, too.

Alo broke in. "Look. We think there are lots of very small discontinuities throughout space. But normally they're too small for us to notice, or measure—they're like the spaces in the weave of a tight cloth. But here the threads are splitting apart, and probably in the heart of the zone there's nothing but a big, gaping hole in the fabric of space."

Panglor nodded. "That's one way to look at it," he

said. "Another way is that in the ocean of reality, there are billions of imperceptible wavefronts of distortion, of aberration. And here they all intersect, reinforcing each other, and it's like a gigantic standing wavefront of distorted reality. In a way, it's like a black-hole singularity, minus the gravitational effects."

Tiki chortled enthusiastically. But most of the men seemed to have trouble following.

Panglor explained again.

After considerable confusion, most of the crewmen began to understand the significance of the discovery—if Panglor's interpretation was correct. "This discontinuity in space and time can swallow ships. It can pull them in like mosquitoes to a trap." Panglor said. "There are probably other zones like this, all through space, that we haven't detected yet. Who knows how many of the ships that have been lost in foreshortening have been swallowed up by discontinuities? Right, Tiki? Alo? Jeeb?" He looked from one to another, fired by the implications. The zones could be the cause of the uncertainty faced by every spacer and every passenger in foreshortening. This was the unknown danger, the mysterious killer. If it could be understood, perhaps it could be avoided.

And here was a real, live Kili, helping them understand it all. Panglor glanced at Tiki and suddenly felt a rush of affection for this alien, whom he barely even knew. LePiep grumbled happily, reflecting and sharing his emotion.

"There's one problem," Jeebering observed, looking depressed. "We can't get off this planet, and even if we could, there's no way to make an insertion out of this system. The collapsing-field's shut down." He cast a neutral glance at Panglor, then studied the backs of his hands.

Alo spoke, digging at the grass roots with her fingers.

"Bet we could start it up again." She pulled up a tangled bit of weed and squinted at it.

Turret, the crewman, snorted.

"Sure," said Alo. "They wouldn't have kept the capture-field going if they hadn't thought maybe they'd want to come back some time, and they wouldn't do *that* unless they knew they could get the collapsing-field going to get home again." She dropped the weed and glanced around. "Right?" she said. Panglor caught her eye and gestured affirmatively. He should have thought of that himself.

No one replied. But suddenly one of the crewmen started choking, with a sound somewhere between a sob and a ghoulish cackle. The others stirred uneasily, but it was a moment before anyone moved to help the man. He was gagging hoarsely, grinning. Finally Turret and another man grasped him by the arms and calmed him. Jeebering gestured for them to take the man back into the ship. Then he faced Alo. "Turning on a collapsing-field is not so easy, you know. Even if the station was left in working order, we don't have the equipment or the trained people to do it."

"So what's so difficult?" Alo said insistently.

Jeebering threw his hands up. "What's so difficult? First you have to control the solar collectors and relays, and there's no telling what condition they're in, and if they're defective you have to go to each one, in close solar orbit, and repair them—which we're not equipped to do. And then you have to control the transformation and transmission to the field generators and radiators, neither of which is located at the station, which is where the primary controls are. And no one here knows how to operate those systems anyway!" He glanced thoughtfully at Tiki. "Unless our Kili friend, here, does."

Tiki rocked back in surprise. "Oh no, no, no. I know nothing of it."

Jeebering sat back grimly.

Alo shrugged, undeterred. "So, we don't *know* that the systems are out of order, and we don't *know* that we can't get them working even if they are, and you don't *know* that there's no one here who knows about these things." She hoisted herself up where she sat, to make herself taller.

"Oh?" said Jeebering dryly. He looked around, surveying his ship and crew. The men who had escorted the ailing crewmember were returning.

"Yes," Alo said coldly. "*Oh.* It so happens I've spent several years living in a waystation, where knowledge of this machinery is commonplace, and it also happens"—she stopped and glared at two men who were chuckling derisively—"it also *happens* that I know a thing or two about tech maintenance and repair—*and* about the operation of the D3 foreshortening system, which succeeded the one here at D1."

"Why, is that truly the case?" said Tiki, rocking in delight.

Alo nodded severely.

Jeebering got to his feet and walked away, scowling. Panglor watched him, feeling strangely relaxed under the orange-and-red sky, lighted by a fiery green circlet of a sun. LePiep crooned. Jeebering suddenly shouted, and Panglor focused, following his gaze. One of the crewmen was flickering in and out of existence, like a film image. A moment later, he vanished completely. Panglor had a sinking feeling. "What's this?" roared Jeebering, wheeling around. Most of the other men growled and jumped to their feet—except for one pair, who were lying on their backs staring at the sky.

"What's what?" asked Tiki.

Jeebering waved his hands. "Where has my crewman gone?"

"He's just walking over here," Tiki said mildly.

"Yeah," said one of the men, lazing near Tiki. He sat up, and his gaze moved slowly past the others.

The vanished man reappeared. He sat down near Tiki, smiling crookedly. Then he disappeared again.

Jeebering sat back down. He looked at Tiki, at Panglor, at Alo. He pressed his lips together tightly and frowned. He cleared his throat and looked at Panglor again. Then Alo. Staring at the ground, finally, he said, "It doesn't matter whether we have any chance of getting the field in operation or not, because we can't lift off the planet. Neither ship can, not from where they sit now. We're stuck here."

They stared at one another in silence.

"True enough, I expect," remarked Tiki.

Alo looked back and forth between Tiki and Jeebering. She shook her head, obviously undeterred. She reached over and ruffled LePiep's fur, and said, "We'll see about that." The ou-ralot hopped into her lap, radiating blissful confidence.

11

"LET'S GO for a walk," Panglor said, rousing Alo and Tiki. Though they were presumably under arrest, no one made a move to stop them. Jeebering sat quietly with an expression of despair; he watched them get up and stroll away.

"Where are we going, Pangly?"

LePiep squirmed and quivered in Panglor's arms. "Nowhere. Just around." He poked the ou-ralot. "Want to run, old girl?"

"Hyoop." She leaped, gliding with spread wings to the grass, then trotted off ahead of them.

"We'd better not go too far, though," Panglor said, glancing back. "No telling what'll happen to these guys if we wander out of sight. Let's keep in view of the ships."

Though he said nothing to the others about it, Panglor was feeling rather strange. He was almost comfortable on this world, at least by comparison with the

Vikken men. And yet, he hated the thought of being trapped here, a prisoner of some bizarre twists of nature. It rankled to be a victim of sleazy maneuvering by Grakoff-Garikoff—who must be quite delighted now, with both *Deerfield* and the *Cur* gone. And he felt bad for the Vikken crew, if not for the Vikken company. Jeebering was a decent fellow, and probably not the only one. So Panglor wanted to leave, or at least to have the choice. Not as desperately as the others, certainly, and not that he had anything wonderful to go back to—probably just more trouble—but he wanted to go nevertheless. Maybe for Tal Jeebering, or even for Alo—or for himself, to take back the news of their discovery.

"What're you thinking?" asked Alo.

"Nothing much," he answered. But his mind filled with images of this strange world they were inhabiting. It occurred to him that perhaps, even as peculiar as things were here, they might not now be at the true heart of the discontinuity. Suppose they were simply near it, wedged in the splitting weave somewhere near the actual hole in the space–time fabric. No telling what might lie in the center, or what would happen to them if they ended up there. Perhaps that was where those who disappeared went—into the hole, perhaps into another reality altogether. Would anything remain as they knew it, there? Would events there be more influenced by mental state, or less?

The thought intrigued, and worried, him. He didn't want to go there. Maybe next trip. Things were quite difficult enough as they were, right here, right now.

His thoughts returned to the present. How to get out of here was the problem. He nudged Alo. "Were you stringing a line back there, talking about how you knew the foreshortening systems?"

Alo didn't answer at once, and he looked up to see that she was grinning too hard to speak.

"Oh, surely, no," said Tiki.

"More or less," she admitted, chuckling. "But you know they're just borrowing trouble. The systems could be okay, and between you and me we ought to be able to get just about anything working, don't you think?"

Panglor arched his eyebrows. He shrugged and surveyed the land. *The Fighting Cur* stood solitary against a line of ridges, and behind them on the other side sat *Deerfield*. The sky was lemon yellow, and the sun was still a green circlet of fire; charcoal clouds drifted in gentle motion across the sky. Ahead, the grass ended in a beautifully eroded rocky bank, and beyond that a lake of misty water gleamed. LePiep was already at the bank, sniffing and whistling tentatively. A number of airfish approached from one direction, and from another a small cluster of aerial crystals, singing faintly like jeweled chimes. "Taking off is the problem," Panglor said.

"Hey," said Alo, "one of those crystals is the same one we saw at first—the one that broke."

Panglor followed the direction of her finger. A rose-quartzlike crystal drifted by that indeed looked just like that first one they had seen. Could it be the same one, brought back to life?

"Ho-la-ruuu!" cried LePiep. She radiated joy at the approach of the airfish. She fluttered her wings and stepped to the very edge of the bank. Two of the airfish nosed down to her.

"Careful, Peep," warned Panglor—but he watched in fascination. The airfish in themselves fascinated him; there was something about them that nagged at his mind, that made him think that he should be noticing something but wasn't. "Where do they come from, Tiki?" he asked.

"The crystals?"

"The airfish."

"Ah. I don't know for certain. They have given me several versions of how they came to be here, and I don't know which is the real one. But I suspect they were aboard a ship that crashed long ago—perhaps they were specimens, cargo, or just friendly companions like your LePiep, to some other travelers. These may be descendants of the originals." Tiki fluttered his hands in the air uncertainly.

Panglor fingered his lips and thought about it. "You suppose they come from a place where they really lived in water, like most fish?"

"Do most fish live in water?" queried Tiki.

"Have you seen fish anywhere else that didn't?"

Tiki skewed his eyes momentarily. "No. I've never seen fish before. How would they stay in the air in normal places? What would hold them up?"

"Right," said Panglor—but now he was talking to himself. He worried his tongue around inside his mouth and watched LePiep. She was pacing the bank, following the direction of the airfish, which had retreated a few meters. "Right. They wouldn't stay up. But they do here." He scratched his neck. "Of course, all kinds of things happen here that shouldn't. But I was just wondering—"

He stopped talking and sat in the grass with his legs sticking out over the bank. Alo sat down beside him and peered at him questioningly.

Airfish. . . .

"Well," he said, "it's just that I thought—how do they know they can swim in the air here? Do they think it's water, or do they know it's air but they don't concern themselves about it?"

Alo peered at him closely.

He forced the thought to continue. It resisted;

something in his mind was ridiculing it even before it was fully formed, but he snagged the thought and dragged it upward, to the surface. "Well, what I was thinking was, maybe the airfish stay in the air because they *think* they can stay there. Tiki, you said that conditions here are sensitive to what people think, or at least to their states of mind, right? Isn't that what you said?"

"So you think—" interrupted Alo.

Panglor raised a finger to silence her.

"Indeed," said Tiki. "The people who couldn't feel at home have always had more trouble and disappeared sooner than the others."

"And we found our way back to the ship without any trouble last time, right?" Panglor looked at Alo. She nodded, her mouth open. "And these airfish—they stay in the air, and look like they love it. Maybe they do think it's water, or maybe they know it's not but they don't care because they want to float in the air. They *want* to float in the air."

He rose and stared at the *Cur*, standing silent against the sky. "Maybe we can do that. Maybe we can fly if we just think like airfish. Maybe if we *want* to get off this planet, we can."

Tiki clicked his lips thoughtfully. Alo stood beside him. "But, Pangly, why did we come here in the first place? We didn't want to," she said. "And those crewmen want to leave, but they haven't."

Pánglor nodded. "Right." He looked around to see where LePiep had gotten to. She was at his feet, peering up at him in response to his growing excitement. "Right," he repeated, picking her up. "They haven't. But they don't know how to. They don't know how to think around here at all. Look at them—it's pathetic. They're breaking down." A grin twitched to his lips. It was a perversely good feeling to be the sane one, watching the others break down. Except for Jeeb, who had treated him well when nobody else had.

"Look, you two," he said.

"Alo," supplied Alo. "And Tiki."

"Yeh," he said impatiently. "I think we can get the old bucket off this planet, even if it is a real planet, which I don't think it is. We could go check out the foreshortening station and then, maybe, go . . . home." He ended on a funny note. Well, they'd go back to D3, anyway, whether or not they chose to call it home.

"Why?" said Alo. She put both hands on her hips and tilted her head back, peering at him through several clinging locks of hair. "Why do you want to?" Her eyes probed his.

Panglor stroked LePiep, who was muttering reassuringly. He opened his mouth. Finally he forced words out. "We don't want to stay trapped here, do we?" He shook his head and tried again. "We should help the others get off, I think." His voice quivered. "It's partly my fault they're here." He blinked and shook his head again.

"Boy," said Alo quietly, brushing the hair from her face. "Never thought I'd see the day." Her voice was strained, and it was difficult to tell whether she was approving or disapproving. "You'll be in big trouble if you go back."

Panglor cleared his throat. Was the little-girl Alo talking or the not-so-little girl? "Well," he said, considering the possibilities. "We'll be bringing a live Kili with us—Tiki, you'll come, won't you? And we'll bring important information back. About the zone here, and the foreshortening hazard. After all—" He stopped and clucked his tongue.

"What?" said Alo.

"I would be delighted to go with you," Tiki piped up in a grave voice.

"We're in the middle of something important here," Panglor said, his voice stretched tight. "I don't know how it happened, but here we are. Who knows what could come of it? Suppose we can fly in this zone, this field. Tiki, you said you went to other worlds like this one. Suppose we could do that in our ships, and control it somehow. Like flying by a daydream. Only it'd be real." He puckered his lips and for a moment was lost in thought, aware only of LePiep's gentle empathic touch.

A touch of another kind brought him back to the present. Alo kissed him on the cheek and said, "Let's go try, then."

"Hoop," LePiep said approvingly. Tiki moved forward to join them. Panglor looked from one to another, not quite believing that he had convinced them. Then he nodded, and they moved off quickly.

The distance to *The Fighting Cur* was short, and they crossed it without attracting attention from *Deerfield*. Panglor didn't want to have to explain what they were doing—he would certainly be thought crazy, and be restrained—so he was hoping that they could at least make a start without being observed. They strolled close to the ship and Panglor noted that a promontory once more ran up to the ship's entry port. They hurried up the incline. There were shouts from across the plain, and several *Deerfield* crewmen raced after them, brandishing weapons.

"Inside!" Panglor shouted. He pushed LePiep into Alo's arms and shoved her toward the airlock with Tiki. He waited at the port to see what the crewmen would do. "Stay back!" he shouted, cupping his hands to his mouth. "We're going—to try—to take off! We're not—trying—to escape!" He looked back to be sure that Alo and Tiki were safe inside, and found them standing right behind him. "What are you doing?" he exploded. "Get inside—"

"Halt there, you!" The men were racing up the promontory now. One of them knelt to the side and took aim.

"Hold it!" Panglor yelled, waving. "Take a message to Jeeb! Tell him—"

"He sent us to make sure you didn't try anything," the other crewman called.

"*Tell* him, please," said Panglor, lowering his voice, "that we think we know how to lift off, but we don't want to risk anyone else until we've tried it. If it works, we'll come back for all of you. Tell him that." He backed toward the airlock.

"Jeeb said—"

"If it works, we'll be back! Now *stand clear*!"

The leading man squinted, toying with his weapon. "Jeeb told us not to—"

Panglor slammed the hatch and locked it from the inside. "Let's go," he grunted, herding Alo and Tiki through the inner airlock door. They hurried to the control bay.

LePiep leaped high onto the console, while Panglor tried to figure out where everyone should sit. There were only two real couches, and he needed to be in one of them. "Alo. No—Tiki. Ah—" He looked around. He started pushing boxes and loose clothes beside the second pilot's couch, then let Alo finish, since she was doing a better job of it, anyway. "Here. Make a comfortable place to sit. If the grav control works, it won't matter. And if it doesn't work—well, we'll all be squashed flat."

"Indeed," said Tiki. "I should sit here, since I'll be of little help in operating the craft."

Panglor hesitated. Tiki was probably the frailest of them, physically—but Alo should be at the controls, too. "Okay," he said. "Peeps, you're with Tiki." The ou-ralot whistled and hopped into the Kili's arms.

Finally Panglor started powering up the ship. The viewscreen produced an outside view. The Vikken crewmen were huddled at some distance from the ship, but not at what Panglor would have called a clear distance. He cursed mildly, but there was nothing he could do except hope that the planet with its bag of tricks would protect them.

When the ship's console was clear, he sank back and sighed. He looked at the viewscreen and looked back at the console. He twiddled the viewscreen to show the sky, now a pastel green. He looked at the console.

"What are you going to do?" asked Alo.

"I'm going to think," he replied.

For some minutes, he did exactly that and nothing else. Alo and Tiki waited silently, as he worked at clearing extraneous thoughts, so that he could concentrate on those he wanted. The thoughts returned relentlessly, however, so he stopped trying actively to rid himself of them. He simply ignored them and concentrated on his mood, on twisting the general flow of his thoughts to the frame he wanted. LePiep's silent empathy relaxed him, coaxed him. Thoughts of Alo and Tiki, beside him, went by; memory of Alo undressed in his cabin (No— let that one go!); the insertion under fire from Grakoff-Garikoff. No—none of that was going to help. Wasn't what he wanted. He wanted to think of the airfish: the quiet, musing creatures drifting at will across the surface of the ponds. Perhaps something existed beneath the surface of those ponds that they didn't wish to see (but no, that's not important, not interesting now, let it slide); he thought of the airfish, fat ones and skinny ones, with funny-looking fins, with their certainty that they could not fall. Perhaps if they knew they should fall they would, and so would die. But they did not know they should; they knew they were at home drifting in the air, communing with the floating aerial crystals, or simply hovering and exploring.

The airfish were at home in the air, as *The Fighting Cur* was at home in space. Their world, their existence was to drift above a vaporous surface, and so was the *Cur*'s proper existence above the clouds and vapors of the planetary atmosphere. The *Cur* should always remain above the atmosphere, no closer than a wide black interval. Black space, carrying in its vastness both the bulging mass of the planet and the trivial mass of the orbiting ship. The ship could reach space. Of course; that was where it belonged, where it lived. He had only to turn on the drivers, *here*, and they would be lofted into space.

He didn't touch the driver control, though. There was a feeling of discontinuity . . .

. . . and the viewscreen was black, except for the stars. He blinked, and touched the viewer controls—and there, turning slowly beneath them, was the partially misted orange ball that was the planet. They were in orbit. In space. "Ulg—" he said. He cleared his throat. His vocal cords refused to work. Finally he gestured to Alo, who was gasping beside him, to check things in the sensor-fringe. "Find out where we are," he whispered.

With Alo moving around checking instruments, Panglor squinting at the screen and readying the driver-controls, LePiep whistling and hooting and radiating pleasure, and Tiki peering gravely over everyone's shoulders, things were confusing for a while. Then Alo said, "Looks like we're in orbit, Pinglo, but we won't be for long, if you don't give us some velocity."

Panglor's voice returned. "Want to be more specific?" Alo grunted and did some things at her board, then fed the results directly to his. "Right," he said, and started the sequencer. The ship yawed a little and pitched up, and the drivers kicked on, jarring, until the grav control caught up.

He grinned in satisfaction. Then a thought occurred, and he frowned. "How reliable were those figures you gave me?"

Alo looked down her nose. "What's that supposed to mean?"

"I mean, how consistent were the different readings? Were they in agreement, or did you tinker an average?"

"Oh. Well, actually—" she said, and then she got up and left the control room.

Panglor roared, "Where the hell are you going?" He jumped up—but realized he couldn't leave the console. "What are you doing?" he shouted. He turned to Tiki. "What is she doing?" Tiki looked mystified.

Alo came back a minute later, carrying three meal-packs and three brew-packets. "Anybody hungry?" She seemed to notice just then that Panglor was choking on his tongue, and she added, "They were all on the beam. The readings, I mean. Seems like we're in the clear, instruments-wise." With a grin, she settled between them and snapped her brew-packet.

Panglor made exasperated sucking noises against his teeth, then *hmph*ed and opened his meal-pack. The first bite he gave to LePiep. She beamed and gulped it. "First thing we got to do," he said with his mouth full, "is find that station." He glanced over the board and nodded. The drivers were running hot and smooth, and the *Cur* already had a stable orbit—contingent, presumably, on the states of mind of the *Cur*'s inhabitants. "Wonder how far out this thing's influence reaches," he mused. He choked, suddenly, with food in his windpipe.

Alo thumped him on the back. "Leave it to me. I'll have that course for you in a couple of minutes."

Tiki said something, which Panglor understood as, "Borka drig limits . . . ulu zone thesla . . . others blik."

He frowned. "Tiki, what's wrong?"

"We must be at the limits of the influence right now," Alo said thoughtfully. "We won't be able to understand him at all when we're outside of it—not unless we learn his language."

"Gah," muttered Panglor. "You any good with languages?"

Alo shrugged and patted Tiki on the arm. The Kili's eyes were sharply crossed. "We'll be okay, I guess. Maybe Tiki will be able to figure out ours."

Well, Panglor thought, at least we have a handy warning system. "Let's get that fix on the station, hah?" he said to Alo.

They worked for thirty-five minutes, then spotted the station emerging from the nightside limb of the planet, a bright gleam that stood out among the stars. Alo got a passive-sensor track on it, then double checked on active. "It's out over a hundred thousand," she said, puckering and blowing through her lips. She squinted at Panglor, and at Tiki. "You want to go back now for your friends? You did promise, if we made it off all right."

"Huh? Go back?" Panglor said. "Oh." He mulled. He didn't much want to turn right around—not yet, at least. He switched on the com and tried to contact *Deerfield*. No success. "Well, hell," he said, switching the com off, "what's the point in going back till we've checked out the foreshortening system? What good would it do?" Alo shrugged; Tiki just bowed in puzzlement. "Okay, then—let's get a course to the station."

Once they had a program worked out for reaching the higher orbit of the station, they settled back to pass the time. They expected to reach the station in twenty hours. Panglor had trouble relaxing, though; the whole situation surrounding the station bothered him. Finally he voiced his confusion. "You know, I wonder where this station was originally, anyway. If the discontinuity existed then, why didn't they know anything about it?"

Alo plucked at her lip. "Seems to me," she said—and stopped and leaned forward to key a question into the library computer. Reading the results, she nodded. "Yah, the station used to be in a solar orbit a couple of hundred million kilometers farther in. The planet, of course, wasn't known at all, mainly because it's not a planet. I expect it was probably far enough away from the waystation not to be detected, but close enough to snare an occasional ship that got flung in its direction. Depending on what orbit or position it held relative to the sun, the trajectory angles of the ships that didn't make it would have seemed pretty random as the waystation moved around the sun."

Panglor frowned more deeply. "How many ships did they lose?"

Shrugging, Alo said, "Enough, over the long run, that people got spooked, and the system was getting a bad reputation. My teacher Urula used to say that they were crazy, superstitious fools—but I guess they weren't, after all. So when they talked about building the D3 station—and D1 was getting pretty old, anyway—a lot of people said, as long as we're going to put a new station over there, and it can do the work of this station, too, well, let's just close down and get the hell out of here before anything weirder happens. And that's what they did. Most of them moved to D3, but some of them went to other places. Took a couple of years to clear the whole population out."

Panglor chewed his lip. "And since then, the station has been drawn out toward the discontinuity, or the discontinuity has moved closer to the station."

"Maybe both," said Alo.

Panglor shook his head, thinking that if anyone had told him all this a month ago, he'd have laughed in the idiot's face.

Panglor napped a while, and later took the watch. Alo curled up in the second pilot couch. "Pangly," she said, "do you still mean to go back for the others?" She cradled her head in her right arm and looked down at the floor. She looked drowsily thoughtful and, Panglor thought, vulnerable. He stirred uneasily. How attached was he growing to this girl . . . or woman?

"What do you figure?" he said, locking and unlocking the fingers of both hands.

"Don't want to figure," she mumbled. "Just want to know."

He gestured awkwardly. "Well, we said we would."

Alo nodded sleepily. Her mussed hair obscured her face. "Think we can land and take off from that place twice?"

"Sure," he said huskily. He cleared his throat. The truth was, he wasn't all *that* sure—and he was even less sure that there was a way to get *Deerfield* out of the zone.

Alo murmured, "Okay," and then she was asleep.

Panglor felt LePiep's gentle, encouraging touch; she was following him with her eyes, from Tiki's lap. The Kili was completely relaxed. "Burr-illl," he said, smiling in imitation of the human expression. Panglor wondered if LePiep had conveyed to him, somehow, what had transpired. Certainly, at least, she had touched Tiki with feelings of peace reflecting Panglor's. Yeah, they'd be going back down to the planet.

Right on schedule, the station grew from a twinkling bit of silver to a respectable, if silent-looking, space station. It was stable, not tumbling; clearly some systems were still functioning on board. Panglor switched on the com and instructed Alo to monitor it, in the unlikely event that they were challenged by a guardian, either human or robot.

They circled the station, inspecting. The structure appeared intact; at least, there was no external damage. Panglor brought the *Cur* to the most centrally located docking port and stopped just shy of the hangar doors. "How are we going to get inside?" Alo said. He glanced at her ruefully. He had just thought of the same question, but he hadn't thought of an answer yet. Normally there would be crews inside to operate the docking facilities.

"Must be a way," Alo said. "Figure they left things in case they wanted to return some day. So how would they plan on doing it?"

"Go over in a suit, probably," said Panglor. "We only have the one suit, though. I'd better go see if I can get in through a personnel lock, and then try to find the main controls."

"You mean leave me to fly the ship in?" asked Alo with a twinkle in her eye.

Panglor pushed a thumb back into the corner of his mouth. His face grew warm as he hesitated. "Well, we probably should check out everything we can, first, to see if there's some automatic system on standby."

They tried. Alo worked the com, transmitting standard approach activation codes, while Panglor searched visually for a manual activator. Neither effort was successful. Finally Panglor, swallowing his reluctance, put Alo at the maneuvering controls and went to the airlock to suit up. He called her through his helmet-com and said, "Okay. You ready there, kid?"

"Say 'kid' one more time and I'll crash this thing," Alo answered gravely.

"Right. Sorry. If you're set, I'm going outside now."

He opened the airlock, hesitated at the lip, and stepped off. He floated weightless, beyond the ship's grav field. He drifted the few meters to the station, worked his way along its exterior, using the handholds, and peered over the coated white skin, looking for any kind of mechanism, even for a small crew entry port. "Don't see a thing," he said. He turned toward the *Cur*'s sensor-fringe, through which he assumed Alo was watching.

"Hold it a minute," said Alo, her voice scratchy through the com.

"What for?"

There was a pause, then Alo said, "Move about ten meters toward the stern, and then wait. Stay close to the ship."

"Why?" he asked, but did as she instructed. Then he faced the sensor-fringe again. "Is it a secret?"

A blue laser beam blinked from the sensor-fringe, striking a small spot beside the hangar doors. The beam flickered several times, with varying time duration and width of focus. The wavelength changed: green, yellow, red . . . invisible.

The station skin began moving; the hangar door was opening. Panglor roared, "By damn! How did you find that?" He watched, astonished, as the bay doors contracted to their limit, exposing an enormous cavern.

"Want to come back aboard?"

Panglor entered the airlock. "You going to tell me?" he asked over the com, as he pulled off the silversuit.

He stalked to the bridge. "Well?"

Alo grinned and winked at Tiki. "I spotted that receptor when you went by it. Figured that it would only respond to coherent light, so it was just a matter of finding the right frequency. Want to take the ship in? I have it lined up." Panglor blinked. She had turned the ship expertly, with its nose pointed straight into the hangar. LePiep was curled drowsily atop the console, as though nothing at all had been going on.

He made a throaty sound. "Think you can handle it?"

Grinning lopsidedly, Alo touched the controls and moved the ship in.

The hangar was an enormous deserted warehouse, large enough to hold perhaps six vessels the size of *Deerfield*. That made it puny compared to facilities at D3, but still awesome and ghostly looking from the *Cur*'s tiny control bay. A few scattered light panels glowed along the walls, chasing back the inky darkness. Alo stopped the ship dead in the gloomy cavern. The question: Was there a functioning airlock docking port? If not, they still faced the problem of getting into the station proper without suits, since the hangar was in vacuum. Using the nightscope, they inspected the hangar walls. There were a number of crossmembers and cargo-access bridges and cranes. Many of the shapes were confusing and hard to identify in the ghostly image.

"Over there," Panglor said, pointing. A fat cylindrical structure protruded from the wall. It was a docking port with a funny corrugated ring at its end. "See if you can mate her up." He no longer doubted that she could, but it would be a tricky maneuver in this hulking old ship.

Alo encountered problems jockeying sideways, but eventually she had the *Cur*'s airlock aligned perfectly with the docking adaptor. "There might be an automatic system here, or there might not be," Panglor said. Nodding, Alo nudged the ship sideways and made contact. Nothing happened. She flashed the laser, hitting several spots that looked like receptors on the wall. Nothing happened. Then she applied force, snubbing the ship, not too hard, against the docking port. The corrugated endpiece suddenly gave way and conformed like soft putty to the *Cur*'s airlock. The ship stayed in place when she cut the driver; something else was now holding it.

She turned and bowed. "Not bad," Panglor admitted. "I'll go check the passage."

He resuited and passed cautiously from the airlock into the mating tunnel. The tunnel was clear and lighted and, best of all, pressurized with safe-testing air. He cracked his helmet seal and took a breath. Stale, but breathable. Returning to the airlock, he unsuited and dressed again. "Seems fine," he called with a surge of excitement. Exploring a long-deserted space station appealed to his sense of adventure.

Alo and Tiki joined him, bringing LePiep. Alo sighed when they entered the station proper. "Let's do this fast, okay?" she said. "This reminds me too much of D3."

Deflated, Panglor shrugged and moved ahead, gesturing for the others to follow.

For several hours, they roamed through the engineering and control sections of the station. A fine, almost oily layer of dust coated everything. Many of the station's systems had been left operational; the vital core systems, such as life-support and electrical power, were running at a minimal automatic level, powered by sunlight collectors. The systems possessed a degree of self-repair capability, but generally the machinery still running was simply of long-life design, and had been running untouched since the station was closed half a century ago.

The control room for the foreshortening field generators they found, finally, three levels up from the main engineering deck. Panglor and Alo examined the instrument panels carefully. Tiki stood nearby, keeping watch on LePiep; apparently he knew nothing of such technical matters. After a while, Panglor began to feel that he and Alo didn't, either. The foreshortening field systems were on, according to the instrument consoles—including both the collapsing-field and capture-field generators. But the collapsing-field was nowhere in evidence. Panglor was trying to puzzle out why this might be so, while Alo worked over some of the main panels to look for a malfunction.

"Now, we know the capture-field's working all right," he said. "And the relays to the collapsing-field are all closed, and the telemetry says there's power going through—but we don't know how much power the thing takes. We know we've got some solar collectors in solar orbit, so that's where the juice is coming from." He clacked his teeth together and picked up the ouralot. "What do you think, Peep?"

"Hluuu," LePiep mourned, wiggling in his arms. Her eyes turned wet.

"Pangly, check the capacitance circuit for me on the third panel?" asked Alo, from behind a bank of gear.

Panglor sucked against his teeth and did as she asked. He was impressed by the technical checks she was running—no question about that—but he didn't think it was the way to find the problem. Something told him it would have to be reasoned out. "What'd you find?" he grunted.

"It's okay," said Alo quietly.

"Trouble is, too much of this outfit is scattered across half the solar system, and the station isn't even in the same orbit it used to be in. Collectors, power relays, generators—we can't get at most of it."

"It's all metered and if we just check through the metering systems, we ought to find the problem," came Alo's voice. She had moved farther down.

"But we don't know the values. How much power is this thing supposed to pull, anyway?"

Alo's voice came back: "We know what the capture-field pulls, right? And it works."

"Yeah, but do they both draw the same?"

For a moment, she didn't answer. Then she reappeared, disheveled and sweaty. "Don't they?" she demanded.

He thought a moment. "Not sure," he admitted. "It seems to me, maybe they don't. I think maybe the collapsing-field draws more, does more of the work." He scratched his head. "Actually, I think it draws a lot more."

"We're in trouble then. There's no more power coming out of the solar units. That's all there is."

They stared at each other. Alo's eyes were sharp and angry. "You mean there's no way to up the power?" he asked.

She tugged at her hair, which was becoming very ratty. "There must be a way."

He thought about it, and shook his head. "No."

"There *must* be."

He thought again, and shook his head again. "I don't think so."

Alo fumed. She curled her lip and went back to the panels. For two more hours she worked. Panglor sometimes worked with her and sometimes stood with Tiki, who looked dejectedly cross-eyed. Alo became more and more frustrated. Finally she barked at Panglor, who had taken a break to play with LePiep. "You know, maybe if you helped a little instead of doing that, we'd get this thing fixed, you know!"

Panglor stopped what he was doing, which was picking up LePiep by her front paws. He fixed Alo with a hard gaze. The ou-ralot suddenly became still, her emanations cold. "I don't think so," he said. He patted LePiep to reassure her and sat down, defeated, beside Tiki.

Alo blinked several times. Then she twisted around and worked at the panels again, glaring. Every muscle in her small body was trembling. Ten minutes later she returned and faced them. She looked more at Tiki than at Panglor. "There's no way to make it work. I'm sure now," she said. Her face was as cold as stone.

"Yah," said Panglor.

"We're stuck here. We can't go back."

"Yah."

12

DEPRESSION HUNG like a fog in the room. Tiki sat silent, erect, eyes crossed so sharply he must have been looking sideways; his brow pulsed nervously. Alo fumed at the floor. Her hair hung limp over her eyes, and her posture suggested a marathoner who had fallen lame just short of the finish. Her eyes smoldered, giving off occasional glints of anger through the curtain of hair. LePiep lay in Panglor's lap, her head hanging over his knee in dejection; every minute or so she sighed loudly.

Panglor felt as though his heart had dropped out of his chest. The station had been their last hope; now they had no hope. They could stay here, or they could go back to the planet. He had made a promise to Jeebering. But he couldn't think about that now; he couldn't think about anything. He sat staring through half-lidded eyes. Waves of depression from the others washed over him. He stared at the floor, at the tracks they had left in the dust.

"God damn," he muttered, later, when he had more energy.

"Kervill mondometzo-brrrr, snik snik, kaffledorf," said Tiki, looking from Alo to Panglor. "Muck muck." Panglor looked at him oddly. "Filge-fick," concluded Tiki.

"Do you have any idea what he's saying?" Panglor said to Alo.

"I don't have any idea why we're here!" Alo muttered coldly. "You and your going after that ship!"

"What do you mean?" he said slowly.

"I mean, you didn't have to do it. You let those criminals push you around, and now here we are because of it." Her eyes turned bright and steely behind the tangle of hair.

Panglor felt a flash of anger. He tried to suppress it, but the feelings boiled up anyway. How could this girl—this stowaway!—say that, when she was the one who had no business even being on the *Cur* in the first place? "Listen!" he growled. "No one asked you to come along, you know!"

Alo jumped up and glared. "And where would you have been without me copiloting?"

Blood rushed in his ears. "Where am I now!" he said savagely.

"Why you—!" Alo cried in fury. "You—you bastard!" Her hair bounced as she yelled, shaking her fist. "I'm not going to help you any more—you can do it yourself! See how far you get!" Whirling, she stormed out of the control room. Her footsteps echoed down the corridor and faded.

"Krilll b-dartz!" Tiki said tremulously. His eyes jumped spastically, and his body went rigid as a statue.

Bah! thought Panglor. She'll be back.

LePiep bounded from his lap and streaked across the room to the doorway where Alo had disappeared.

"Hyo-lo-lo!" she cried, peering down the corridor. She stood there for several minutes, then slowly walked back to Panglor, head low, radiating severe dismay. She crouched silently at his feet.

Christ, he thought.

And the trouble was, she was right. He was to blame for everything that had gone wrong—for their coming to the D1 system in the first place, for *Deerfield's* coming along after them, for their failure to find a way home. He felt a burning in his chest as he thought about it. What was he supposed to do now, for chrissake?

He waited, not moving, until the iron band around his lungs eased its grip. He became acutely aware of the whisper of induction-circulated air. Finally he sighed. "Tiki—want to come look for her? For Alo?"

"Snirrveff," answered the Kili, blinking in response to Alo's name. LePiep responded, too; she jumped into Panglor's lap, then sprang up and out, spreading her wings, and swept in a tight circle around the room. She landed at his feet, then jumped into his arms again, emoting happily.

They explored the corridor Alo had taken, calling her name, but hearing only their own echoes. They followed the corridor around a bend, through two large archways, and into a high-ceilinged lobby fifty meters long and twenty wide, lighted gloomily by scattered squares on the walls. The chamber was barren. Corridors branched off in every direction except to the right, and on that side a long staircase, perhaps provided for architectural novelty, ascended to a balcony. Panglor thought a moment, then led the way up the staircase. It seemed the sort of direction Alo would take.

The balcony proved to be a deep, dark area that might once have been a lounge or hearth. Panglor squinted into the gloom. Finally he hollered, "God damn it Alo! Where are you?" His words reverberated in the space.

Alo's voice returned, faintly. "Over here." He turned in annoyance, trying to decide where "here" was, and finally spotted her, standing at the far end of the lounge. LePiep perked up in his arms. Panglor led the way over.

"What are you doing?" he asked as he approached, but the answer was obvious. She was standing before a wide viewport, looking out into space and downward at the bright ochre-brown crescent of the planet. Panglor said nothing more. He gazed at the sight—at the enormous calico crescent grinning in the darkness. He could not quite think of it as a planet, and yet could not envision it as anything but. It was their zone of discontinuity, their locus of wavefront aberrations, their frayed hole in the fabric of what they were accustomed to thinking of as reality.

The sight instilled a peculiar awe. Something down there, some set of conditions, had responded to his thought and to his will. How many times in his life had that happened?

But there were people down there, trapped, who were his responsibility.

"Mus-nu choka-loka mmmffsss," muttered Tiki.

"We're stuck," Alo said. "Might as well go back down. No point in staying here." She cleared her throat noisily, then lifted LePiep from Panglor's arms.

Panglor grunted. The view, even without her anger, gave him pains—straight in the chest, like the stab of a knife. LePiep grumbled, sweeping him worriedly with her eyes, sharing his distress. His guilt.

He suffered silently, not letting it reach his face. He felt dizzy, felt LePiep's silent waves of empathy soothing the pain, lessening it, and yet making him dizzier still with confusion. The view of outer space seemed to sway drunkenly, and his thoughts whirled, revolving about the edges of his vision, spinning and falling forward into the black hole of all the worlds and possibilities he had ever lost.

And the idea struck him broadside, smashing the pain into splinters. LePiep yipped audibly, encouraging him. "My God, why not?" he muttered foggily, and the pain vanished in an rush of exhilaration. The notion bloomed full in his mind—

"Hey!" he said.

Tiki turned at once. Alo rolled her eyes toward him and restrained the excited ou-ralot.

"Why didn't I think of it before?" Panglor cried. He put both hands against the glass and leaned forward and stared out into space, down at the strange world whose nightside was curiously distorted to his vision, as though cradled not quite correctly by the glowing crescent of dayside. "Yeah," he said softly, convinced now because his idea was so logical it hurt, and so outlandish he scarcely dared to speak it.

"Yeah, *what*?" Alo said impatiently. LePiep was purring with excitement.

"Why not use the planet?" he said, his face to the glass. "The zone, I mean. If that thing out there can reach ships in foreshortening and grab them and pull them out like a capture-field—well, maybe it can work the other way, too. Maybe it can put them *into* foreshortening."

"Are you crazy?"

"Well, why not?" Panglor said, turning to face her. "We got off the planet right? The zone responded to our thoughts, our frame of mind, I don't know what."

"Yah," said Alo. "Tiki said the behavior of things changed according to stresses and moods."

"Right. So when we wanted to lift from the planet, it worked. Before that, it brought us to a safe landing. We assume it will bring us to a safe landing again. So why not assume it could do more?"

"Never worked for anyone else, did it?"

"Naw, probably not—but who knows? Probably no one knew how to do it. Probably never even occurred to anyone else. The poor sons of bitches just go crazy down there."

Tiki rotated his eyes in a circle. "Fffessss-llbrinth," he whispered.

Panglor squinted, wishing that he could communicate with the Kili. Then he shrugged and looked back at Alo. "Sure—they're all going crazy. It would never cross their minds that they could drive their ship right through the zone into foreshortening."

Alo opened her mouth slowly. "Drive *through*?" She clawed at her hair. "Why not just think—or whatever—our way into foreshortening?"

"Well, we need velocity, of course."

"Yeah." Alo nodded, thinking. "The trouble is—if it didn't work, we'd be splattered all over down there, wouldn't we?" Her eyes flickered and danced between her friends. "Well—wouldn't we?"

That was hard to argue with; but for Panglor's idea to work, they would need a high velocity for the plunge into foreshortening. A collapsing-field worked by compressing the interstellar space fabric in a shockwave surrounding the ship—effectively shortening the distance the ship traversed between stars. But even compressed, the distances were so vast that high entering velocities were required, on the order of $.01c$. So they had little choice; if they were going to try, they would have to make a very fast dive directly into the zone. He gestured helplessly. "What have we got to lose?"

Alo's eyes softened, and she shrugged. "Okay. I'm in. How about Tiki?"

The Kili was smiling blissfully. Whether that was

some Kili expression, or Tiki's own translation to the human, Panglor couldn't guess. "I think we'd better wait until he understands us again, when we go back down."

"Hyolp!" said LePiep. She jumped from Alo's grasp into the arms of a startled Tiki. She beamed happily, nuzzling the Kili, who bobbed sideways in evident contentment.

"We're still going back for them, then?" said Alo.

"Said we would. Besides what do you think they'd say to us back at D3 if we came back alone?"

Alo made a noise with her tongue. "Okay. What are we waiting for?"

They walked back through the empty halls. Eventually they made their way back to the hangar and *The Fighting Cur*. They boarded, sealed the airlock, and made ready to depart. Panglor took the controls and applied thrust. The ship vibrated, but failed to move.

"Pangly, we're stuck to the hatch," Alo said.

Panglor cursed. He shut off the drivers and stared at the outside of the hatch structure in the viewscreen. "Any ideas, kiddo?" he said, finally.

"Naw," said Alo, squinting at the screen. She went to the laser control and beamed various frequencies at likely looking targets. That effort was futile.

Muttering, Panglor returned to the airlock to suit up again. He was getting tired of this, because when he changed clothes he remembered how much he was beginning to stink. Helmeted, silversuit-field on, he went back into the docking tunnel and looked for a manual release switch. He found a panel but no controls. He ripped off the cover and scrutinized the circuitry. With more intuition than certainty, he tripped several relays with the lightbeam of his unitool. At the end of the passage, a dark ring appeared as the ship separated slowly from the docking port. *Hhmph*ing, he pocketed the unitool and leaped easily into the *Cur's* airlock.

When he was dressed again, he hurried back up to the bridge. Alo was already moving the ship out of the station.

The return trip took half a day, ship's time. They took turns using the mistshower, and rested. Their destination grew steadily as they dropped toward it, a great ochre-red ball. Panglor gazed at the "planet" and tried to envision it as nothing more than an elaborate collapsing-field placed here by the fates—a curious hole in space, a threadbare spot in the fabric of the continuum that they could fall through if they chose.

"What're you thinking, Pangly?"

He clicked his teeth. "About how crazy this is, that thing out there. It's demented. The whole idea is demented, the thought that anyone could fly through that and come out the other side in foreshortening. Everything that happens near this thing is demented, and I think we're demented, too."

Alo hoisted herself up onto one of the front consoles. She looked a lot better now—scrubbed and clean, with her hair combed. She was wearing one of Panglor's shirts, with the sleeves rolled up, and it hung on her like an enormous bag. Panglor nodded. "Yeh. Demented. That's why I'm naming the place right now. Planet or not, it needs a name. It deserves one."

"Yeah?"

" 'Dementia.' That's what I'm calling it." Rising, extending both hands toward the image in the viewscreen, he bowed. "I dub thee 'Dementia'—you earned it." He raised his eyes. "What do you think?"

"Pangly," she said, shaking her head, "I'm worried about you. Really, I am."

There was a scrabbling noise. LePiep poked her head

out of her corner stash of junk and regarded them each in turn, her eyes pulsating, reflecting their sense of anticipation.

The landing went much as it had the first time. Alo seemed relaxed and Panglor tried to pretend that he was. The *Cur* slipped toward Dementia's atmosphere with both position and velocity wholly ambiguous. Panglor kept his hands off the controls and tried to think negligently in terms of safe landing, and he glanced at Tiki, who appeared nervous. "Don't worry," he said.

"I don't worry about the landing," said Tiki. 'It's what comes after that I worry about."

"Why? We're going to take off again and try to get back home. We're going to dive right into the zone."

"That's what I thought," said Tiki, crossing his eyes. "I know one other—a Daco—who tried that. I never saw him again."

"He probably made it home, then."

"Or he crashed and obliterated himself."

There was a queer, wrenching discontinuity . . . and when it ended, the *Cur* was standing upright in a meadow, in easy view of *Deerfield*.

"I wish you hadn't said that," Panglor said to Tiki. He made a complete sweep with the viewer. Things had changed. The landscape was greener and the sky was orange, with a chocolate sun. Stands of exotic trees cropped the ridges. He hooked a thumb toward the exit. "Let's have a look." He caught LePiep and led the way, hoping there would be a convenient promontory for them outside the airlock.

There was. They started down, surveying as they descended. Things had changed, all right, but not necessarily more than they might have in a single "night" here. Panglor wondered how much time had passed for the *Deerfield* crewmen.

"Hallo there!" he heard—from behind. He turned. One of the *Deerfield* men stood in the airlock, where they had just emerged.

"How did you—"

The crewman shimmered like a ghost and faded. Panglor swallowed, remembering: *Dementia.* Right. The crewman appeared at the bottom of the slope. "My God," Panglor said, "I hope they haven't all turned to wraiths since we left. We'll never be able to get them to stay in the ships." LePiep muttered uneasily in his arms.

Crossing the meadow to *Deerfield* they passed a finger of a long, shallow lake of crystalline water. They could see, moving about in the water, the shadowy forms of large fish. LePiep craned her neck and watched them intently. "Uh-oh," Panglor muttered. Had the airfish taken to the water? That could mean . . . what?

"Maybe they just wanted water for a change," Alo suggested, reading his thoughts.

"Mmgh!" he grunted. Well, it didn't matter. It was the *idea* of the airfish he had to keep in mind; what they did with their own lives didn't concern him.

Several *Deerfield* crewmen emerged, wild-eyed, but not hostile. One of the men appeared not to recognize them, but he was nevertheless very hospitable, inviting them into the ship. "Is Jeebering around?" Panglor asked, gazing about.

"Inside, inside—sure," chorused the other two crewmen.

They went in. The ship's interior was gloomy, the passageways musty. They found Jeebering in the commons, just aft of the bridge. He looked pale and unwell, and he was staring into a mug of stale moke. He looked up, his eyes dull. "Hullo," he said. "Where've you been? Has it been a long time?"

Panglor winced at the broken voice. The mental deterioration of these men was even worse than he had feared. "Don't know how long we've been gone, your time, Jeeb," he said. "We got to the space station all right. But we couldn't get the collapsing-field working." He looked closely at Jeebering, to see if his words had penetrated.

LePiep stepped from his arms onto the table and nosed close to the officer. "Hyoll?" she muttered.

Jeebering shook his head, but his eyes glimmered with understanding. Panglor sighed in relief; the man wasn't completely gone. "You tried, hey, Balef?" Jeebering said. "Well, I give you credit for that. You tried. And you came back. The captain would appreciate that, if he were conscious. How long have they been gone, Tregs?"

A crewman emerged from the shadows and saluted solemnly. "Well, sir, that's hard to say. Some say just a day or two, others say over two weeks."

"And what do you say?" Jeebering asked, not unkindly. His voice was tired, but he glanced at the ouralot and a smile flickered at his lips.

"I make it about three days," said Tregs. "Sir."

"Jeeb," Panglor said urgently. "I didn't finish. I think we have another way to get out of here. Without the collapsing-field."

"There is no other way," said Tregs.

"We think we have a way." Panglor glanced at Alo, who gave him a thumbs-up sign. LePiep rumbled encouragingly.

"Sure. You have a way," Jeebering said, nodding. "Trouble is, I hardly have any crew left. They're disappearing all over the place."

"I know—we saw some of them."

"Did you see Captain Drak?" Jeebering asked, raising his eyes. "He's one of the ones who's gone."

Panglor's breath caught in his throat. Jeebering's gaze was haunted. "Aw—Jeeb—" Panglor said, struggling for words. What could you say to a man who'd lost his captain, especially when the man probably considered it your fault?

Jeebering's eyes sparked and hardened as he refocused his attention on Panglor. "What was your idea, Balef?"

"Right." Panglor coughed. It was one thing to propose something like this to Alo or Tiki but quite another to say it to Jeebering without sounding like a madman. "Well—"

Jeebering blinked.

"Well—Tal, we were going to take off again, in both ships this time, and—and—"

Alo nudged him, with another thumbs-up.

"Right. We're going to dive the ships straight into the planet—the zone—Dementia, that's what I call it—it's not really a planet. We're going to dive at insertion velocity, and aim just as though we were making a foreshortening insertion, and—"

"Boom!" said Jeebering, throwing up both hands. "Get it over with right away, huh?" He grinned both ways at his crewmen, most of whom chuckled blackly.

"No, Jeeb—we mean it. We think we can make it work. Use the zone the way we took off in the *Cur*." Panglor glanced from one man's eyes to another's, trying to keep his voice even. LePiep barked mournfully.

Silence enveloped the commons as the Vikken men perceived that Panglor was serious. He spoke quickly, explaining his idea. In the end, no one would say that it was impossible, and after the proposal had rolled off enough tongues, it began to sound like an intriguing notion—a tall-tale escape from a ludicrous situation.

An all-hands call went out, to return to the ship.

Wandering outside, Panglor felt sure that none of these men had the slightest inkling of what he proposed to do. He also suspected that if he succeeded, he would bring home a shipload of madmen. But that was better than nothing, he supposed. He tried not to think about what he would say to the authorities at D3, if he ever saw that place again.

Alo, however, had other worries. She pulled him away from the confusion around the ship. They walked across the grass toward a blossoming broad-leaf tree. "I don't know what kind of shape this *Deerfield* is in," she said, glancing back at the freighter, "but one thing I do know is that none of those guys is in any condition to pilot. They'll never even get into orbit, much less pull off the rest of it."

That question had been bothering Panglor, also. "Well," he said, watching LePiep scamper up into the tree. "I dunno." Suddenly taking Alo by the hand, he led her under the tree and sat down on the grass. The return pressure of her hand made him self-conscious; but he shrugged to himself, thinking, Balef, she's only a girl. A part of his mind was quaking at such proximity to a female who liked him, even one as familiar as Alo. LePiep, sensing his confusion, peered down at him from the lowest branch and chirped.

"Pangly, are you—?"

"What we've got to do," he said, cutting her off because he thought she might say something about—

"Pangly," she said, looking him in the eye. "You're awfully cute." She locked her hands behind his neck and leaned forward to kiss him.

"Come on, now!" he cried, lurching evasively. "We have to decide how we're going to—"

"Coward!" she growled, and quickly planted the kiss on his lips. LePiep hooted.

Panglor blushed and tried not to focus on the sensation he'd just felt, of her lips at his, and the pressure of her breasts against his arm, and the light pleasant smell of her close to him. Instead, he thought about what she'd seemed like earlier—insolent, arrogant, looking no older than sixteen (except when . . . she'd been undressed . . . back there in his cabin). "Listen," he said, shifting his position to hunch forward, cross-legged, over his knees. She beamed at him. "How are we going to get that ship off? We can't take them back in the *Cur*—there's no room unless we put them in the cargo hold, which might not be such a bad idea."

"So we'd better all go back in *Deerfield*," Alo said.

"What? No. How can we do that? What about the *Cur*? We can't leave her here!"

"Pangly, Pangly!" Alo chuckled. She rubbed his thigh and slapped his knee. "The *Cur* is not the only ship in the universe. Why do you care if it stays here— it's falling apart, anyway. Look." She ticked off on two fingers: "You and I are the only ones here capable of flying a ship off this place and doing that bit into foreshortening."

"You?"

"If you can do it, I can," she said with a shrug.

Panglor scrutinized her. "How old are you?" He noticed that her hand was still on his knee.

"Nineteen, maybe. Twenty. Twenty-five. Who knows? Why?"

"Just wondered. You insulted my ship, and I wanted to know whether I'd be killing a minor if I squashed you flat."

Alo snorted. "One of us has to fly *Deerfield*, Pangly, and that'd be me. Now, you can either leave the *Cur* here and do it with me, or you can leave me with all those men, half of whom are psychotic, and bring your precious ship back yourself."

Panglor thought hard. Obviously he couldn't send her with the *Deerfield* crew, and he didn't want to leave her alone with the *Cur*, either. But to abandon the *Cur* would practically be a betrayal. That ship and he had been through a lot together. But she was right; they would all have to go in *Deerfield*. Curling his lip, he said, "Witch. I wouldn't leave you with those men—it wouldn't be human. To them, I mean."

Alo lunged, knocking him back flat, and was on him in a second. "Witch, eh?" she howled, sitting on his stomach. "Witch, is it?" She started thumping his chest. "I'll beat you to a pulp!" Panglor chuckled and grabbed her arms and rolled her sideways, making her struggle to stay on top. Alo fought back, grinning, her breasts visible down the front of his oversized shirt; and suddenly Panglor was getting a terrific erection, which he knew she noticed at once, because she started twitching her rear. That flustered him; he hadn't meant to get quite so serious. He held her arms tightly, giggling, trying to make her stop, and that only increased his arousal. LePiep swooped down out of the tree, whistling with excitement. The sound made him light-headed.

Alo shimmered and vanished. His hands closed on emptiness.

The world went dim, and he felt himself falling, LePiep clutching at his right arm. The world turned about him in a blur, like the rushing of the wind, like the wheeling of the stars, like the vast rotation of the galaxies. Turning . . . falling through an incredible tunnel . . .

Damn! he cried silently. Not now—no!

—and he became aware of voices, human and inhuman, screams and whistles and clicks and *brrrr*ing rasps, and he squinted and thought he saw a layering in the world as it passed around him, a kind of wide latticework, glistening strands crossing and crisscrossing all around, with dark emptiness below him, as though Alo's analogy of a hole in the fabric of space had come to life around him. Well, he thought dazedly, spinning. Is this how it ends?

He seemed to be falling down through the hole in the lattice, but slowly now; he could gather his wits without rushing or panicking. And he could accept.

His arousal of moments ago—threatening unstoppered emotions—had that dumped him into this free space?

. . . falling . . .

LePiep comforted him by huddling alertly in his arms. His arousal was gone now, that was for sure. Perhaps the world would turn solid around him again, beneath him. But he still heard voices . . .

. . . turning in the lattice, dropping . . .

The ou-ralot perked her head up, radiating recognition, concern. "Hyoop," she said quietly, straining her neck to see something in the distance.

"What, Peep, what is it?" Panglor muttered, and his own voice echoed around him in a vast reverberation. All he could see were shadows against the gloom, and the pale gleam of lattice strands, and . . . as though through a window, the figure of a man, a human being, a *Deerfield* crewman. He strained to focus. It was Turret. Was he one of the men who had disappeared?

Panglor took a breath to shout, and then realized that Turret had already seen them and was in fact struggling to move toward them. LePiep mewled—and Turret moved more frantically. He looked so small, almost lost in the vast lattice, a tiny man swimming through nonexistent waters to reach them, a pathetic creature moving against elements he could not possibly understand.

The ou-ralot purred, hardly disturbed at all by the transformations around them, by the disappearance of Alo, of the landscape. Take a hint, Panglor thought; she knows. And without urgency he decided that really what he wanted was to move closer to Turret, and perhaps give him aid. Even as he made the decision, he realized that he was already closer; he was falling or drifting in the curious streams of this existence.

Turret calmed visibly as they closed upon him, as LePiep's chirping encouragement washed over both of them. Turret's eyes were blinking erratically, twitching; but that, too, subsided as Panglor reached out and seized him by the arm. "My God—" Turret gasped. "I thought we were both—but are we—?"

"No, we're not," Panglor said, his head pounding but his self-assurance intact.

"Purrrl," said LePiep, as though to confirm Panglor's sentiments.

Light suddenly flooded the world, and it tilted queerly as the latticework vanished, and the ground became solid beneath them. Panglor heard Alo shout: *"Pangly!"* and then he stumbled and fell to the grass beside Turret. He was just picking himself up when Alo collided with him, seizing him in a bearhug, and they tumbled to the ground again with LePiep scrambling out of the way.

"Pangly!" Alo cried, wiping away tears. "You were gone! What happened? You disappeared, just like the others! Where did *he* come from?" She sat back and looked at Turret, perplexed. She sniffed and rubbed her eyes.

"I'll explain later," Panglor said weakly, urging them both to their feet. "I think we were closer to the center of the discontinuity, and I think things are starting to fall apart here, and I think we'd better get to the ship and be ready to take off."

Turret took a deep breath. "We're back. He—brought me—back."

"Hrrrrl," said LePiep warningly.

"Yah. Let's get to the ship," Panglor said. Alo took his arm and kept a cautious eye on Turret as they walked back.

The *Deerfield* crew was in chaos, but most of them were inside the ship. Jeebering and Tregs stood near the open port, apparently trying to make a count of those who had returned and boarded and those who had vanished like ghosts. "Sir, they're gone for good, I fear," Tregs was saying, as they walked up.

Jeebering socked a fist into his open hand in frustration. He nodded unhappily to Panglor, Alo, and Turret. "Four men gone," he said. Then he noticed Turret. "Wait. Aren't you one of them?" He turned back and forth. "Wasn't Turret one of the men missing? Where were you?"

Turret shuddered.

Panglor shoved him gently toward the port. "I found him, Jeeb. He was in trouble. Now look—we're all getting shaky here—"

Jeebering interrupted him. "Captain Drak. You haven't seen him, have you?"

"Uh—no," Panglor stammered, losing his train of thought. He clucked somberly; damn it all, the captain was still missing. "Jeeb," he said, "Jeeb, I've—we've—been thinking about this, about the best way of taking off." He hesitated, chewing his lip, knowing that it sounded terrible—as though he were suggesting that they go ahead and leave the captain and the others behind. But actually, he *was* suggesting it. What else could they do?

"Jeeb, it looks as though we'll all have to go in your

ship, if you don't mind. And Alo and I should do the piloting, I think—you know, just to make sure."

"What?" Tregs said, glowering.

Jeebering looked skeptical. "You and Miss— Miss—?"

"Castley. Right. Jeeb—not meaning any disrespect, but you know, we did this once already—"

"You and Miss Castley."

Panglor nodded, swallowing. He explained what had just happened in his rescue of Turret, emphasizing the need for the proper state of mind, and the kind of intuitive control that seemed necessary to influence events in the discontinuity. Jeebering listened, and smoothed a tic at the corner of his mouth. "Just as well," he answered. "My men are all damn near crazy, anyway. Not one of them's competent to fly, that's for sure." Panglor eyed him, and he added, "Very well, then, Balef—you are First Pilot of *Deerfield* until further notice, and you can make use of such assistants as you choose." He paused broodingly. "We'll have to go without the captain. It's what he would have ordered—for the crew's safety."

Panglor's breath caught, but he nodded. "If we don't go soon . . . How are your food supplies?"

"Adequate. Right?" Jeebering turned to Tregs for confirmation. "We're missing five people. Four? I don't know. We'll leave some supplies for them, in case they're still alive."

Panglor grunted sympathetically. "Sure. They might show up yet." Clearly it was possible; but if the men failed to return, it did not necessarily mean they were dead. They might, perhaps, have moved farther into the discontinuity or even out of this universe altogether . . . perhaps still living, still aware. Tiki had traveled to other discontinuities and returned. But how many others had returned? Waiting here would only serve to put more men at risk. "Well," Panglor said, "we'd better go pack some gear from our ship." His voice trembled, filled with a sudden flush of nervousness that he had not meant to let out of its cage. He cleared his throat and hummed.

Jeebering nodded and turned away.

With Alo, Panglor hurried back to *The Fighting Cur*. He went through all the ship's compartments, packing items into his duffel. Alo, meanwhile, gathered food supplies to bring along. She waited impatiently as he tarried in the control room, blinking as he took a last look around. Then they went out through the airlock and he turned and squinted at the ship, tears misting his eyes. Stupid; it's just a ship. Used to hate the thing. Alo poked him, her eyes glinting with sympathy. He nodded. Right. He saluted the ship, and then turned and walked straight away from it.

The sky had darkened to a muddy orange, and the sun was a dancing yellow ring with a black center. It felt as if a storm were brewing. "Where's Tiki?" Panglor muttered, looking around. He hadn't seen the Kili in some time.

"He was with some men over by the lake," Alo said.

They went and looked, but no one was by the lake.

One *Deerfield* crewman stood at the port; everyone else was in the ship. "Is Tiki inside?" Panglor asked. The man blinked dreamily. "Tiki," Panglor repeated. "The Kili. The alien."

"Oh, him," the man said. "I don't think so."

Alo's eyes filled with anxiety. "We have to find him, Pangly."

Jeebering's voice echoed through the port. "Set, there, Pilot? Let's make ready for space."

"One minute, Jeeb," Panglor shouted back. "We have

to find Tiki." He moved away from the ship with Alo and began calling. "Tiki! *Tiki!*" LePiep twittered nervously as they looked in all directions. Jeebering shouted for them to hurry. "TIKI!" Panglor called desperately.

"Pangly, he's not coming." Alo was on the verge of tears.

"Damn it, Tiki!" he bellowed. Where could the Kili have gone?

The storm in the sky broke. Torrents of sparkling rain swept across the meadow toward them, like a shower of liquid jewels. Panglor's heart sank. "Better get inside, I guess," he said dismally. "Before anything more happens. I guess we should take off." He chewed his lip, drawing blood. LePiep huddled miserably against his neck. Despair washed over him.

Alo turned to protest—and then screamed happily. She pointed. There, in the heart of the "rainstorm," was Tiki—dancing and leaping, appearing and disappearing, and waving. "What's he doing?" cried Panglor. "He's waving to us. Isn't he coming?"

Alo pointed again. "The airfish! He's dancing with the airfish!" Panglor squinted. She was right. The Kili was capering madly, blinking in and out of existence, dancing around several large airfish that moved lazily toward the ship. LePiep perked up and watched the strange dance, which lasted about a minute. Then Tiki vanished—and popped into the air beside the ship. He bowed, side to side, to Alo and Panglor. The ou-ralot hooted. But Panglor and Alo smiled uncertainly. Had the Kili decided not to come with them after all?

Tiki turned, eyes crossed, and spoke to the airfish. "Good-bye!" he said. The storm and the airfish retreated, leaving behind a pink sky. His eyes still crossed, Tiki turned back to this human friends. "I'm ready now. I had to tell my friends that I might not be back."

"You'll be back sometime, I'll bet," Panglor said, through a thick throat. He didn't know why he had said that, but he was touched by Tiki's display of affection for the creatures of Dementia.

"Perhaps so. I brought my most important objects." Tiki held up a tiny satchel. "May we go, then?"

"Hyolp," said LePiep.

Liftoff in *Deerfield* differed from their previous experience only in the degree of confusion. The bridge was a madhouse until Panglor appealed to Jeebering to clear the room—and to have tranquilizers administered to all of the crewmen. There was no telling what effect their crazed minds would have on the liftoff. Panglor felt better once the men had been quieted.

When he and Alo and Tiki were set, and relaxed, and thoughtful, he switched on the ship's main power. "Look okay?" he asked, watching the indicators flicker meaninglessly. LePiep peered over the top of the console, watching him intently.

"Sure," said Alo. The control layout of *Deerfield* was considerably more sophisticated than the *Cur's*, though it was nothing they couldn't handle. Of course, none of the indicators could be trusted as long as they were in Dementia's field of influence.

Panglor half closed his eyes. He had to be ready to hit the drivers for power when the ship returned to space. But for the moment, his object was to create the proper mind-set for leaving the zone. "All right, kiddo," he said softly. "Peep, ready for a ride?" He focused wryly on an image of the spaceship sitting in the meadow, and thought of the meadow disappearing, leaving only the empty vacuum of space. LePiep warbled contentedly. That was too easy. He went through it again, deepening the image and sharpening the focus; he gazed through half-closed eyes at Alo, hoping that she was formulating similar images. *Deerfield*: gleaming undamaged ship full of cargo and men. Powerful under the flaming yellow sun and clay sky, as strong-willed as airfish floating happily, riding the updrafts and currents that moved beneath the tricksy veils of the discontinuity. *Deerfield*, beside *The Fighting Cur*, shimmering like a ghost and then no longer there but somewhere else—the meadow gone, the sheer emptiness of space where the meadow used to be, and to one side the huge curved surface of the planetary ball, orange and brown in the light of the distant sun, D1. His thoughts blurred, and there was a thrill in his gut of dreamy déjà-vu, and a shiver streaked up his spine . . .

. . . and he blinked, shaking free of the wrench at his thoughts, and he focused on the multiview scanner. LePiep hooted and another rush went up his spine. They were in space. "Get me something on that orbit," he said to Alo. He began checking his own instrumentation, but he couldn't expect accuracy yet. The ball of the planet was growing visibly. Under the ou-ralot's eye, he checked the ship's attitude and hit the drivers, then made adjustments. There was no sensation of acceleration at all. The ship had excellent grav-control, much better than the *Cur's*.

"Here you go, sir, Captain sir," Alo said cheerfully, transmitting data to his screen. "Give it to her hard, or we'll be right back where we started."

"Right," Panglor said, adjusting the thrust vector.

Alo said, "We're starting to get some consistency here. I think we're moving out of the zone. Orbit's firmed up."

"What's happening?" Jeebering asked.

Panglor looked up in surprise. He had forgotten that Jeebering was on the bridge. "We're out," he said.

"Doing fine. Heading up for a high orbit now." Jeebering smiled, and Panglor realized that Jeebering had tranquilized himself, as well as his crew. That was good. He hoped there was plenty of the stuff left for the dive back down.

For half a day, they drove steadily outward from Dementia.

Twelve hours and seventeen minutes after the start of the outward climb, Panglor turned the ship and reversed the direction of thrust—first breaking the speed of their climb, then beginning their dive, slowly, then faster, at steadily mounting speed dropping straight toward the silent ball and the stars behind it.

Precision was something of a problem in terms of their insertion trajectory for D3. They really didn't know what the characteristics of Dementia's "collapsing-field" would be, assuming it worked at all. Panglor figured to fly by the seat of his pants in the final insertion, and trust the quirky effects of Dementia to pull them on line.

Alo, tonguing her teeth thoughtfully, watched the planet growing in the screen and said, "This has to be the funniest stunt I've ever tried. If it doesn't work, there won't even be two molecules of us stuck together anymore."

"Brilllicka," said Tiki. He had remained silent throughout the maneuvers, though he had watched everything with shining eyes. Now he fiddled for a moment with a small, dumbbell-shaped object he had brought from his ship, and he said, "Good show. When hit?" His eyes danced.

Panglor arched his eyebrows. Apparently the object was a translating computer. *"Hit?"* he said. "You had to say *hit*? We go through in about three hours." He tapped his teeth, glanced over the board again, and nodded.

"Hloops!" cheered LePiep, scrabbling around behind the couches. She radiated a great wave of confidence.

The three hours passed quickly enough. They ate, but stayed clear of the ship's commons, because the crewmen were beginning to act strangely as the tranquilizers wore off. Panglor suggested that Jeebering give the entire crew another stiff jolt. Jeebering took a look in the commons and the corridors and gave the order. He took another dose himself, and sat reigning benignly from the command seat on the bridge.

Alo massaged Panglor's neck muscles as he made final course adjustments. The sight of Dementia is now awesome and frightening in the screen, an enormous reddish-orange globe filling a quarter of the sky. The globe swelled with each passing moment. "Why are you doing that?" Panglor asked, gradually becoming aware of Alo's fingers moving pleasantly at the top of his spine.

"Dunno," she said. She went to her own station, touching LePiep behind the ears on the way and winking at Tiki.

Panglor grunted and remembered the sensation of the fingers, now absent. It had been nice. He finished the final adjustments and sat back. "Ready," he said, pressing his lips together. The planet was growing very fast, as *Deerfield* drove downward, and the instruments were beginning to show aberrations. Tiki stared intently at the screen, Jeebering stared contentedly at nothing, and Alo caught Panglor's eyes, then looked at the screen. LePiep whistled excitedly.

"All right, you mother!" Panglor howled, bursting with energy. He locked his gaze onto the screen. "Whooo*eeee*!"

The ochre surface mushroomed. Waves of devilish excitement washed over him and whirled in his heart.

Panglor grinned at the ou-ralot and pictured a hole right in the center of that image, in the heart of the zone of strangeness. A hole they could streak through like a bull's-eye. A hole in the planet that wasn't solid—that wasn't a planet. The hole was a bit too small to see just now, but it was there all the same. *Deerfield* accelerated, plummeting, and Panglor smiled, comfortable in his seat. And thought of the ship dropping through the hole in space, twisting into foreshortening, streaking down the compressed taffy of space . . .

. . . and suddenly remembered again the touch of Alo's fingers at his neck, softly kneading. And remembered her kiss, back on the world, and the press of certain parts of her body . . . the same body he'd seen . . . no, no, this wasn't right, these were subconscious thoughts washing up, not what he had to think of . . . he had to fly the ship, zero on shooting straight through the bull's-eye. But this was nicer, and nobody was reading his mind except LePiep in her own way, encouraging him, hooting softly. The thoughts . . . what was it he wanted to picture? . . . Alo? . . . no . . . yes . . . the soft parts of Alo, the woman qualities . . . it wasn't really helping, he knew, with that enormous red area mushrooming in his screen, opening; and the thing was he had an incredible hard-on at this moment, a bursting erection, thinking . . . of the woman in the girl, the firm small features in the woman he'd glimpsed . . . waves of LePiep's excitement reflected his own, agitated him further . . . the hormones were truly out of control now, rampant, and he focused on the image of the world closing around him, swallowing him, and all he could think of was that desire . . . and the world totally surrounding him and his ship . . . and there was a *shift*, a discontinuity, and a rift yawned in the planet, black with spangling stars; and the ship fired through the opening like lightning, and everything visual went milky, and Panglor ejaculated just before losing consciousness, his last thought an instant of embarrassment as LePiep hooted and a ghostly airfish winked at him and vanished.

13

THE FIRST thing he felt was a wave of appreciative pleasure from the ou-ralot. The second was an abrupt draining of energy, and the third was dampness at his crotch.

Alo's eyes were on him when he came out of the fog.
He blinked, and had trouble focusing; but not so much
trouble he couldn't see Alo's eyes twinkling. She had
followed everything that had happened to the ship, to
the planet—and to him. Flushing, he blinked hard and
stared into the scoopscope—grimly feigning calmness.
There was no sweat soaking his back, no wet spot at his
crotch; no. But there *were* drifting white speckles in
both eyefinders of the scoopscope. The main screens
were blank, blue.

They were in foreshortening.

There was an incredible tension, like a vacuum, in
his chest. He reached out to touch LePiep, still crooning
happily on the console. "Jeeb!" he said, trembling, raising his voice without turning. "We're on our way!

Don't know where, for sure, or when we'll get there—
but we're on our way."

"Wonderful," said Jeebering. He sounded pretty
stoned. That might be embarrassing later; it wouldn't do
to remind him of it. Ever.

Panglor felt Alo's gaze on him. He glanced at Tiki.
The Kili yodeled in his native tongue, then consulted
his device and said, "Good job. Splendid. Did it work?"

"Yop!" said Alo, cutting off Panglor's reply. "Pangly
did it. Of course, whether he could have done it without
me is debatable." Her voice sounded satisfied and
faintly amused. Panglor knew that that may have been
his imagination, but he damn well was not going to
look at her face to find out.

There wasn't a lot they could do on the bridge now.
Only time would tell of their ultimate success or failure.
Panglor ran through a complete check of the ship's systems and finally set the emergence warning alarm.
"Jeeb, I think it'd be a good idea to keep the others off
the bridge for a while," he said hesitantly. "Until you're
sure they're okay."

Jeebering nodded placidly. He seemed content to sit
and survey the bridge. "You are relieved," he said.

Panglor shrugged, scooped up LePiep, and gestured
to Alo and Tiki. They left the bridge together. Tregs
was coming out of the commons, just outside the
bridge, and Panglor stopped him in the passageway.
"Are there some empty cabins?" he asked.

Tregs looked startled. His eyes filled with questions
and a hint of hysteria, but outwardly he was relaxed; the
tranquilizer was still working. He pursed his lips. "Cabins thirteen and fourteen. I don't think any others—"

"Right," said Panglor. "Thirteen and fourteen." He
started to move away.

Tregs seized his arm. "What happened? Where are
we?" The hysteria was finding a grip in him, after all.

Panglor thought a moment. Let Jeeb tell them, he decided. He nodded. "Thanks. I think—"

Jeebering's voice broke in, on the shipwide com. "All hands! This is the bridge—Jeebering in acting command." A long pause followed. Panglor nudged Alo and Tiki down the passageway, while Tregs listened to the com. "We are in foreshortening," said Jeebering's voice. "We are bound, we hope, for Dreznelles Three."

Panglor ignored the rest of the address and searched for their quarters. They found cabins thirteen and fourteen at the end of the passageway, near the cargo bulkhead. Panglor hesitated. Which took precedence—giving a private room to the female or giving it to the guest alien? While he debated, Alo said, "Tiki ought to have his own room, so I'll stay with you—okay, Pangly?" She caught his eye soberly.

Panglor nodded. He felt dizzy, with blood thundering in his temples. Without a word, he went into the second cabin, leaving Alo to show Tiki his room. He let LePiep down on the bunk. The cabin was small, with a single sleep bay, a tiny personal alcove—and—what was he thinking, sharing this with Alo? Unless—

But how could he?

And how could he take time to worry about this, when he had foreshortening to worry about? They could be on their way to limbo right now, all of them . . .

But no. He didn't think they were.

His mind was filled with strange and unfamiliar tensions. He was frightened of foreshortening, and he wasn't. The fear was lessened . . . or rechanneled . . . because he could not spring his mind loose from her: the girl, the woman, Alo. Alo. He'd thought he had rationalized her into the daughter, the sister he had never had. But other pathways kept opening, sparking new feelings: unsuspected affection, lust, embarrassment, and boiling among all of those, fear. Something in him resisted involvement with so sharp-witted and caustic a young woman, who could inflict more pain than any other woman he had ever known. The tension, the fear, the desire branched out, and reached down into his body somewhere near the sternum, and tugged sharply. The girl was intelligent and capable and commanded his respect. So why such a feeling wrecking his equilibrium and twisting his desire with pain? The physical desire, the emotional need, both existed in a swarm of electrons alive in his mind, caught in a bind of magnetic energies, threatening to collapse like a foreshortening field.

Shaking his head, he tossed his duffel into the sleep bay beside LePiep. The ou-ralot padded along the edge of the sleep bay, trying to calm him with waves of reassurance, poking at him with her nose. His chest was so tight he could hardly breathe. He could faintly hear Alo, talking to Tiki in the next room. Deciding quickly, he stripped and stepped into the personal alcove and turned on the mistshower. A fine, vaporous spray billowed around him, soothing and cleansing him and gradually, after a fashion, relaxing him. He lingered—and finally, reluctantly, turned off the mist and turned on the dryer. He felt better.

Alo was sitting in the sleep bay when Panglor came out, adjusting his clean jumpsuit. He avoided her gaze and looked around the cabin, poking at his duffel. Finally he glanced up. Alo stared at him with dark, grave eyes. He swallowed uncomfortably. LePiep was touching him with waves of anticipation. "Well—we did it. Everything went all right, I guess." He looked away.

Alo set LePiep aside and stood up. "Pangly," she said. "Who were you thinking about?"

His throat thickened. "What do you mean?"

Sighing, she moved closer, facing him. She pressed her palms to his ribcage, then squeezed his sides, holding him. The pressure was familiar, warm, and terrifying. She gazed at his shoulder. Tension was in her eyes, too. "You know what I mean." She turned her gaze down for a moment—and he felt a stirring in his loins—then she met his eyes nervously. "Pangly—" she started, and he couldn't tell whether she was taunting or pleading. "When we went through . . . when you. Oh, Pangly!" There was anguish in her voice—and tears in her eyes. "Who were you thinking of?" she cried.

Part of his breath went out with a hiss. The rest stuck in his throat. Nerve endings fired randomly through his body, making him twitch, and his vision clouded. "How—old—did you say—you were?" he grunted, past the huge obstruction in his throat.

"Old enough!" she cried, muffling her face against his chest. She hugged him, pressing her breasts against his stomach; then she straightened and kissed him, making a quiet crying sound. He struggled to overcome the tension in his arms. His heart was pounding. LePiep purred quietly, somehow making it easier. Somewhere, in the branches and roots of his mind, he made a decision. He closed his arms around her head and neck and cradled her as she kissed him, and then his instincts awakened as his excitement eased past the tension. He ran his hands once over Alo, and then quickly lifted her into the sleep bay.

Some time later, Alo gazed down at him and sighed happily, her eyes sparkling. "You still haven't told me who you were thinking about," she accused gently.

"Did you tell me how old you are?" He closed his eyes, relaxing blissfully.

"Told you, I don't know exactly," she said, settling down close to him, fingering the sweat on his chest. "Haven't even begun to figure in the relativistic effects."

"Mmf. Can't recall who I was thinking of, either. We

must have been traveling too fast." Very fast, he added silently. Fast enough to blow aside a lot of memories of failure. Where was the last woman he'd made love to? Veti IV? Good-bye, whatever your name was.

Alo had no comeback. She was asleep, her cheek resting against his bare chest.

Panglor blinked his eyes open. Alo mumbled sleepily, her eyes closed. He rolled over and squinted to check the time; nearly ten hours had passed. LePiep tiptoed gingerly along the edge of the bunk and peered into his eyes, radiating soothing alertness. And contentment. *Alo*, Panglor thought, closing his eyes with a sigh. He blinked them open again, touched LePiep on the nose, and shook his head wryly. Who would have thought it?

He rolled quietly out of the sleep bay, feeling drowsy but restless. He felt a curious sense of rightness as he studied Alo, still peacefully asleep, with a hint of a smile on her lips. Nodding to himself, he started dressing, while LePiep walked back and forth across the narrow bureau ledge, watching him. LePiep whistled, and a moment later he heard a mumbled, "Morning, Pangly." He turned. Alo sat up, blinking and tugging back her hair. She smiled crookedly and gestured for him to come closer.

It took them a while, but eventually they went to the commons for breakfast, with Tiki. They ate in an uncomfortable, eerie silence—watched by several crewmen, who, with nervous gestures and eye movements, betrayed contradictory emotions of fear, resentment, and respect. Panglor had the uneasy feeling that the *Deerfield* crew didn't know what to make of them. But he thought it would be a good idea not to linger here. He and Alo finished their meal (Tiki had declined ship's food), and they left as they had entered, in silence.

The bridge was quiet, and it was a moment before

Panglor realized that Jeebering was present, on watch. "Things all right?" Panglor asked, approaching him.

Jeebering turned slowly. "There have been no problems on the bridge, Pilot Balef. However, I am concerned about the crew, and I think it best that you keep apart from them, for the present. Therefore, you will stay on the bridge or in your cabins, and meals will be served to you there or here. Understood?"

"Sure," Panglor said. It was probably just as well, if strangeness was still running strong on the ship. Lovemaking was one thing, but half-crazed shipmates was another. Suppose they didn't make it back, after all? Suppose he ended up in real limbo, with an honored Kili guest, a woman to love, and a ship full of madmen? He shivered and glanced back. "Jeeb? Is something else wrong?"

Jeebering was scowling, and for a moment appeared not to have heard. Then he looked up. "I thought I saw Captain Drak."

"What? When?"

Jeebering shook his head. "In the zone. At the moment we dived through, in the very center. I saw the captain in the screen, and I believe I also saw one of the missing crewmen. Adams." Sighing, Jeebering rocked almost imperceptibly in his chair, his eyes clouded with thought. "They both seemed alive, and conscious—but I don't know what that means, or if I simply imagined that I saw them."

Panglor silently took his seat, but swiveled back to face Jeebering. "Maybe you did see them. I was thinking earlier—they may have simply moved deeper into the discontinuity—into the heart of it, if there is such a place. Possibly a gate leading right out of our reality. They may be safe, at least after a fashion, wherever they are." At least I'd like to think so, he added silently.

Jeebering pressed his lips together thoughtfully, and nodded.

With Alo's help, Panglor began checking over the control consoles. When he next looked around, he was surprised to see Jeebering sound asleep in his chair. Good lord, Panglor thought, he must have been up on watch ever since we left. Shaking his head, Panglor turned back to the consoles, determined not to let Jeebering down—or the rest of the crew, either.

Not that there was anything he could do now; it was all in the hands of fate. The instruments could provide no clue to the ship's condition with respect to the outside universe.

"Will we—" asked Tiki, consulting his translator in mid-sentence "—arrive?"

"Hope so," said Alo, eyeing Panglor.

Panglor nodded.

Five shipdays passed. Panglor chafed at the passage of time—wondering, scrutinizing blank instruments, talking in subdued tones with Alo and Tiki. Crew tensions remained high, but Jeebering allowed a few of the better-adjusted men to return to their duties, though the bridge remained mostly off limits. Alo, Tiki, and Panglor spent most of their time on the bridge.

Tregs brought them their meals. He had become more friendly toward them; he seemed awed because they had flown through a planet into foreshortening. During the sixth day, distributing breakfast trays, he asked, "Mr. Tiki, are you sure I couldn't bring you something?"

Tiki declined graciously. "No—no—I am quite well." He had bundled up in a thick turtleneck robe, saying that he found the human ship uncomfortably cool.

Tregs clearly was disappointed. As he turned to go, Alo said, "Hey, why don't you stay and eat with us?"

"Well, I've already eaten," Tregs said apologetically. "But—if you wouldn't mind—" He looked at Panglor and at Jeebering. "I'd like to offer something to your ou-ralot. I was wondering if I could make friends with it—her." He shuffled his feet.

"Sure," said Alo. Panglor nodded.

Tregs set down the tray and lifted a small cover, exposing a portion of a muffin. "Where is she?" he asked anxiously. Panglor pointed. At the end of the console, in the corner, Panglor's duffel and several other bags were strategically piled. A tail stuck out on one side. Tregs approached cautiously. He knelt and called, "Ou-ralot. LePiep. Will you come out?" He held out the muffin.

The tail pulled in. There was a faint scratching sound, then silence. Tregs looked around. Chuckling, Panglor called, "It's all right, Peep."

There was another scratching sound. Tregs edged closer, peering. A snout appeared in a dark hole in the pile. Tregs held the food close. The mouth opened, took the muffin gingerly, and withdrew with it. There was a faint whistle, then silence.

Tregs stood up, gesturing uncertainly. Panglor struggled to keep from laughing; but Tregs looked so discomfitted that he finally chuckled, "It's all right. She likes—"

A bell chimed. The EMERGENCE light winked in the view scanner.

Panglor leaped to the binocular scoopscope. Adrenaline rushed in his veins. Peering, tuning the scope, he focused on a peculiar clustering of pointillist dots against a greenish-gray background. The configuration was unusual, but clearly suggested the beginning of a change in the foreshortening field. The dots shifted and arranged themselves into discrete, but unaligned, planes. Not normal. Was this the signature he'd always dreaded—the signature of a ship about to pop out into limbo?

Alo poked at him urgently. He let her have a look. "What's this mean?" she said. He nudged her aside and looked again. The planes that the dots occupied shifted, *twisted*, and suddenly dissolved. The dots reappeared and clustered into curved surfaces. Unusual.

Frightening.

"What's happening?" Jeebering demanded, standing behind him.

Panglor shivered. "Don't know for sure," he said, keeping his face to the scope. This was totally aberrant.

A terrainlike contour fell into focus, milky against the background. The binocular element was working— two individual patterns, combined into one field by his eyes and his brain. "Wait—" he said.

"What's happening?" Jeebering roared.

"Pangly?"

A chime sang, and a twisting, vaguely erotic sensation rushed through his body, and for a moment he was dizzy and could do nothing except cling to the scoop-scope housing. Then he sat back and focused on the viewer.

The first thing he saw was a vast starfield. The second thing, in the rearward screen, was a capture-field shrinking away behind them. The third thing was the spectral ID—*Dreznelles 3*—flashed up by the computer. And the fourth thing was Alo, hollering triumphantly in his face, clutching him; and LePiep, bounding bright-eyed at him, whistling; and Jeebering and Tregs roaring in astonishment. He grabbed Alo and LePiep and hugged them, and blinked and blinked at the wetness blurring his vision.

14

PANGLOR RELEASED Alo and got LePiep free of his neck in time to hear Dreznelles 3 Waystation Control come on-com. Tiki chittered excitedly over the general bedlam, and it was hard to tell what anyone was saying.

"QUIET!" Jeebering bellowed, and after that it was easier.

D3 Control wanted to know who the hell they were, why they weren't on the capturing roster, and why they had just narrowly missed colliding with another ship popping out of the field. Panglor listened to the com with a clammy feeling—not only because of the ship they'd just missed, but also because here in the D3 system he was still a criminal—discoveries and alien guest or not.

Jeebering sent D3 Control a telemetry pulse of *Deerfield*'s identity. That kept them happy for a little while, and then they came back, asking for a voice confirmation.

Panglor glanced nervously at Jeebering. Giving no sign of his thoughts, Jeebering keyed the com and stated: "Dreznelles Three Control, this is *Deerfield*. We confirm, we are Vikken freighter *Deerfield*, First Mate Tal Jeebering in temporary command. We have returned from the Dreznelles One star system under unusual circumstances, and request escort to the station."

D3 Control came back: "*Deerfield, can you give us more information on that, please? We do not copy. Did you say Dreznelles One?*"

With a glance at Panglor, Jeebering said, "D3, affirmative. We will tell you everything when we arrive. We have several passengers bearing important scientific information." Panglor held his breath as Jeebering added, "Two of our guests are human, a Pilot Panglor Balef and a Miss Alontelida Castley."

Control responded: "*Pilot Panglor Balef, did you say? Wait. . . .*" Silence ensued for a number of seconds, during which Panglor's face grew numb, and then Control said: "*Is that Balef, pilot of the freighter, Fighting Cur?*"

"Affirmative," Jeebering said. "His ship was lost in the D1 system. However, he piloted our return. And aboard, as *his* guest, we have a . . . Mister, I guess . . . Tiki . . . a distinguished representative of the *Kili* race." For an instant, merriment flashed in his eyes. "We request protective custody for our guests."

D3 Control advised that escort was en route.

"Did you have to tell them we were aboard?" Panglor said uneasily.

Jeebering gazed thoughtfully at Panglor. "It was either now or later. We'll just have to see how things work out." He stared at the screen. "For you—and for my men. I don't know what the psychs will make of my men." His face betrayed apprehension.

* * *

The waystation was the same glittering beehive that had greeted Panglor once before, but it had travelled more than halfway around its sun. Nearly half a standard year had passed here since their departure. Flanked by escort ships, Panglor docked *Deerfield* in a specially designated mooring, some distance from the commercial traffic. Minutes later, the ship's corridors were aswarm with uniformed officers of the Waystation Authority. Several officials stepped onto the bridge and looked back, as though awaiting someone else.

Soon an older man appeared, flanked by two assistants in government uniforms. He introduced himself as Jonli Bertrecht, Deputy Secretary of the Office of Extrasolar Affairs. After the initial greetings, he formally welcomed Tiki on behalf of the waystation and humanity in general. "Is it true, sir, that you are a member of the race we call 'Kili'?" he asked. "We have found many of the worlds your people once inhabited, and we have sought contact with your people for many years."

Tiki consulted his translator and performed a series of gestures. "As nearly as I can answer, yes," he replied. "I am graciously pleased to greet you, too."

Bertrecht smiled and said, gravely, that he anticipated a long and mutually profitable friendship between his and Tiki's peoples. Tiki blinked and consulted his translator again. "Indeed," he answered, obviously confused. "I trust that your bodies water well, and your tongues do not stick." Suddenly he brightened. "Let me show you now my fine good friends Panglor and Alo and LePiep, who brought me here to this world. They survived discontinuity." He held LePiep up, beaming.

Bertrecht scowled ever so lightly. "Yes. Pilot Balef and Miss Castley, we are sure that you have a great deal to tell us. However, I am afraid that for the time being you will be under the custody of the Waystation Authority." One of the uniformed officers stepped forward as though to take charge.

"Now, wait a minute," Panglor growled. LePiep scrambled from Tiki's arms into his and huddled, radiating displeasure. "We stay with Tiki or we don't go."

Tiki agreed, suddenly becoming agitated. "No, no, yes! They must—"

"Hold it!" Jeebering interrupted. Bertrecht looked at him questioningly. "I am still commanding this ship," Jeebering said. "I told you that these two have important information to offer, and that the Kili is here as *their* guest, and as mine. Now, will you give them protective custody—in *your* department—or not?" He gazed sternly at the D3 officials.

Bertrecht met his gaze. "Very well," he said finally. "They will be provided with joint quarters, under the auspices of my department, on my authority." His gaze shifted to Alo, then Panglor. "However, you understand that you will still be required to answer to the Waystation Authority?"

Panglor nodded. You play it straight and we'll play it straight, he thought. Let's all play it straight for once.

Shortly afterward, they boarded a shuttle and flew to the waystation. Panglor felt a variety of emotions at the sight of the gleaming, intricate world: relief, pleasure, apprehension about the future. Alo squeezed his hand, and LePiep gave an encouraging squeak. The shuttle circled the station and docked in a government-restricted sector. They were processed quickly through decontamination, ahead of the *Deerfield* crew, and conducted to their quarters. Two officials took preliminary statements, and then left them alone.

The quarters were impressive: three adjoining luxury rooms, with a common room in the center dominated by a small decorative pool and sumptuous furnishings. They would be comfortable, all right—except for the locked exits and the guard outside. Tiki looked around thoughtfully. "We are guests of honor, then?"

"Guess you could say that," Panglor sighed. "We're the guests of *your* honor. If you weren't here, we'd be in the slammer." He wondered gloomily what would happen at the debriefing session, set to begin in six hours, at 0800.

"Horrrrl," said LePiep, radiating unease.

The buzzer sounded, and almost simultaneously the door paled. Panglor looked up to see a pale, blond-haired man enter, carrying in his right hand a small glass cage. "Pilot Balef?" he said. "My name is Gometz, and I'm from the Office of Extrasolar Affairs."

"Yeah?" Panglor said grouchily. "It's not 0800 yet, it's only 0700. What's that you've got in your hand?" He did not at all like the looks of this man. LePiep hopped into his lap, radiating distrust.

Gometz half-opened his mouth but hesitated, hefting the cage in his hand, before he spoke. "I apologize for the disturbance—and for what I have to tell you. But my orders come to me from the Department of Health, through the Office of Extrasolar Affairs."

"What orders?"

Gometz cleared his throat. "I am afraid that we must take your pet, the ou-ralot, back to the veterinary section for quarantine and examination." Panglor rose, blood rising in his face. "She has been with you to a world of which we know nothing," Gometz continued, "and this is a precaution against any pathogens or viruses—"

"What pathogens or viruses?" asked Alo, entering the room with a yawn.

"Cock-and-bull pathogens and viruses," Panglor said. He glowered at Gometz and held LePiep protectively.

Gometz displayed no emotion. "Please understand, it

is a matter of legal necessity," he said, handing Panglor a small plastic card. "That's a health warrant, issued to anyone bringing in an animal without Known Planet Clearance. It was only an oversight, in the confusion, that you weren't served with this on your arrival at decontamination. But it's necessary now, and we all just hope that it goes smoothly."

Panglor frowned at the warrant. It looked authentic and confirmed what Gometz had said. Alo peered over his shoulder and snorted. "If LePiep carried any viruses, why wouldn't we be carrying them too?"

Waving negligently, Gometz said, "You have been cleared. But our scanning procedures for humans are faster than those for animals we see infrequently—such as ou-ralots."

"Aahh," Alo said deprecatingly. Panglor remained silent, thinking.

"I assure you that your ou-ralot will be well cared for—I'll see to it personally." Gometz pointed to the com-console. "Why don't you go ahead and verify that warrant? It might make you feel more comfortable if you confirm its authenticity."

Alo took the card from Panglor and padded over to the console. "Fine thing," she muttered. "Come home and be harassed like this." Panglor watched her, thinking, True—but we're in enough trouble with the law as it is. If this is for real . . .

"Pangly, it checks out," Alo said, frowning, turning from the console.

"According to the computer," Panglor growled, trying not to believe it.

"Yeah, well—but why wouldn't it be right?" said Alo. "I mean what would anyone gain by falsifying it?"

Panglor shrugged and faced Gometz appraisingly. Not that he trusted this joker, but what could he do? He had probably dodged as many laws by now as he was going to get away with. "All right," he said. "But I'm coming down there with you. I want to see where you're taking her."

Gometz cleared his throat. "Ordinarily I would say yes, but the problem is that you have to be at your debriefing in a few minutes and, well, I've been asked to remind you to be there on time. They'll be sticky about it, I'm afraid." At Panglor's scowl, Gometz added, "But please don't worry. Your ou-ralot will be fine. And now . . ." He touched the side of his glass box, and the top swung open.

Panglor hesitated, but saw no alternative. Lifting LePiep carefully, he studied her dark pulsating eyes. "Old friend, you've got to go off for a bit while they check you over. Okay? You be good, and we'll have you back here soon." He looked up at Gometz. "Right?" he said tightly. Gometz turned his palms up.

"Hrruuu," said LePiep, quivering. She seemed uncertain and unhappy, but when she touched Panglor with her emotional radiance, their bond was as secure as ever, and her trust of his actions was complete. She peered at Alo, too, and warbled.

"Okay, bub. See you soon," Panglor whispered. He carried her to the box and set her inside. Then he closed the lid himself. "All right, Gometz," he said rising. "You can take her to the meds now. But I want you to remember this: If anything happens to her, I hold you personally responsible. She comes back safe and happy, or I am going to break your neck. Is that clear?" He glared, his temples pounding.

A spark of emotion lit Gometz's eyes, then faded. He's afraid, Panglor thought. Good. Gometz picked up the cage and walked to the door. "She'll be fine. I'll bring her back just as soon as I can," he said. The door paled before him and opaqued behind him when he was gone.

Panglor turned helplessly to his friends. Tiki had just come into the lounge, and as Panglor was explaining to the Kili what had happened, the buzzer sounded again and the door paled. A guard entered to escort them to their debriefing.

The debriefing panel consisted of a semicircle of examiners, some in the flesh and some as holacrums, led by an Undersecretary of Extrasolar Affairs, a middle-aged woman named Dr. Barthollo. She introduced the government officials, the Vikken Lines representative, and the scientists on the panel and then said, "We have several purposes in conducting these hearings. First, to learn exactly what happened in the Dreznelles One system, how you met our Kili guest, and how you managed to return. Your preliminary report is astonishing, to say the least—yet you are here, and so is your friend Tiki. We also wish to interview Tiki, of course; but we are honoring his request that we speak with all of you together, at least for now. Finally, and I address this particularly to you, Pilot Balef, there is the matter of certain events in D3 space, culminating in your insertion to the D1 system with *Deerfield*. That question will be deferred until the end of the inquiry; however, it will not be left unasked." She caught his eye for a moment, then said, "Very well. Let us proceed."

The session lasted all day. Panglor and Alo related everything that had gone before, and answered a multitude of questions. The scientists on the panel listened with skeptical interest to their descriptions of the world they called Dementia, and to their laymen's conclusions that Dementia was a zone of discontinuity in the fabric of space. What prevented outright disbelief, Panglor thought, was their simple presence here—especially Tiki's. The Kili was the sensation of the inquiry, and during the second half of the day, most of the questions were directed to him.

Through it all, Panglor fretted and sweated and wondered what the vet crew was doing to LePiep. He tried to convince himself that LePiep was all right. When they were conducted back to their quarters at the end of the day, he asked the guard if he could be escorted down to the quarantine area. The guard, a young man, said affably enough that he would have to check.

Alo and Tiki were in the other rooms when the door buzzer sounded. Panglor turned, assuming that it was the guard, with an answer. To his surprise, Gometz entered, carrying the glass quarantine cage with LePiep.

Panglor hurried to release her. Gometz stood with both hands in his pockets, a tiny smile at his lips, as Panglor scooped LePiep into his arms. "Babe, how are you doing, bud?" Panglor cried, lifting her to eye level. LePiep muttered uneasily, looking dazed. She radiated groggy confusion and seemed to have trouble focusing her eyes. Panglor turned a hard gaze upon Gometz.

"She's a little woozy from the anesthesia, I think."

"The—"

"Mr. Balef, we must talk," said Gometz. His hand moved in his pocket, and suddenly the air shimmered and they were surrounded by a privacy-shadow, enclosing just the two of them. Panglor glared, but before he could open his mouth, Gometz said, "Now, Balef—the first thing to understand is that if you make any aggressive move toward me, your animal will die. Instantly."

A sick feeling invaded Panglor's stomach. "What are you talking about?" he said slowly.

The smile on Gometz's face was suddenly an atrocious sight against the shimmering privacy-shadow. "Yes, Balef, I'll explain. And you'll listen, won't you? Your brawny threats will be quite ineffectual here. If you will please examine the left side of your animal's neck, tell me what you see."

Panglor scowled as he looked. LePiep squirmed, but he saw enough. "You cut her, you bastard!" he hissed. He edged forward ominously.

"That's far enough, Balef," said Gometz, raising his chin. "My hand is on a trigger." He moved his right hand in his side pocket. "There is a capsule in your animal's neck, containing a dose of 34-cymid. One touch on my trigger, and the capsule releases the poison into her bloodstream." His eyes glinted, meeting Panglor's. "Actually she won't die instantly. Over a period of several minutes, all of it with her in agony, her own enzymes will convert the 34-cymid to a-cymidine. Then she'll die—when the a-cymidine reaches a lethal level."

Panglor was so stunned he scarcely heard the rest. ". . . to know exactly how your animal dies." He suddenly focused on the words. "It doesn't have to happen, Balef. She can live. You simply tell the Waystation Authority, when they ask, that you stole the ship you left in, as the report shows. You make no mention of your employers. In fact, you can't even remember who they were. You stole the ship and you made a run against *Deerfield* to spite your old employer, Vikken. Anything you might have already told them was a lie."

So. The miserable son of a buggered rat worked for Grakoff-Garikoff. Or . . . what was their name? . . . Barracu Transport. "You want me to protect those bastards?" Panglor answered, laughing coldly, knowing his words held no power. It all made sense now. Garikoff had to cover himself; he could be in deep trouble if the truth came out at the inquest, and the truth was exactly what Panglor intended to tell.

Gometz shrugged. "If you tell the inquest board anything else, the animal dies. If you breathe a word about what I've just said, she dies. Painfully. Is that what you

prefer? I understood that you cared for the animal."
Gometz chuckled faintly.

"What proof do I have you're telling the truth?"
Panglor said, scowling. Instinctively he held LePiep
closer; she was beginning to stir, to become alert, to radiate waves of distress.

"Want to put it to the test?" Gometz said tauntingly.
His hand moved again in his pocket.

Panglor silently measured the distance between
Gometz and himself, and wondered if he could reach
the bloodsucker and squeeze the life out of him before
he could press the trigger. It seemed unlikely.

As though reading his thoughts, Gometz said, "Never
mind thinking about me." He took his hand out of his
pocket and held it out, palm empty. He laughed. "Mr.
Garikoff has another trigger, and he's in another part of
the station. If I don't return on schedule he'll kill your
animal anyway, without another thought. And if you
open your mouth at the inquest, she dies for sure. It's
your choice." His face was smiling, ugly, and Panglor
longed to smash it like a pumpkin.

"How," Panglor said carefully, trying to keep his
voice even, "do I know Garikoff really is here at D3,
really has a trigger, or that there really is a poison capsule? Or that he won't kill her even if I do keep quiet?"
As he spoke, he gently probed LePiep's neck. His fingers passed over a small bump under her skin, just below the ear, near the incision. His hopes vanished.

Gometz shrugged, smiling. "As I said, it's your
choice."

Panglor stared, silent and defeated. What choice did
he have left but to go along with them for LePiep's
sake? "Tell Garikoff I want to see him in person," he
said, but it came more as a whine than as a demand. "I
want to see him in person, and I want him to assure me

personally that he'll leave us alone if I do what he says."

Gometz arched his eyebrows, "I'll ask him, but don't count on it. Now, then . . ." and as he spoke, the privacy-shadow vanished and he stepped back. Nearby, Alo and Tiki were watching in puzzlement. "Remember," Gometz warned. He picked up the empty cage and headed for the door.

"Tell Garik—" Panglor started then cut himself off. He glanced at Alo, then at Gometz again, beaten, humiliated.

Gometz nodded, eyes steely, and left the room.

"What was that?" Alo asked. "Is LePiep all right?" She reached out to take the ou-ralot from Panglor, and looked puzzled and hurt when Panglor resisted angrily. LePiep herself was wide awake now and crying softly, radiating waves of fear and dismay.

Panglor was silent for a long time. Alo did not move, waiting for him to reply. Finally Tiki spoke. "Your . . . LePiep . . . is hurt?" He looked back and forth between the two of them.

At last Panglor found his voice. "That," he said softly, "was a Grakoff-Garikoff stooge. *And if you're listening to me now, Garikoff, it doesn't matter—they already know.*" Alo's brows furrowed sharply. Panglor, speaking in a strained voice explained. "It could be a fake, a bluff," he admitted afterward. "But they weren't faking when they put bombs on the *Cur*."

Alo reached up gently and took LePiep from him. She touched the lump beneath the incision and looked at Panglor gravely. "We can't let them kill LePiep," she whispered. Panglor shook his head. He sat down, a little apart, and stared silently at the floor. No, he couldn't let them kill her.

But could he give in to Garikoff, as he had once before? That was what Garikoff counted on—that intimidation, having worked once, would work equally well again.

That night Panglor did not sleep. He paced. He sat. He stared at LePiep. He cursed. He imagined what he would do to Garikoff if he could—and to every one of the bum's henchmen, especially Gometz. He looked at LePiep, at her dark, uncomprehending eyes, and he felt his heartache reflected in the ou-ralot's puzzled misery, her fright and her pain. And he knew that he had to protect her—and if that meant giving in to Garikoff again, well, then, it simply had to be. But if he protected Garikoff, then he would be taking the blame himself for the *Deerfield* incident. Still, LePiep would be alive. But for how long? How long would either of them stay alive?

Part of the night, Alo sat with him in silence, part of the night, Tiki filled the silence, speaking softly, nostalgically about Dementia. Part of the night, they left him alone—to think.

He sat numbly through the next day's debriefing, speaking when spoken to, but not always without prodding. Asked by Dr. Barthollo whether anything was wrong, he shook his head and muttered about the strain of the trip. LePiep lay quiet, curled tightly in his lap. When they returned to their quarters after an all-day session, he hardly felt that he had left. The same thoughts went wearily round and round through his head. And soon, he knew, the panel would begin asking the questions he could not answer.

Alo knelt by him, stroking LePiep. She stared at him silently until he met her gaze. "Whoh-ee?" LePiep quailed softly, lifting her head.

"It's the filthiest trick I've ever seen," Alo said quietly. "They must have worked their way into the station's main computer system, if they're bugging the hearing room—and getting phony IDs and orders."

"Probably," Panglor muttered. His head hurt from lack of sleep. After all they had been through at D1—to come back to this! "They must be expanding their illegal operations into the Dreznelles—why else would they penetrate the station's computers?—and we came back in the middle of it." His voice was little more than a whisper. *"Damn!* They're so bloody buggering sure of themselves! He twitched, and realized that he had unconsciously balled his fists.

"Pangly—"

"The computers, though—the *damn computers*." He focused on Alo. "What if—?" Suddenly his heart beat quickly. "Listen, how long do we have before the next hearing?"

"Till morning. We're supposed to be sleeping. And you really should—"

"No sleep. Forget sleep," Panglor said tightly. He leaned close to her ear and whispered, almost inaudibly, "You're about to outdo everything you've ever done on a computer system. First see if they've got a bug on us through the com-console. If they do, kill it. Then we're going to falsify a few programs of our own."

As he explained, Alo's brows knitted in fierce concentration.

Panglor put Tiki to work calming LePiep, then he tackled the mechanical job. He opened the access panel of the com-console and sat on the floor, staring at the internal components of the terminal, balancing his unitool in his hand, thinking. He looked up at Alo, waiting for her to finish at the board, wanting to scream to relieve the terrible tension in his chest. Alo stared at the board, brow furrowed. Her fingers moved, slid, danced across the board. Panglor peered back into the works of the console and poked tentatively with his unitool.

Alo looked down. "Okay, Pangly, the bug program is

blocked. And this is set to go as soon as you cross those circuits."

Taking a long, deep breath, Panglor reached into the console and disconnected several hair-fine light-fibers in back, then several more in front. The cross-circuiting was no easy job, and by the time he was finished, he had clipped out several circuits altogether and used the fibers as extensions for the ones he needed to rearrange. "Okay," he grunted. "Send."

Alo fiddled. "It's done. The med section will receive the alert for a cymidine poisoning case, starting in half an hour, appearing consecutively on every cardiac display in the department."

"You're sure Garikoff couldn't monitor that through the bug on our sender?"

"Pretty sure. Not unless they're smarter than we think they are. I sent it out as a coded telemetric pulse through the central system."

"All right, let's get that other message ready." Panglor cut six circuits and reconnected one. "Go ahead." Then, as Alo worked, he began dismantling several unrelated components under the console. Alo was already finished when he finally sat back, holding several units in his hands. He looked at LePiep, then spent the next forty minutes assembling and recircuiting, and when he was finished, he had two pieces of equipment in his hand. One looked like a piece of barnacled toast with horns, and the other looked like a tiny spaceship trailing a wire.

"Tiki," he said, holding up the barnacled toast, "you keep that close to LePiep at all times. Maybe you can hold it under your robe." Tiki took the instrument and held it for LePiep to sniff. Then he carefully placed it under the front fold of his robe and held LePiep to his breast. "I don't *know* if that thing will jam the signal from Garikoff's trigger," Panglor said—his words scarcely conveying the fear in his heart—"but it might. I hope it won't be put to the test."

"Excellent," said Tiki somberly. "A difficult situation."

Alo was staring at the other device. "We have to test this," Panglor muttered. It was the transmitter-laser from the com-console; with the use of extra components and fibers, however, he had attempted to step up its power. He reached into the console and connected the power line trailing from the device. Then he pointed the instrument across the room and touched a switch. A hairline beam of light jumped out; smoke hissed from the opposite wall. Panglor disconnected the laser and went to inspect the damage. He had burned a small hole into the metal-matrix wall. "Right," he said, and his stomach grew tight. The laser worked. So he was going to go through with the plan. There was a chance that it would fail—that he would watch LePiep die. He turned, feeling a numb weakness in his legs. LePiep was watching him from Tiki's arms, and her sorrowful fear washed over him.

"That's it?" Alo asked. She cleared her throat; she understood.

Panglor nodded, closed up the com-console, and handed the laser to Tiki. "Can you hide this in your robe for a minute?" Tiki clucked, and the weapon vanished under several folds of cloth. "Okay," Panglor said and went to the door.

When Alo nodded from the com-console, he pressed the door signal. The door paled, and the guard peered in. "Yes?"

"Um . . . there's a message here on our console you need to see," Panglor said. He indicated the com-console with his eyes. "You're to let us go for a while."

The guard looked dubious. "I'll look," he said. "But listen—I don't like to use this—" he pointed at Panglor with his right forefinger, the tip of which glittered with the tiny muzzle of a grafted-on-nervie "—but if I need to, I will."

"Right—sure," Panglor said and stood well back as the guard crossed the room and glanced at the com-console. His eyes widened in surprise. "You see?" Panglor said. "I wasn't kidding." He joined the guard and looked at the screen, to see what message Alo had trumped up.

The message read: "BY ORDER OF THE DIRECTOR'S OFFICE OF THE DEPARTMENT OF EXTRASOLAR AFFAIRS, THE FOLLOWING PERSONS:

PANGLOR BALEF

ALONTELIDA CASTLEY

TIKI

ARE INSTRUCTED TO PROCEED TO THE MEDICAL ARRIVAL AREA, FOR CONFERENCE WITH ACTING COMMANDER TAL JEEBERING OF FREIGHTER DEERFIELD. THE ABOVE-NAMED PERSONS MAY PROCEED UNESCORTED, AND DUTY GUARD IS HEREBY INSTRUCTED TO REMAIN AND GUARD QUARTERS IN THEIR ABSENCE. PER AUTHORIZATION, WAYSTATION AUTHORITY, 543:11.24: 2210."

The guard scratched his upper lip. "I'll have to confirm this. I can't imagine why they didn't notify me in the usual way." He squinted for a moment; Panglor could see his throat move slightly as the guard operated his implanted transceiver. Panglor crossed his fingers. The guard grunted and reached out to the com-console terminal. "Something's wrong with channels. I'll have to try for a confirmation on here."

"That must be it," Panglor said. "I wondered myself why they would contact you this way. Probably some difficulty in the other systems." He glanced at Alo behind the guard's back. If she knew how to set up a block in the security-com system from here, it was no wonder she had always been in so much trouble at the station.

The guard cleared the board and punched in a request. The word "CONFIRMED" appeared in the screen, followed by the same message. The guard scratched his head. He used a different code. The result was the same. The guard appeared at a loss; he was obviously not completely convinced.

"Is there a problem with this?" Tiki said suddenly, moving to join them. He was still holding LePiep. He addressed the guard, his eyebrows dancing. "I do not understand. Is it usual for you not to trust messages from your own human people?" He spoke in a tone of voice that was soft, and yet not so much gentle as persuasive, conveying the disappointment of one who has trusted and been let down.

"Well, it's not that, sir, Mr. Tiki. It's just that well—this isn't usual, and I think I should wait." The guard bit his lip. "If it's really important, they should send a messenger down."

Tiki made a sorrowful hissing sound. "We have been summoned to a friend," he whispered. "We are needed. Do you not believe this?" Panglor felt a curious wave of lightheadedness. He was suddenly afraid that all was lost; and yet, he wanted very much to believe what Tiki was saying, with all his heart. Of course, he would anyway—but this was different. Suddenly he recognized, in a tiny corner of his mind, that he was being gently hypnotized. Tiki was still talking but Panglor could not quite understand what he was saying.

Tiki's words became clear as he concluded. "We have been summoned to our friend, and we really must go." The guard nodded and agreed. His hands dropped to his sides and he smiled.

Panglor blinked, then gestured toward the door. He followed the others out, glancing back only once. The guard was watching them, looking vaguely unsettled. When they were in the corridor, Panglor took his weapon back from Tiki and hissed, "How long will he stay that way?"

"Why, I don't know," said Tiki. "As long as he remains convinced of the rightness of my words, I expect. I did not command him. I merely persuaded."

"Well, if he changes his mind," said Alo, "there will be plenty of confusion. I planted a bulletin that we've been seen escaping on the far side of the station. That should give us time to do this, if we can do it at all."

"Yah," said Panglor, scowling. He touched LePiep, in Tiki's arms. "You have to help us now, babe. It's for you and for all of us. Can you lead us to those scum? Can you tell us when we're getting near?"

The ou-ralot perked her ears sadly. "Hyool?" she said mournfully, emitting soft waves of misgiving.

"It's to save you, buddy," Panglor said urgently. "Tiki, you can talk to her pretty well. Can you get across to her that we just want her to reach out, to feel for the presence of that bastard, wherever he is?"

Tiki hissed softly and murmured to LePiep. The ou-ralot purred in return and radiated soft waves of hopefulness. Panglor took that as assent and started down the corridor. "They can't be far away, because I don't think their transmitter could function through too many walls. This whole section's half deserted, anyway. They've probably set themselves up in one of these empty rooms."

As they passed the first doorway, Panglor watched LePiep for any sign of reaction. She simply looked at him with wide eyes. They moved on. Panglor glanced up and down the corridor nervously, knowing that security scanners must be tracking them; he hoped Alo's program was successfully feeding the monitoring center a picture of an empty corridor.

"Which way, Pangly?" Alo stood at an intersecting corridor, peering both ways. "I see someone way down at the end, there," she said, pointing to the right.

Panglor caught up with her. "This way," he said, pointing left. Besides avoiding company, he wanted to circle around the block of rooms that included their quarters. "Any idea what's on the levels above and below us?"

Alo spoke as they continued walking. "Above—that's where they're interrogating us. I don't think Garikoff could infiltrate that very easily." She glanced at LePiep. "She looks a little nervous now, doesn't she?"

"She grows uneasy, yes," said Tiki, gently stroking the ou-ralot in his arms.

Panglor felt his own nerves tighten. "What's below us?" he asked, striding forward again.

"Government offices, I think. Maybe the guard headquarters. I'm not sure," Alo said.

Nodding, Panglor eyed every doorway they passed and glanced back for any indication from LePiep. Nothing happened until they turned the next corner; then LePiep began emoting plaintively. Panglor hesitated, then reached back to scratch her lightly on the head. "We gotta do this," he murmured, his throat thick. "Wish you could understand why." He gripped his laser more tightly and moved ahead.

A man rounded the corner ahead and strode toward them. He wore the uniform of a Waystation Authority guard. "Uh-oh," Panglor muttered. "Tiki, do you think—?"

The Kili swept by him silently, with astonishing grace and speed. As the guard approached, he appeared to recognize them and quickened his pace. Tiki, however, intercepted him and spoke to him in a voice too low for the others to hear. The man looked puzzled for a moment, then visibly relaxed. He nodded to Tiki, and to Panglor and Alo; and then he walked on by and disappeared around the corner. Panglor, breathing more easily, pulled the laser out from behind his back. Tiki beamed. "I told him we had been granted freedom of the corridors for exercise. Who would disbelieve an honored guest-alien?"

"Especially when he uses his voice to hypnotize," Panglor muttered gratefully.

"Really, friend Panglor, I only use my voice to increase the persuasiveness of my words. Still," Tiki admitted, "it is a useful ability. My evolutionary ancestors used it—"

"Tiki, let's just—"

"Of course." Tiki turned and glided down the hallway. After passing four doors on his left, he stopped and cocked his head. Panglor hurried to his side.

"Hrrrrl," LePiep said, bristling. She radiated dismay and . . . *hatred.* She peered unhappily into Panglor's eyes.

"You feel them up ahead?" Panglor whispered, his limbs turning to lead. "That next door?" His voice caught; he was unable to breathe for a moment. Meeting Alo's and Tiki's eyes, he steeled himself and walked forward to the shimmering, opaqued door. This appeared to be the room located just about exactly behind their quarters. LePiep's waves of fear cascaded against him. Fear—and hatred—of someone beyond that door. She growled throatily in Tiki's arms. Panglor touched her to shush her. His hand trembled. He steadied himself with a sharp, silent command.

Gripping the laser, he nodded to Alo. The girl worked with incredible speed; in seconds she had the service plate removed from the door-lock mechanism. Panglor unwrapped the threadlike power line from the laser and, squinting, attached it to the power supply inside the door mechanism. The laser-charging components came to life. He nodded again to Alo, and she probed at the door-actuating mechanism. Panglor stretched out his power line; he had about a meter of free movement— enough to get inside the door and take aim.

Alo moved something, and the forcefield door changed almost imperceptibly, without paling. Panglor crouched and edged closer. The door's field was weakened just enough to allow sound to leak through. Blood rushed so hard in his ears he could barely think, and he exhaled slowly, steadying himself.

Voices were barely audible through the still-opaque door. For a moment he could not distinguish words. Alo modified the field a hair more, and suddenly the sounds became clearer and he heard Gometz's voice, bored and grumbling. Someone else spoke, a familiar, slightly hysterical voice. That was interrupted in turn by another . . . one full of gravel, saying, "All right. So the tap's down. Don't worry—he's in our hand."

Panglor fought down a wave of dizziness. Garikoff's voice jumped out of his memory; it was the voice he had just heard. It was true, then; he was here. Vertigo gave way first to anger, then rage. Panglor glanced at Tiki, who was holding LePiep. The ou-ralot was quaking silently, radiating terror; she recognized Garikoff's presence, all right. "Tiki," he whispered. "Hold that gadget I gave you right in front of her." He blinked hard and gripped his laser tightly. Someone in the room shouted: "Hey, the guards have a bulletin out! They've escaped, and they're halfway across the station!"

"What?" growled Garikoff.

"Now!" Panglor hissed.

Alo tripped the door lock, and the door-field vanished. Panglor sprang into the room, crouching, leveled the laser, and bellowed, "FREEZE, YOU BASTARDS, OR YOU'RE DEAD!" Three men leaped out of their seats in astonishment and panic. Lousa Garikoff rose to his short, stocky height and turned to stare at Panglor. His hairpins glinted and his eyes smoldered. "You sons of bitches!" Panglor snarled. "Hands where I can see—"

Gometz's eye made a movement to the left. Panglor glanced and saw a man in the corner raising a weapon. *"Freeze, I said!"* he screamed and triggered the laser and swung it in a fast arc. A thread of light swept across half the room. The man in the corner howled in pain and fell backward, dropping his gun. Panglor swung the other way, cutting empty air. All of Garikoff's men were on the floor. Panglor lowered his sights and swept again, but with the beam cut off. The smell of burnt flesh touched his nostrils.

The first man was not the only one moaning in pain. The laser had slashed Garikoff and Gometz both. Two men on the right were crouched on the floor, staring in fear. Panglor squinted at them and at Garikoff, who was pushing himself up from the floor, clutching his abdomen. "Balef!" he said hoarsely, his voice filled as much with surprise as with pain. "You'll wish—"

Panglor snarled and fired again. Garikoff's left hand had closed over a small, squarish object that had fallen to the floor. Garikoff grimaced, squeezing, as Panglor's needle of fire seared across his hand. Garikoff barked and dropped it. Panglor swept the beam three times across his chest and then cut his fire. "Bastard!" he hissed. Garikoff fell back to the floor, gasping. Panglor carefully covered the room with the stilled laser. From behind him, Alo darted into the room and disarmed the Garikoff men, tossing their weapons to the door.

A bell was clanging inside Panglor's head, filling him with pain—and then horror. "LePiep!" he cried. Tiki swept to his side, holding the ou-ralot close. She was rigid in Tiki's arms, eyes hard and glazed, radiating wave after wave of pain. "Peep!" Panglor whispered, touching her with his fingertips. She could not respond; she could only radiate pain. *"Alo!"*

His cry was unnecessary. Alo was already at the room's com-console, shouting to someone that an emergency poisoning case was on its way to the med section. She whirled and caught Tiki's arm. "I'll take her; I can run; I know the way!" she said in a single breath and reached for LePiep.

"Lead," hissed Tiki, keeping LePiep in his arms. "I can follow faster than you know!"

"GO!" Panglor screamed.

Alo's gaze flashed from Tiki to Panglor. Then she sprinted out the door and down the corridor. Tiki followed with LePiep, moving like a frightened breath of wind.

Panglor stared after them helplessly, his heart pounding. He whirled to keep his prisoners covered, and it was all he could do to keep from lashing them over and over again with laser fire. Gathering up the hand weapons, he jerked on the power line to disconnect his laser, crossed the room to the com-console, and called the Waystation Authority. Then, trembling with emotion, he waited.

15

BY THE time guards arrived, Panglor was nearly incoherent with rage and fear. No matter how fast Alo and Tiki had gotten to the meds, there was very little chance of saving LePiep's life. He was no expert, but he knew that cymid was a deadly killer. Garikoff and Gometz were both unconscious on the floor now; Panglor had blasted them both with a nervie when Garikoff tried to rise again. Panglor wished that the bastards were still conscious, so that he could blast them again. But it wouldn't save LePiep or bring her back.

One of the two uninjured men, he realized, was Grakoff, partner to Garikoff. He was a pathetic-looking man, fat and frightened.

Panglor turned over his weapons but it took frustrating minutes to explain to the guards why they should arrest everyone here and let him run to the medical section.

The med-section was buzzing when he burst in with

two guards dashing after him. "Where is she?" he cried. A medical worker, startled, pointed to the veterinary area. Panglor charged into the next room. Finally he spied Alo and Tiki clustered around a screen with several medical and veterinary people.

Also saw him coming and urgently waved him over. Heart ready to burst, he looked to see what they were watching. It was a video image of a surgeon working on LePiep's small, still form. "She's going to be all right!" Alo cried softly, seizing his arm and squeezing him until her nails dug into his flesh.

"How do you know?" he hissed weakly. If she was still in surgery . . .

"It never went off, Pangly! The capsule never got triggered!" Alo was shaking him.

"But you saw her! She was—"

"She was reacting to us, and—when you burned those guys, those bastards—she felt it, she couldn't help reacting to *their* pain!" Alo shook him harder. "Pangly, she was never poisoned!"

Relief washed through him like a flood of tears. He struggled to keep from going to pieces. "You mean . . . what are they doing in there, then?"

They both looked back at the screen, where the surgeon was finishing. "Taking the capsule out. They really did put one in there, they meant to do it. Either you shot him before he hit the trigger or your jamming gadget worked. I don't know which, and who cares?" Alo was crying now, still clenching his arm.

"I'll be damned," whispered Panglor. He looked at Tiki, who was swaying drunkenly from side to side in pleasure. "I'll be *damned*."

The days that followed were a bewildering blur. LePiep was released from surgery in good health, and with a cheery sendoff from the veterinary staff. The inquest board began an immediate inquiry into Panglor's involvement with Grakoff-Garikoff, and the alleged criminal activities of that company and its officers. Not all of the story, as it turned out, was a surprise to the Waystation Authority.

The Garikoff ship which had fired on *The Fighting Cur* during its insertion run with *Deerfield* had been captured by the Traffic Patrol. The pilot of that ship had been willing to talk, and had actually told some of the story before dying suddenly and mysteriously while in confinement. Garikoff, it seemed, was in the process of establishing a territory for his business in the D3 system; and while he had penetrated the government computer-bureaucracy to an alarming degree, he was also more closely watched than he probably had realized.

As to Panglor's role, the panel rendered no immediate judgment, saying that their present interest was in learning the facts, and only after the entire inquiry was concluded would they return to the issue of possible criminal charges.

Eventually the inquiry was put back on its original track, and attention shifted from Panglor to the zone of discontinuity and to Tiki. Panglor and Alo answered questions until they were weary, but Tiki showed no signs of tiring. By this time, evidence supporting Panglor's account of events had been provided by Jeebering and several of the *Deerfield* crew and by the *Deerfield*'s instrument recorders. Once the majority of the scientists had conquered their initial skepticism, they began to grow excited. Suddenly there was talk of an expedition, of a return to the D1 system by a science-equipped ship and crew.

The inquest sessions blurred altogether. At some point, Tiki was invited to become the Kili ambassador to humanity, with D3 as the initial contact and trade point representing human peoples. Tiki responded with enthusiasm and delight—until asked for help in locating the Kili people. At this he crossed his eyes and stiffened. Finally Panglor nudged him, and he blinked. "Of these things I know nothing," he said mournfully. "Really, I am only a poor Kili, considered—" and he consulted his translator for the first time in days "—blellicka . . . by my fellows." He stared solemnly at the ceiling. "How else may I help you?"

Undersecretary Barthollo appealed to Panglor for help. Panglor sat mute, realizing suddenly that the panelists did not yet understand that Tiki was considered . . . not sane . . . by his own people. Alo came to Tiki's rescue, however. "He's not a space pilot," she explained. "He doesn't know the answer to your question." The undersecretary looked at her with skepticism, but at least for the moment, dropped the question.

Eventually they were given a day off, though they were still confined to their quarters (under improved security). Panglor could hardly rest, though, wondering as he did what the judgment of the inquiry board and the Authority would be. LePiep groomed her wings and purred soothingly, reflecting only a hint of his worry; she was pleased to be safe again, not having to face the likes of Garikoff. Tiki talked about his preliminary diplomatic exchanges, and how he had given the board still more details on the shipwrecks of Dementia. "Humans are vain about their brand names, even in their shipping companies," he reported. "That upset them. But most of them, you know, thought their missing ships were done in by ships of different brand names. Surprised to learn differently."

Jeebering stopped by for a visit, the first time they had seen him in days. He looked tired, but good color had returned to his face, and his eyes were clear. He wore a clean, smartly tailored uniform. "How are you, Jeeb?" Panglor asked, glad to see him.

"Okay," Jeebering said, accepting a mug of hot moke from Alo. "Wasn't what I came to talk about, though."

"How are your men?" Alo asked.

Jeebering blew across the top of his mug and sighed. "The psychs and meds have their hands full with some of them," he admitted. "But some of them are coming around." His eyes flickered. Panglor felt a sour taste in his mouth and wondered what to say. Nothing, maybe.

"Hope they'll be okay," Alo said quietly.

"Yup," said Jeebering. Suddenly he smiled. "Hey, that wasn't what I came to talk about, either. I've heard some rumors—nothing official, but my sources are pretty reliable—that you're going to get some good news."

"Oh?" Panglor raised his eyebrows.

"They were quite pleased by your testimony against Garikoff," Jeebering said. "They think they've got a good case against them, and perhaps they can nab those two from—what was it, Barracu?—while they're at it. Garikoff will be indicted as soon as he recovers. I don't think they'll press charges against you, though—either Vikken or the Authority."

Panglor's head was light and his stomach tense all at the same time. Jeebering added, "They'll probably go after that useless pig Grakoff, too, though he was basically just a stooge."

Panglor's mouth opened, then closed. He recalled his capture back on Veti IV. "You know," he said, "I never understood those two. Garikoff told me that Grakoff was his brother, but not exactly—or something like that. I wondered what the hell that was supposed to mean."

Jeebering chuckled and shook his head. "I'm surprised you never heard about them while you were spacing for the lines. They're pretty notorious. Grakoff is Garikoff's younger clone brother. I don't know how much is rumor and how much truth, but they say that when Garikoff's biological mother became sterile—not a bad thing, considering her son—she had an illegal clone made of her young son, Lousa. It was a typical backroom lab job, and they botched it—the clone came out not-quite-right. Garikoff hates him, has nothing but contempt for him. But there was a time when Garikoff was broke and hurting, and Grakoff had money to put up, and so they formed the Grakoff-Garikoff Shipping Line."

Alo wrinkled her forehead. "So why don't they have the same name?"

Jeebering sighed. "Grakoff suffered early mental and speech deficiencies. Or anyhow, the story goes that when he was young, he couldn't pronounce his name right—it came out as *Grakoff* instead of *Garikoff*—and he just kept his own version. Who knows? It probably became a symbol of some imagined autonomy from his domineering brother." Jeebering toyed with his mug. "Well, anyway—"

"Mmm," grunted Panglor.

"I just stopped by to tell you I think things are probably going to go your way. Those scientist guys are all hepped up about this zone of yours." Jeebering laughed. "I don't know why I think of it as being yours, but I do. Probably because you were right in your element there." He chuckled and glanced at Alo. "Anyhow, they didn't believe you at first, but all the ship's records were there. And they seemed to trust me because of my stripes or something, and I told them all about your crazy scheme of diving through that planet—"

"Not a planet," Panglor protested.

"Right. Whatever. I told them you did it and it worked, and all the records verify that. And you brought a real live Kili with you, and—to keep it short—they're pretty impressed by the implications there. First I thought they'd just be happy to know where all the ships were disappearing to, but no, they're blathering now about theoretical possibilities, just like regular damn scientists. Talking about new theories of the nature of reality, blab, blab. Cripes. They're saying maybe some day we could fly through these things as a matter of routine, going from one zone to another the way Tiki talked about. Fly right through the zones into another reality, steering with mental images the way you did. Daydream-flying!" Jeebering shook his head. "Maybe in some other century. Anyway, I told them you were the ones they should be talking to, not me. We were just bystanders." He fell silent and drank his moke.

Panglor was touched more deeply than he would have believed. "Jeeb," he said, embarrassed. "That was nice of you." When the hell had anyone ever given him credit for doing something useful, for being capable where others weren't? He scarcely knew how to reply to the compliment.

"Hah?" Jeebering said. "Ah, hell no. I just told them the facts." He set down his mug. "Got to go. So long."

After Jeebering had gone, Panglor sat in silence, gazing at Alo. He couldn't think of a thing to say.

In the morning, Jeebering's rumors were confirmed officially, when the inquest panel delivered their preliminary summation. In view of the extraordinary information brought back, and the courageous actions taken to bring *Deerfield* safely home, and in consideration of the testimony rendered against Grakoff-Garikoff, no charges were being considered against Panglor for the sabotaging of *Deerfield*'s insertion. Or, for that matter, for the breach of security and the assault against Garikoff and his men. Panglor stared at the panel, unable to voice his relief.

Then a man named Elbright, who seemed to be chief of the scientific phase of the inquest, took the floor. "Now that that's out of the way," Elbright said, "we have an offer to make—a request, really. Will you return with a scientific expedition to the D1 system? We're formulating plans to outfit a research ship to investigate, er, Dementia, and we want you two to come along as special consultants."

Alo stirred suspiciously. "Do you mean consultants or insurance?" she asked. "Or test animals?" Panglor shot her a cautioning look; she ignored him and eyed the scientist.

Elbright was startled, but he did not seem offended. "Maybe all of that," he admitted. "But we'll pay you consultants' salaries—twenty thousand a month—although the psychs will be wanting to observe you, as well. They'll be observing everyone, including themselves."

"I'm not so sure I want to rush right back there," Panglor said.

"I wouldn't call it rushing," Elbright said. "It will take time to prepare, and if we get appropriations for a ship carrying its own foreshortening-field generators—to be on the safe side for the return—it could take a year, anyway."

Panglor blinked and sat back.

The scientist added, "We'd like you to be available as consultants right away, though. Salaried, of course."

That impressed Panglor even more.

Later he discussed the matter with Alo. Tiki joined them and said that he had been asked to go along, too—if it would not interfere with his ambassadorial duties. The scientists wanted to return with him to his wrecked ship; they hoped to find and decipher, with his help, locational coordinates for the Kili worlds. "Will go if you go," said Tiki. "Flillik." He was dressed in a

new robe with tassled trimmings, tailored to his specifi-
cations by his waystation hosts. Panglor chuckled. The
Kili was taking his new job seriously, but not without
flair.

"So, Alo, what you say?" Panglor asked. Alo was ex-
amining the door's opaque-field mechanism. Panglor
didn't know why, because they were no longer being
held under tight security. "We go back there," he said,
"that's what drove the poor bastards from *Deerfield*
crazy. Even Jeeb."

"Because they weren't crazy enough to begin with,"
Alo said, without turning.

"Belllri-brikk. True," said Tiki, blinking.

"So do you want to go back?"

"Sure," said Alo. "Why not?" She turned from the
door and went to the mantel under the holo-screen,
where LePiep lazed, chin hanging over the ledge. She
rubbed the side of her finger against the ou-ralot's
snout. "You want to go?" she asked, looking back finally at Panglor.

"I guess so." He felt a strange pressure in his chest,
like a balloon inflating. He wanted to go if she did, but
otherwise not. "Sure. We could bring the good old *Cur*
back."

"This is good, then," said Tiki. He rose, swaying. "I
must go now and meet with the people I said I would
meet."

"That's the life of an ambassador," Panglor said with
a wave. Alo followed Tiki to the door and patted him as
he left. Then she fussed with door for a moment and
came back, grinning.

"It's settled, then," she said and sat in his lap, strad-
dling and facing him.

"Right," he said, breathing faster. Alo was quite
attractive at the moment; she wore a close-fitting,
flared-cuff jumpsuit, open just an inch or two at the

throat. Her hair brushed his face as she bent and kissed him. "Wait—" he mumbled, when their lips parted. "Those scientific joes are coming in a few minutes." He didn't want to get involved in something here he would hate interrupting.

"No, they're not," Alo said slyly. She kissed him again, for several long seconds this time, and pulled back to watch his expression. "I jimmied the door closed."

He gazed at her suspiciously. She nodded evilly.

"Hyoolp!" LePiep whistled.

About the Author

Jeffrey A. Carver is the author of a number of thought-provoking, popular science fiction novels, including *The Infinity Link* and *The Rapture Effect*, and most recently *The Chaos Chronicles: Neptune Crossing* (Vol. 1), *Strange Attractors* (Vol. 2), and *The Infinite Sea* (Vol. 3). His novels combine hard-SF concepts, deeply humanistic concerns, and a sense of humor, making them both compellingly suspenseful and emotionally satisfying. Carver has written several successful novels in his "star-rigger" universe, *Star Rigger's Way*, *Dragons in the Stars* and most recently *Dragon Rigger*. *Panglor* is the book that sets the stage in Carver's future-history for the later events in the Star Rigger universe. Recently, Mr. Carver has hosted an educational television series about how to write science fiction. He lives in the Boston area with his wife and two daughters.

TOR
BOOKS The Best in Science Fiction

MOTHER OF STORMS • John Barnes
From one of the hottest new names in SF: a shattering epic of global catastrophe, virtual reality, and human courage, in the manner of *Lucifer's Hammer*, *Neuromancer*, and *The Forge of God*.

THE GOLDEN QUEEN • Dave Wolverton
A heroic band of humans sets out to save the galaxy from alien invaders by the bestselling author of *Star Wars: The Courtship of Princess Leia*.

TROUBLE AND HER FRIENDS • Melissa Scott
Lambda Award-winning cyberpunk SF adventure that the *Philadelphia Inquirer* called "provocative, well-written and thoroughly entertaining."

THE GATHERING FLAME • Debra Doyle and James D. Macdonald
The Domina of Entibor obeys no law save her own.

WILDLIFE • James Patrick Kelly
"A brilliant evocation of future possibilities that establishes Kelly as a leading shaper of the genre."—*Booklist*

THE VOICES OF HEAVEN • Frederik Pohl
"A solid and engaging read from one of the genre's surest hands."—*Kirkus Reviews*

MOVING MARS • Greg Bear
The Nebula Award-winning novel of war between Earth and its colonists on Mars.

NEPTUNE CROSSING • Jeffrey A. Carver
"A roaring, cross-the-solar-system adventure of the first water."—Jack McDevitt